## Praise for Girl-O

D1246035

From the *School Library Journal* An[illegible]

“ADULT BOOKS FOR YOUNG A[illegible] category

“Books reviewed are considered noteworthy in their appeal to young adults for pleasure and/or research and are chosen for their literary merit and their ability to inspire, challenge, instruct, and/or entertain teens. Because these books were written for adults, readers must assume they may contain mature themes.”

Excerpt from the *SLJ* review for **Girl-On-Fire**:

“The strength of this book is in the rich details of Native American culture in the 1870s. The smell of wood smoke and simmering stews; the ‘tidy efficiency’ of a tepee with its inner drape, rawhide trunks, and willow-slat beds; and the sounds of the language and songs all encourage readers to experience the human complexities of tribal life. Even teens reluctantly fulfilling a dreaded historical fiction assignment should become caught up in the protagonist’s bittersweet adventure with a people who will soon face many tragic losses of their own.” —Dori DeSpain, reviewer

*School Library Journal,* January, 2000 (review begins page 158)

“**Girl-On-Fire** is a wonderful, well-constructed novel combining adventure, matters of the heart and a strong young female character. The combination of these elements is rare and well worth the read. I particularly appreciated Werkley’s perspectives and clarity on gender and cultural differences. Carrie, as the central figure, is very real, compelling, and instructive. Through her eyes, the reader learns of the lives of Comanche women and of the sexual politics that both bound and empowered them. Through her eyes, the reader learns about the process of acculturation that transforms Carrie from victim to willing participant. I will certainly share the book with my daughters and recommend the book to young female patients who are discovering their own power and learning to live their own adventures.” —Paula J. Jean, Ph.D., Virginia

Licensed Clinical Psychologist

Specialist in Women’s Issues; Teacher of Women’s Studies

“I want to thank Vicki Werkley on behalf of the Comanche people for using our Comanche Language. These are little words and phrases, but these little words come from our ancestors, and we are proud of our heritage. As I read this book, I felt like I was right there, feeling Carrie’s feelings, smelling the wood smoke, seeing how everything was arranged inside the tipi. I enjoyed this book very much!”

—Kay Weryackwe [Horse In Motion], Oklahoma

Comanche Tribal Princess, 1968

## More Praise for Girl-On-Fire:

"Growing up as an inner-city kid in a decidedly non-Indian environment, nearly every film or novel I was exposed to about Native Americans made them look inferior and pathetic. Getting hold of **Girl-On-Fire** would have made my day!"

—Vena Pontiac (Odawa), California

"This story is both a thrilling adventure and an interesting insight into the lives of pre-reservation Comanches from a young woman's point of view."

—Anita Codopony, Oklahoma

"When I read this book, I could envision everything I was reading about. It was like I was there. This is a great book! I'll probably read it again."

—Glenna Kaudle-Kaule (Chibitty family, Comanche)
Intake Specialist, JTPA [Job Training Partnership Act]
at the Comanche Tribal Office, Oklahoma

"I work in a school district Native American office, and we maintain books and other materials for use throughout the school district's curriculum and for student checkout. **Girl-on-Fire** is a definite 'must' for our library. Vicki Werkley's book weaves together a girl's emotions, fears, changing maturity, resilience, determination, and strength of endurance with a mystery; while at the same time preserving tradition, culture and history of a Native American people. Interesting reading! Do take the time to enjoy this outstanding book!"

—LaVerne Cabell, Bilingual and Native American Office
Montezuma-Cortez School District, Colorado

"In **Girl-On-Fire**, Vicki Werkley has written the female version of Gary Paulsen's *Hatchet*, a book that teaches girls and young women that they are their own best resource—strong, capable and complete.

"But she's done much more than that.

"Turning the 19th Century abduction novel on its head, she's produced a new, improved heroine in Carrie, whose red hair gives her the Comanche name, Wehanaibi or Girl-On-Fire.

"Carrie, thinking, stereotypically, that she's entering a world of 'savages,' finds herself instead in a nuanced society of harmony and order the likes of which she's not previously experienced.

"Like Daniel Quinn's *Ishmael* and *My Ishmael*, **Girl-On-Fire**—in its authentic treatment of the Comanches, their culture, language and traditions—forces us to reassess just exactly what so-called 'civilization' is, given the predominant culture's unwarranted co-option of the term. The first time Wehanaibi enters the balanced interior of a Comanche tepee, she discovers an almost Feng Shui-like perfection, the antithesis of the settlers' sod house she came from, and she takes another step toward understanding exactly what it means to become *Nuhmuhnuh,* or one of the People, as the Comanches call themselves."

—Gary Peterson, Youth Education Coordinator
New Beginnings School / New Beginnings Youth Program
Big Valley Rancheria (Pomo), Lakeport, California

# GIRL-ON-FIRE

Vicki Hessel Werkley

Haven Books

This is a work of fiction. Names, characters, places and incidents are a product of the author's imagination or are used fictitiously (except historical facts as specifically noted). Resemblance to actual persons (living or dead), events or locales is purely coincidental.

All Rights Reserved
Girl-On-Fire ©1999 Vicki Hessel Werkley
First Printing: December, 1999
Second Printing: March, 2000

No part of this book may be reproduced or transmitted in any form or by any means, electronic or mechanical, including photocopying, recording, or by any information storage and retrieval system, without prior written permission from the publisher. Contact:

Haven Books ◈ www.havenbooks.net
10153½ Riverside Drive /North Hollywood CA 91602

Author website: http://home.earthlink.net/~starwerks/

Werkley, Vicki Hessel.
Girl-On-Fire / Vicki Hessel Werkley. -- 1st ed.
p. cm.
LCCN: 00-90078
ISBN: 1-58436-400-9

1. Comanche Indians--Fiction. 2. Oklahoma--Indian Territory--History--Fiction. 3. Indian women--Oklahoma--Indian Territory--Fiction. I. Title.

PS3573.E667G57 1999 813.54
QBI00-279

◈ Cover Design and Beadwork by Vicki Werkley ◈
◈ Cover Art by Mary K. Helsaple ◈
◈ Editors: Gayle HighPine and Jean Laidig ◈

Published and printed in the United States of America

# Dedication

This book is dedicated to every single person who—over the years—has read, listened to, critiqued, typed, dreamed about, helped with, corrected, researched, contributed to, kept alive, prayed for, visualized, argued over, supported, cared about and/or believed in this story
(you know who you are!)
but most especially:

**Bob Winn,**

who had no idea what he was getting started

and

**Gayle HighPine,**

who made me listen and then drew me into the Native American women's world and became my teacher.

# Acknowledgments

This author is grateful for the assistance and encouragement of so many people over the years, it's impossible to include everyone by name. In the early years of **Girl-On-Fire**, those participants were mainly residents of the Mendocino Coast, especially colleagues and students in the Mendocino Schools. If I were to try to list them all, I'd be sure to overlook someone, so I'll just say "Thanks!" to you *en masse.* But I do tip my hat to the folks who were part of the creative writing group where **Girl-On-Fire** was born and first fostered—especially **Dianna Morgan**, who typed the very first draft and is **still** helping…body, mind and spirit….

More recently, I've been grateful for invaluable
insights and corrections of factual details from
(among others cited elsewhere in this list):
**Joshua Bryant, Madeline Hartmann,**
**Virginia Knowlton** and **Lynda Sappington**.

In addition to the priceless contributions of **Gayle HighPine**, the following provided extensive editorial comment: **John Bear, Julia Bershenyi, Ann Bouricius, Marian Gibbons, Richard Hessel, Christine Menefee, Sandra Smith Segebade** and **Lil Sibley.**

And a big thank you to **Jean Laidig**, proofreader *extraordinaire*, for wading through last-minute corrections via telephone till three in the morning.

Thanks to all the libraries that provided materials (especially the staff of Redbud), to **Brett Cruse** at the Texas Historical Commission and to **Heather Lanman** of Palo Duro Canyon State Park (Canyon, Texas).

For preproduction internet/computer/printing assistance, I owe a big debt of gratitude to **Bruce Jividen, Todd Andrews** and especially, **Bruce Clawson**.

Other preproduction thanks go to the staffs of the following Clearlake, California businesses: **Shelley Graphics, Perfect Printers and Smith's Postal, Etc.**

As for the book's physical creation and publication —not to mention support, encouragement and guidance —deepest appreciation to everyone who's part of **Haven Books** (which made it all possible at last), especially **Reya Patton**. Thanks to **Mary K. Helsaple** for her dedication to realizing my vision for the cover artwork, as well as for her skill and talent. And to **Bill Leahy** for his lay-out and printing expertise.

For "peripheral services" I'm very grateful to:
the **Onstad** family, **Laurie Grant, Bonnie Price, Bette Wilgus** and **Darryl Johnson** (and not just for those sugarfree, caffeinated peppermints!).

Very special thanks for gifts that can't be defined or quantified: to my husband **Tom the Longanimous**, to my mother **Bobbe Hessel** (who's waited a long time to see it), to the memory of my father **Bill Hessel**, who taught me to write (and to edit!)...if only he could be here to share this with me...and to **Dr. Ivan Schwab** of the UC Davis Ophthalmology Department for giving me back my vision, as well as my eyesight.

Heartfelt thanks to the Comanche Nation, including all the unnamed elders and Comanche speakers and family members who answered the questions of those who served as my sources. For the gift of time, attention, personal knowledge and wisdom, I thank:

**Diana G. Sovo, Margie Sovo, Kay Weryackwe, Dwight "Ike" Pocowatchit, Carney Saupitty, Sr., Anita Codopony,** and my manuscript-wrangler at the Tribal Office, **Jolene Jimenez Schonchin** — whose Comanche name Thekwane means One Who Likes to Talk.

It's impossible to measure (or express the depth of my gratitude for) the contributions of **Barbara Goodin** and other members of the Comanche Language and Cultural Preservation Committee (see page 219), especially **Richard Codopony, Jr.**—and his wife **Anita**—who took great pains to help me get the Comanche language correct. Richard is a linguistic student at Cameron University (OK) and an apprentice speaker, who in February, 1999 received a prestigious award from the United Nations for his work preserving the Comanche Language.

**Ura!**

# Nʉmʉ Tekwapʉ (Comanche Language) Pronunciation Guide

## Vowels:

| | | |
|---|---|---|
| **a** | ah | **a** as in father |
| **e** | ay | **e** as in weight |
| **i** | ee | **i** as in tipi |
| **o** | oh | **o** as in hope |
| **u** | oo | **u** as in you |
| **ʉ** | uh | **u** as in circus* or **a** as in sofa*<br>Could be compared to a schwa (ə) |
| **ai** | eye | **ai** as in haiku |
| **oi** | oy | **oi** as in noise |

**aa, ee, ii, oo, uu, ʉʉ** = prolong vowel sound.
NOTE: **ee** is a drawn-out ā not ē
and **oo** is a drawn-out ō not o͞o

**a e i o u ʉ** Whispered (unaspirated) vowels are underlined.
These are often almost inaudible.

## Consonants:

| | |
|---|---|
| **b** | similar to **v** in having* |
| **h** | **h** as in happy |
| **k** | **k** as in skip* |
| **m** | **m** as in meat |
| **n** | **n** as in neat |
| **p** | **p** as in speech* |
| **r** | **d** as in rider* or **t** as in writer* |
| **s** | **s** as in same |
| **t** | **t** as in stop |
| **w** | **w** as in weather* |
| **y** | **y** as in yet* |
| **kw** | **qu** as in quit |
| **ts** | **ts** as in beets |
| ʔ | glottal stop as in Uhʔoh! |

* see next page....

# Numu Tekwapu Guide (continued)

* Asterisk notes sounds not readily described in English. The **p** strikes many people as somewhere between an English **p** and **b**; the flapped or rolled **r** as between **d** and **t**; and the **k** as between **k** and **g**.

## A Few Examples:

ALL CAPS = main stressed syllable, usually the first.

- Girl-On-Fire: *Wehanaibi* — WAY-hah-nye-vee
- Comanches ("The People"): *Numunuu* — NUH-muh-nuhh
- Comanche Language: *Numu Tekwapu* — NUH-muh TAY-quahp
- Greetings; Hello (Literally: "Tell it to me.")
  - (to one): Ma ruawe – Mah duh-ah-way
  - (to many): Ma ruaweka – Mah duh-ah-way-kah

NOTE: A different, older greeting is used in the story.

- Good-bye (Literally: "Maybe I'll see you again."): *Nah nu tuasu u punitui* — Nah nuh tuh-ah-suh uh poo-nee-too-ee
- Thank you very much: *Urako* — U-dah-koh (Thank You: *Ura*)
- No: *Kee*–KAYY
- Yes: *Haa*–HAHH
- Maybe: *Nahkia*–NAH-kee-ah
- Don't! (to one): *Keta*–KAY-tah! (to many): *Ketaka!*–KAY-tah-kah!
- Pemmican: *turayapu* — TUH-dah-yahp (Mixture of dried meat, fruit, nuts sealed with animal fat)
- ↘ Travois: *wutaràa* — wuh-ta-DAHH

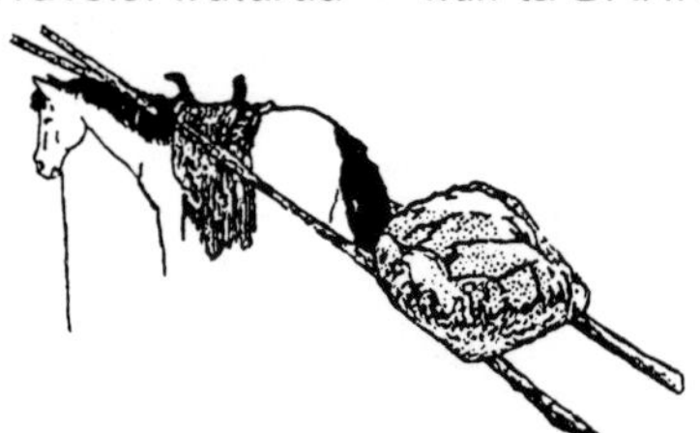

- ↑ Parfleche (rawhide) storage envelope: *wosa* — WOH-sah

**NOTE:** As with immigrant Americans registering at Ellis Island, Native American names were often Anglicized and spelled for the ease of others, so many present-day Comanche names are written with letters not found in the official alphabet adopted for the Comanche language in 1993. For example: Codopony was originally Korabunitu (Brown Eyes).

# COMANCHE COUNTRY

Map compiled by Vicki Werkley © 1999

# Girl-On-Fire

# BEFORE IT HAPPENED

## Texas ◆ July, 1874

Carrie felt the hot blush creep up the back of her neck...up from the white lace of her collar and into the roots of her red-gold hair, which was braided and pinned around her head like a crown. She'd wished, as always, she could wear it loose —like a cascade of copper silk down her back, long enough to sit on—but Aunt Emma, as always, had insisted she wear it up "as a proper lady should."

*I wish Danny could see it down,* Carrie thought. *I bet he'd like it that way.* Without turning her head, she let her eyes slide to the right so she could just barely glimpse—yes, he was still watching her. Realizing he could see her blushing made her color deepen, and she quickly brought her eyes back, unseeing, to the prayerbook in her lap.

Preacher Tate's voice reverberated dramatically throughout the small wooden church, but Carrie heard none of the words, for her mind was still crowded with thoughts of Danny Bonner. She'd been thinking about kissing. Wondering what it was like, how Danny's lips would feel pressed against hers. That was when she'd first glanced over at him, just to remind herself how handsome he looked in his Sunday best and found him gazing at her, the way he did every time he looked in her direction, as if he could drink in the sight of her with his eyes. Something she saw in those grey eyes made her think he might be reading her thoughts—or perhaps he was thinking about kissing too. She had quickly looked away, feeling the blush begin.

Carrie McEdan had always been tall for her age and willowy, and at sixteen, she was so full of life and energy, she sometimes felt as if she might burst right out of her body. She had a strong face with a pleasant, honest smile and wide eyes—the color of new spring grass—that danced when she laughed and flashed green fire when she was angry. Her skin was very fair, quick to pinken from the sun and even quicker to take color when she was embarrassed.

She sat staring down at the prayerbook gripped so tightly in her hands, waiting for the blush to fade away. Just when she felt she couldn't bear it if she didn't peek again at Danny—she *had* to know if he was still watching her—a rude elbow jarred into her ribs, and her older brother Wesley, sitting to her left, made a small noise that both expressed his disapproval and warned her to pay closer attention.

Preacher Tate was to the high point of his sermon, the part about "eternal damnation." *Strange,* Carrie thought, *no matter what the subject or scripture, he always somehow ends up shouting about eternal damnation.*

"And so, brothers and sisters," he was exhorting now, "I appeal to your finest spiritual instincts—to put those unclean thoughts of the flesh as far from your minds as possible and pray to be delivered to a higher plane where—"

The voice went on, but Carrie couldn't concentrate on the words because it took so much effort to keep from giggling. She daren't look at Danny now. She heard Preacher Tate finish with final resounding vehemence, and several voices cried out "Amen!" The loudest belonged to Aunt Emma, who sat three seats away on the other side of Wes and Papa.

Carrie rose with the congregation, added her sweet voice to the next hymn. But she sang the words automatically, for her mind was crowded with old questions: *Surely that isn't all there is to God—eternal damnation? Surely a God who created such a beautiful, miraculous world wouldn't be so petty to punish people just for taking pleasure in it?*

Carrie believed in God—wholeheartedly and unshakably. She couldn't remember a time when she hadn't believed. She prayed to Him, finding her prayers always answered—though sometimes in unexpected or puzzling ways—and was sure it was He who sent the dreams to her: vivid scenes in brilliant colors to liven her drab life. Sometimes the dreams answered questions she pondered; sometimes they told her things that were going to happen; sometimes they were just exquisite images of power and beauty that left her, on waking, with a sense of having almost solved some great mystery.

Like last night's dream. Much was lost upon waking, but she remembered a huge black horse with eyes of fire asking her to make a decision of some kind. Carrie guessed she'd dreamed that because she had horses and riding on her mind so often lately—ever since she'd finally gotten Wesley to let her ride one of the mares Papa brought from Kentucky. That Wes! Eighteen years old and tall as a tree but scared to death of Aunt Emma, knowing how she felt about horses in general and "young ladies riding astride" in particular. But Carrie had used her wits and gotten her way in the end.

Again Wes's elbow jarred her attention back to the present, and she followed him from her family's church pew and out into the hot July sunlight. When she had shaken hands with Preacher Tate, she moved to one side, knowing Aunt Emma would have plenty to say to him.

A sudden gust of prairie wind surged around Carrie, whipping the skirts of her best blue dress and teasing free some wisps of hair. Her hands took control of the skirts—a gesture now automatic after nearly two years on the Plains—and released them just as automatically when the breeze relented. She smoothed the lines of her dress, brushed at her hair and straightened the chain of her silver locket as she stood looking about for a glimpse of Danny while seeming only to be enjoying the day and the view.

On one side of the church, in the shade of the pecan trees, long tables were being covered with tempting dishes: boiled hams and baked chickens, garden vegetables, fresh homemade breads and pies. Just thinking about Maysie Ward's green-tomato pie made Carrie's stomach growl.

In that moment Danny stopped to speak to her. She felt sure he must have heard the unladylike sound of her hunger, but he was much too polite to show it. Gravely courteous, he doffed his Stetson—let the sun fall on all that black curly hair as he almost-bowed. "Good day, Miss McEdan. Did you enjoy the sermon?"

Their eyes met, and she saw it then, the smile in his eyes he was not allowing on his lips. She thought of the sermon and permitted herself the smallest of smiles as she nodded and said, "Yes, Mr. Bonner. It was…most instructive and…and… inspiring."

The smile escaped his eyes and touched his mouth. Carrie felt her heart begin to beat in that most uncomfortable way, as if it would rise to a place in her throat and make breathing impossible.

How handsome he was! That wild black hair and sun-browned skin—was it true his mother had been Mexican?—wonderful, wide cheekbones under smoke-grey eyes. And an endearingly crooked smile that haunted her waking thoughts ...and her dreams.

When Danny glanced away from her, Carrie followed his gaze and saw his father, Buck Bonner, talking with some other ranchers nearby. As soon as Buck Bonner realized who was standing with his son, he excused himself and moved toward them like an ominous raincloud across the prairie.

Danny's eyes caught and held hers in a way that told her to listen carefully. "Hope the weather's not too warm for you, Miss McEdan. Nothing like a cold drink of well water after a piece of Maysie Ward's green-tomato pie."

Buck Bonner had reached them now, eyeing them both suspiciously. He was the wealthiest and most influential of the local cattlemen. Was it any wonder he disapproved of his only son showing interest in the daughter of a homesteader?

In public he referred to them as "nesters" and "pesky sodbusters," but she could guess he used stronger terms in private. Even worse, her papa was rather a leader among the small landholders and had managed to lay claim to the choicest piece of property available in the valley—second only to the spot Bonner himself had chosen for his ranchhouse thirty years earlier.

Grudgingly polite, Buck Bonner touched his hatbrim, said, "Miss McEdan."

She nodded solemnly. "Mr. Bonner."

He turned to his son and told him, "Hank Davis has some news of Quanah." Then to her, "You'll excuse us?"

She watched them go, wondering what Danny had meant. To meet him at the well after she had eaten? She sighed in exasperation. A voice inside her said, *How silly that we have to be so secretive. Why can't our fathers act like grown-up men and get along?* Then the other voice spoke up—for there always seemed to be at least two voices inside her—reminding, *Because there's land at stake. Grass and water. And no two things are more important in this wild country.*

*And beyond all that,* the first voice reminded, *it makes it more romantic...a little like Romeo and Juliet.*

"Carrie!" Aunt Emma's voice jolted her back to the moment. "Come help!"

Moving to the food-laden table, Carrie took the knife she was handed and began to slice the loaves of bread.

"What makes it worse," Maysie Ward was saying, apparently continuing an interrupted conversation, "is that his mother was *white!*"

"Who?" Preacher Tate's wife asked as she joined them, echoing the question in Carrie's mind.

"That Quanah. The Comanche chief who refuses to go to the reservation." Maysie knew quite a lot about Comanches because her husband Josh had lived among them for a time, and she was obviously enjoying being the center of attention. "Quanah's mother was Cynthia Ann Parker. She was captured as a child—only nine years old—and made to live as a Comanche." The women shuddered, almost as one, at the thought. "Became the wife of a warchief. Bore three children. Ten years ago she and her baby daughter were finally rescued and returned to her family."

Mrs. Tate added in horror, "I heard she was so demented, she even stole horses and tried to go *back* to the Comanches!"

It was Josh Ward's voice that spoke up now, for the men were drifting to the table to fill their plates. "She was happy with 'em," he said, clearly relishing the fact he was horrifying the women. "Said she loved her husband and her sons and wanted to return to 'em."

Everyone fell silent for a moment, remembering with embarrassment that Josh Ward had once been a Comanche captive himself, spending several years among them before he was ransomed back to civilization. He never let anyone forget about it, was constantly recalling those years—and the others he'd spent as a frontiersman—to any and all who would listen.

In public, he aimed mainly to shock and appall his listeners. But in private, Carrie knew, he would drift into softer reminiscences of those times. Josh and Papa had quickly become close friends. Though Carrie thought of Josh as an oldtimer, she came to realize he wasn't much older than her father's mid-fifties; the hardships of frontier life had taken a heavy toll on him. But he loved to talk about his experiences and often spent long hours in Carrie's own home, telling his stories to Papa and Wesley while Maysie and Emma caught up on their sewing and gossip. Carrie—who was always still occupied with one of the seemingly endless chores of homestead life—could only listen as she worked, finding herself sometimes horrified but always fascinated by what she heard.

Not to be outdone by her husband, Maysie spoke right up again. "Imagine though! An Indian chief—half white—brutally murdering people of his mother's race."

Several voices spoke up then, relating the most recent tales of Quanah's campaign of murder, theft, and mutilation across the Plains from eastern Texas to Colorado. There was allusion in these stories to other acts, carefully not mentioned in the presence of ladies.

A feeling akin to panic rippled like heat waves around the gathering, and Preacher Tate, obviously wishing to soothe his ruffled flock, said, "I'm sure we'll all be safe enough. This valley's proven to be in our Lord's protection. Why, there hasn't been a single Comanche incident around here for almost thirty years."

"That's true," Josh Ward agreed, stabbing a huge slab of ham with his fork. "It's strange, but they seem to stay clean away from this area. Prob'ly got some superstition about it."

Carrie felt the mood lighten a bit as the people around her clung to that shred of reassurance...and to the bold predictions of a few, like Hank Davis, who declared, "Colonel MacKenzie's soldiers are hot on Quanah's heels. They'll have him whipped in no time."

Thinking, *He seems as eager to convince himself as anyone else,* Carrie filled her own plate and sat eating while she listened to the fragments of conversations around her. Comanches, and Quanah in particular, continued to be the main topic. Some people spoke more sympathetically than others.

Carrie was surprised when a rancher—Buck Bonner, no less—remarked, "The government's broken its promises again. Treaties set aside all that land between the Arkansas and Canadian rivers just for Indian hunting, but no one does anything to stop hidehunters from moving their slaughter there."

"Buffalo hides bring three dollars apiece," Hank Davis pointed out. "It's difficult to fault a man for wanting to make that kind of money."

Bonner frowned. "But a good marksman can kill two hundred buffalo a day with one of those new Sharps rifles. They only want the hides; they leave the meat to rot. No wonder the Comanches are mad."

"You're right," Preacher Tate admitted. "It *isn't* fair."

"What isn't fair," piped up young Wiley Todd, "is the government making promises it won't keep and the rest of us paying for it with our livestock and our lives."

In the end, it was Papa who summed up the feelings of the three groups of churchgoers—ranchers, homesteaders and townsfolk—who hardly ever agreed on anything else. "Land is land," he said. "The Indians don't really *use* it, and we need it to provide for our families."

Carrie looked down at the piece of green-tomato pie on her plate, and before she even knew she was going to speak, she had asked, "But whatever happened to Cynthia Ann Parker?" And her voice, though very quiet, was heard by all in a momentary lull in the conversations.

Josh Ward cleared his throat, told her, "They say she never smiled again. After she'd been back three, four years—let's see, that'd be 'bout six years ago now—her little girl died of the fever, and she never got over it."

In the silence that followed, it was Danny Bonner's voice that finished the story: "Cynthia Ann Parker starved herself to death." A few people nodded, for it was a well-known story on the Texas frontier, but then a kind of uncommon quiet fell over them all.

"You folks aren't doing justice to these fine pies!" Mrs. Tate exclaimed suddenly, and her husband chimed in: "Y'all cheer up now. I'm sure Quanah and his heathens will remain many miles from here. We needn't fear, for we are God's children, and surely He protects us in this blessed valley."

Carrie, no longer hungry, pushed away her uneaten pie and left the table. The people around her seemed relieved to take their conversation to lighter ground, but she found herself filled with a strange sense of melancholy.

She walked away from them all, around to the other side of the white-painted church, where the worshippers' horses and wagons stood waiting near the Tates' small stable. Except for those animals, and a stray dog sniffing at the buckboard wheels, the area was deserted.

Hearing a sudden sound, she glanced to her right, and her heart speeded up as she saw Danny Bonner come around the other end of the church. He walked not toward her, but to the well, moving with unhurried grace, not looking in her direction at all. He drew up a full bucket and drank slowly from the dipper, his eyes making a careful survey of the area, assuring their privacy.

As his right hand lifted the dipper to his lips, the sun flashed on the ring he wore—a gleam of silver against his brown skin. He took a long, leisurely drink, and replacing the dipper, finished his seemingly casual study of his surroundings. Then he looked directly at her, walked to the stable and disappeared inside.

Standing frozen, Carrie gazed down at her hands gripping each other at her waist. What if she didn't go? Would he think she had rejected him entirely? He was certain to be embarrassed later, and so would she.

Unclenching her hands to convince herself there was no reason to be nervous, she grasped instead the silver locket—a gift from Papa marking her sixteenth birthday. Surely there was nothing to fear being unchaperoned with Danny? She drew a deep breath, glanced around to make certain they were still alone, and then went slowly to the stable.

Danny reached for her hands as she entered the dimness, drew her into an empty stall. She was wearing her good kidskin shoes from St. Louis, and she had to step carefully in order to avoid the mounds of horse manure. Usually, she enjoyed the odors of horses and hay, but her nose told her Preacher Tate needed to clean his barn more often, especially in the heat of July. One of the voices inside her noted wryly, *How romantic!*

"Carrie," he breathed, drawing her closer until only their clasped hands separated them. Danny gazed at her with so much emotion in his eyes she had to glance away—down at their hands—trying to find a way to slow what felt like a situation moving much too fast for her.

Her eyes found the gleam of silver on his finger, and she said from her very dry mouth, "What an interesting ring!"

He looked down at her a moment, wonderingly. Then perhaps sensing her unease, he allowed himself to be distracted, told her, "It's Mexican silverwork. My grandmother gave it to me."

Then she really *was* interested, curious about the design. "It's hard to see...." she told him.

He twisted his hand a bit so she could see it better, explaining with a little laugh, "Can't take it off anymore. Been on there so long and I've grown so much, I guess."

She could see then the tooled pattern: an arc with waving lines falling from it and a darkened half-circle. "What an unusual design...."

"Carrie?" She didn't look up when he spoke, but swallowed and continued to stare at the ring, waiting. "We have to talk."

She looked up at him then, saw his unsmiling mouth, his hungry eyes. He started to say, "I want—" but stopped abruptly, unable, it seemed, to find just the words he needed. Instead he drew her even closer—slowly, so she could resist if she wanted, and when she didn't, he leaned down and kissed her.

Carrie felt herself fill with a tender yet poignant sweetness beyond all of her experiences...or even her dreams. She sensed an awakening in every fiber of her body, a kindling of some bold and mysterious fire.

It was Danny who drew away, and they both stood breathless in the damp straw, their eyes saying many things to each other, while a voice sang inside Carrie, *I'm in love! I really am!*

"We need to talk," he said again. "I think we should get married."

*Yes!* Carrie cried inside herself, but she said nothing aloud, because she hadn't been asked, exactly.

"We need some time alone together," he told her earnestly, "so we can talk about our families and make some decisions without them poking and prying."

She nodded, briefly wondering, *Families?* What relatives did he have besides his father? But then wasn't Buck Bonner—and how he felt about Papa—more than enough?

"When and where?" Danny asked.

"Thursday," she said suddenly. "We were all planning to come into town to meet the freight shipment. Papa's new stallion will be with it, and Aunt Emma's ordered some more things for the house."

"Could you stay home...by yourself?" Danny asked.

Her heart skipped, and she considered—thinking how adamant Emma was about not leaving her alone. But she thought also of the pressure of Danny's mouth on hers and nodded, thinking, *I just have to make them leave without me.*

"We'd better go before we're missed," he said, and she wondered if he always had to be so practical. He leaned to kiss the top of her head, where her captive hair was braided and pinned. "I bet this is even more lovely when you take it down," he murmured. And then he was gone, past her, out into the sunlight.

She waited a bit there in the dimness, letting her heart slow to a more comfortable rhythm, hugging herself a little despite the heat, feeling at the same time both very fragile and very strong.

She thought she must be the luckiest girl in the world—or at least in all of Texas—to be proposed to...almost...by Danny Bonner. For not only was he handsome and educated and wealthy—Aunt Emma would have to admit Carrie was "bettering herself," no matter how Papa felt about cattle ranchers—but she'd seen enough of Danny to know he could also be tender and thoughtful, articulate and very witty.

She smiled, remembering Sundays when the picnic conversations had been lighter in tone. Thinking how Danny was often a center of attention among the local young folks and frequently delighted his listeners with devilishly true impressions of people they knew: Josh Ward, Preacher Tate, and even her own father. She knew she should feel annoyed by this behavior, but she just couldn't. It wasn't malicious, and Danny had so brilliantly captured Papa's Kentucky accent, that little frown he carried always between his eyebrows, the way he jingled coins in his pants pockets as if he never stopped thinking of gambling.

Yes, Carrie thought with another smile as she touched the locket, it would be difficult at first. Papa and Buck Bonner would be dead-set against the match, but she was determined nothing on earth would keep her from becoming Danny's wife, if he really wanted her.

An hour later, still thinking about that encounter in the barn, Carrie sat in the back of the buckboard, packing the picnic dishes and utensils in a wicker basket. Up front on the wagon seat, Papa sat holding the reins, and his sister Emma perched beside him like some long-necked bird as they said their farewells to Josh and Maysie Ward. Carrie shifted uncomfortably on the hard wooden bench—wishing she could ride, instead, on one of the mares as Wes was allowed to do—and looked up to see Danny Bonner ride by. He sat his fine bay stallion Pirate with the ease and grace of one born to the saddle. As he tipped his hat, his grey eyes danced above his unsmiling mouth. "Good day, Miss McEdan," he said, his voice a perfect imitation of Preacher Tate's most grandiloquent tones. "Hope to see you again soon." And then he rode on.

The buckboard lurched into motion accompanied by final good-byes. Wes rode up beside the wagon, mounted on the blaze-faced sorrel mare called Brandy. He studied Carrie's face for a long moment, a troubled frown caught between his thick eyebrows. He leaned from the saddle so his voice wouldn't carry to the buckboard seat and whispered, "Just what's going on with Danny Bonner?"

*That Wesley!* Carrie thought. *So protective and pious!* She gave him an affectionate smile and said, "He's only being polite."

Wes straightened in his saddle, harrumphed a good imitation of Aunt Emma, and nudged Brandy so she moved ahead of the buckboard at an easy canter that left Carrie itching to ride her again.

Carrie closed her ears to Papa and Emma's continuing conversation about Comanches. She had more important things to think about than Comanches.

Once she was well out of sight of town and no longer felt the need to behave as a "proper lady," she slipped out of the kidskin shoes that pinched her toes and moved to the tailgate of the wagon where she could sit swinging her feet like a kid. She unpinned, then unbraided, her hair. She thought about kissing, and she thought about Thursday. As she used her hands to comb out her long, russet hair—like rivers of silk between her fingers—she smiled and began to hum.

# CHAPTER ONE: WAITING

*Damn!* Carrie thought the word, even if she wouldn't say it aloud. She grimaced as the snake, having slithered over her bare toes, struck with surprising swiftness at one of the many small openings in the wall near the cookstove. Successful, the snake began to swallow—head first—the hapless field mouse that had dared to venture out into the room.

Carrie fetched the broom, thinking for the thousandth time that there were definite disadvantages to living in a house made of earth. The sod-block walls—cut from the top layer of the prairie's rich, black soil and choked-to-bursting with the sturdy roots of buffalo grass—were two feet thick, providing a comfortable home for tunneling mice and beetles and so, too, the snakes that preyed on them.

By the time Carrie used the broom to push the unwelcome diner outside onto the porch, the mouse had disappeared except for its long pink tail, which stuck from the snake's mouth like an impudent tongue. Carrie swept the snake off the cottonwood planks and into the dirt. Then, becoming aware of the change in temperature, she reflected there were, likewise, *advantages* to sod houses, for within the thick walls it was much cooler than out here on the porch.

Yet she lingered in the heat, searching the prairie as far as she could see for a sign of Danny Bonner. It was Thursday, and she was tired of waiting.

Early that morning she'd put on the newest of her everyday work dresses—crisp brown calico, still smelling of lavender soap. But already, two hours before noon, the Texas heat had dampened it so that it clung uncomfortably along her spine and under her arms and beneath her breasts. She fanned herself with one hand, thought of pinning up her long hair to cool her neck, but Danny would soon arrive, and she wanted to look her most appealing.

Her eyes grew tired of squinting against the glare, so she took the broom and went back into the house. Cooler than the porch did not mean comfortable. Today was a scorcher, for sure. She unfastened the top three buttons of her dress, so the white lace of her Sunday-best camisole showed and the locket resting against it. She wore the necklace always, but had tucked it inside because the buttons on this dress snagged the chain. She sternly reminded herself to fasten those buttons back up when she heard Danny arrive. What would Aunt Emma say?

She smiled, not quite ruefully, as she thought of how she'd outwitted that poor old stork of a woman once again. Growing up under the rule of others—especially those fostering different beliefs about what was right and proper—Carrie had long ago found creative ways to get what she needed without openly defying those holding power over her life.

When she'd announced at breakfast that she wanted to stay home, pretending she was "unwell," Emma had immediately blushed and frowned at her with faded blue eyes reproaching Carrie for speaking so in front of the men. Nervously, Emma said, "Nonsense. You can't stay alone with all this Comanche business going on."

Carrie pinched her own hands under the table until she brought tears to her eyes. Papa stared around the table at Emma looking flustered, Carrie trying to look wan and teary-eyed, and Wesley blushing bright red, shocked by the allusion to "women's trouble." Papa made a noise of exasperation and exclaimed, "For God's sake, Emma. Let her stay home. There's no danger here from the Comanches. They never raid this valley, remember?"

Emma stared down at her plate, her face even redder after her brother's reproof, and insisted, "There are other dangers. Bandits, drifters...."

"She's practically a grown woman," Papa pointed out in a more kindly tone as he tried to soothe his sister's fears. "Mrs. Todd is only seventeen, and she's alone at home all day while Wiley's at the store in town. Anyway, we'll leave one of the guns for you, Carrie—though I'm sure you won't need it."

Carrie leaned the broom against the wall just inside the door now, and touched the rifle where it hung, loaded, within easy reach. Before they had ever left Kentucky, Papa insisted she learn to use it with ease and accuracy, despite all of Emma's protestations about what was proper behavior for ladies.

*I won't be needing that gun today,* Carrie thought, smiling. *Not for Danny Bonner.* Where was he anyway? Could he possibly have forgotten? Had his father found out and prevented him from coming? Or was Danny only teasing her all along?

She sighed and said aloud, "It'll do you no good to vex yourself with questions." It was a worrisome habit she had, for she was a girl with always too many questions in her mind. School had been a treat for her, though she'd often taxed her teachers' patience with her unending curiosity. A diligent student in all subjects, she'd shown a quite astounding talent for learning languages and was quickly fluent in all that were available: Latin, French, Italian and Greek.

*So here I am now,* she thought, *in a land where the second language is Spanish, and how am I using my learning?* She stood wondering which of the numberless chores she should choose to occupy herself until Danny arrived. For she who had lived her first fourteen years sheltered—perhaps even pampered—in a big city home with servants, now found her life filled with little more than perpetual housekeeping.

Well, the broom was ready by the door, so she decided on the continual battle to keep the floor swept. Her mother's heavy old carpets had been laid over the packed-earth floor and were subject to a rain of debris—tiny dirt clods, wisps of dry grass, mouse droppings, dead insects—that constantly sifted down from the sod roof. This shower fell not only on the carpets, of course, but on the beds and dishes, and even—unless great care was taken—into the food cooking on the woodstove.

At least it wasn't raining, Carrie thought gratefully but not without a twinge of guilt. She knew she should welcome any rain that fell—everyone was worried because this summer had been so dry—but when the roof became saturated with the heavy rains, it leaked muddy water in more places than they had utensils to put underneath, and it soaked the carpets or turned the earth floor to slippery mud.

*What would Mama think if she could see her carpets now?* Carrie wondered. And for a moment, she allowed herself to feel the old sorrow she usually kept well locked away. She still missed her mother greatly, though that sweet and fragile person had been dead nine years now, buried beside the baby boy who'd also died a few hours after the difficult birth.

Carrie reflected how different her life might be if her mother were still alive. Even though this was a far cry from anything Mama had ever known, quite possibly Carrie would still be here in a sod house in Texas. For her mother had loved Papa enough to follow him anywhere, and she'd never been able to restrain his bold gambling.

Certainly their new life in Texas was a direct result of his last wild betting on Kentucky racing horses. It did seem ironic he should leave his old community after *winning* instead of *losing*, but the threats and political pressure from an influential neighbor—who turned out to be a very poor loser—had made life uncomfortable in Kentucky.

However, the winnings had also allowed them to take up homesteading life with many more luxuries than was usual among their neighbors—and to invest in blooded stock that would ensure success for his dream of breeding the best horses in all of Texas. Papa promised they would have a real house again someday, but for now, horses came first, and any money he paid out importing lumber must first go for corrals and barns.

Yes, she still might be here in a soddy, sweeping this same carpet, but other things would be quite changed. How different Mama was from Aunt Emma, who had joined their family eight years ago, after she convinced her brother—Papa—he was incapable of rearing two children, especially a young lady. It was true Papa had never been quite the same person since Mama's death. He seemed to have withdrawn half-a-step from the life all round him, thinking of little besides horses and gambling. Wesley, at least, got to spend time with him because he was a boy and shared the same kinds of work.

Carrie was honest enough to admit she was a little jealous, and it wasn't only because of Papa's attention that she envied Wesley. If she'd been born a boy, she could ride horses and round up stock, build fences and force the plow to cut long furrows in the rich, black earth instead of battling the ever-reborn legions of weeds with a rusty hoe. Or scouring stains from mountains of laundry—which probably needed mending too—or cooking endless meals followed by the washing of an equally endless parade of dishes. And, of course, all the time she was laboring at these uninspiring tasks, she had to keep company with Emma McEdan, who seemed to possess not a glimmer of joy or humor or love of life in her dry old body.

Yes, when Carrie thought of Wesley riding the spirited Kentucky mares, she wished she had been born a boy. But then she'd think of Danny Bonner: the way he looked with his head tilted back to drink from the dipper at the church well, the dark silk kerchief knotted around his neck and his Adam's apple sliding slowly up and down in his brown and slender throat. Then she was very glad she hadn't been born a boy after all.

Thinking of Danny made her feel even warmer and out of breath. Why wasn't he here yet? She began to think, *If I go out on the porch right now, I'll be able to see him coming.* She could picture him in her mind, riding up into the yard on that big bay Pirate, smiling down at her with lips that had made her dream last night of more than just his smile.

Again she leaned the broom against the wall near the rifle and pushed her bare feet into the kidskin shoes waiting by the door. They were pretty but uncomfortable, and she usually left them off until the last possible moment. She put them on now so there would be no delay in going to meet Danny.

The porch was on the north side of the house and so in deep shadow, but the heat engulfed her like a wave as she stepped out, squinting to search the horizon for a lone rider. There was nothing but dry, yellow grassland stretching toward the line of distant hills.

In the yard, a few chickens scratched listlessly in the shade of the farm's single oak tree. Their ancient collie Shep lay twitching in his sleep and did not wake even when one of the hens pecked a flea from his tail.

Carrie became aware of a strangely hushed atmosphere all around her. It felt almost eerie to find the air so still, for the wind—somewhere between a howling gale and a breeze that only pushed the heat and dust around—was a constant companion on the Plains. Its absence added to the growing tension in her, as if the universe itself were holding its breath. She wanted to throw back her head and laugh aloud, she felt so near-to-bursting with anticipation in the hot stillness, but she stopped herself without understanding why.

*Something's going to happen!* she thought, and her blood seemed to hum in her veins like singing fire. *Oh please, God, send him to me now. Don't make me wait any longer.*

But the Plains remained empty, and still the feeling grew in her until she felt she would just fly apart unless she did *something*. Searching for the most adventurous act she could think of, her mind returned to—seized upon—the horses.

She thought of the pretty little sorrel mare called Brandy. She was the same red-gold color as Carrie's hair and seemed to possess an admirably balanced nature, both calm and alert. And according to Wes, who had been lucky enough to ride each of the mares, she was the fastest.

"Damned if this one can't run!" Wes had said that day—almost two weeks ago now—and Carrie, standing outside the corral, had gazed with longing at the mare.

Feeling very annoyed with Wesley, she'd thought, *He wouldn't be so brave saying "damned" if Aunt Emma weren't ten miles away.* Right then the plan began to form in her mind, and she said, "Wes?"

"Now, don't beg me, Carrie," he pleaded. "You know I can't let you ride her. What would Emma say?"

Carrie made a face at him, leaning her arms on the top rail of the corral and watching Wes brush the mare's coat till it shone like polished copper. "Who cares what Emma thinks?" she asked, feeling her usual exasperation with his more timid side. "She'll never know."

Half-serious, Wes told her, "Oh, yes, she will. All the way over at the Wards', she'll forget about Maysie's fever. She'll sit up sudden-like—making that face that looks like she just bit into a green persimmon—and she'll say, 'I declare! That wild girl-child is sitting *astride* a horse! I feel it in my bones!'"

Carrie laughed with him, but she was not to be diverted so easily. She pleaded, as she had many times before, for him to let her wear a pair of his jeans, to saddle a horse for her, so she could learn to ride in the western way. Wes stubbornly refused her, growing more and more flustered and guilty-looking as she begged and cajoled him. And then very quickly, she said, "I bet I can ride her without a saddle and without your jeans."

Wes laughed, shook his head. "You couldn't even get up on her in that skirt."

"If you're so sure, then let's make a real bet. If I can get up on her, will you let me ride her?"

"In the skirt? Without standing on anything?"

Carrie nodded.

He studied her, weighing the odds. He was the son of a betting man. "Done," he said.

She was down off the fence and into the corral, reaching for the reins. She spoke to Brandy, touched her shoulder. She'd watched Wes swing up on the horses many times. How was it done? She grasped the long red mane at the withers and swung her right leg up toward the mare's back. It didn't work at first—it certainly wasn't as easy as it looked, and the skirts were definitely a hindrance. But Carrie was a strong girl who regularly lifted heavy loads and beat embedded dirt from carpets, and her tall frame was blessed with a natural grace and ease of movement.

So it was, at last, she found herself atop the sorrel mare—who had stood patiently waiting all this time—and watched Wes's eyes get big and scared. "Carrie...." he began.

Looking down at him, suddenly filled with tender sympathy for her brother, she promised, "I'll stay in the corral"—though she had long dreamed of this moment and how she would ride at a gallop all the way to the hills and back.

She rode about the corral, learning the differences between this and her few experiences riding sidesaddle with a different kind of bit. She had never shared her mother's fear of horses…a fear that had—even before the influence of Aunt Emma—severely limited Carrie's riding experiences but not her brother's. Boys—men—*had* to be able to ride.

Carrie spent some time, too, practicing swinging up, hampered some by those damned skirts, but she found a way to lift the hem just so and grinned at her brother in triumph. Wes watched her mournfully; it was clear he'd no longer be able to keep her from riding if Emma was away or if any other opportunity presented itself.

*Like now,* Carrie thought in the dim oven of the porch, waiting for Danny. *I could go to the barn and get the bridle and swing up on Brandy and ride out to meet him.* Or she could be really daring and take one of the others: Pearl, maybe, or Nyota. Flyer or Belle or Duchess. Eventually, she would ride them all.

As if her thoughts had brought them awake in the hot, still morning, two or three of the mares whinnied from their corral behind the house.

*Danny!* she thought, her heart beginning to race, and her eyes searched for the bay stallion the mares had called to. But she saw nothing more than heat shimmer. A long moment passed. Then another. Still no sign of him. But the horses remained restless. Carrie could hear them whickering to one another, and in the stillness, the sound of their uneasy hooves came to her clearly.

*Where is he?* Carrie wondered, her jaws clamped together until they ached. Suddenly the old collie Shep came totally awake, gave a creaky bark and eased to his feet. His nose tasted the air. Then he began to bark in earnest, moving stiffly toward the corner of the house, heading for the corral in back.

*Of course!* Carrie thought. Danny must have circled around to approach the farm from the rear. That way he would be able to make sure the buckboard was gone and the coast was clear. Aware how annoying a barking dog can be to welcome guests, Carrie shushed the old collie and called him to her in a voice barely above a whisper. He came reluctantly, glancing back several times as if convinced he should be dealing with the arrival behind the house. "Good boy," Carrie said softly, stroking his head as he came up on the porch beside her. "You be quiet now. I don't need protection from this visitor." Surely there was no need to feel nervous meeting a young man without a chaperone—especially not someone as well-known and respected as Danny Bonner.

It was hard for her to wait there on the porch, tugging her clothes into smoother lines, fastening those buttons she had loosened in the heat, patting at her red hair.

*What will happen? What will happen?* The phrase ran through her mind again and again as she waited. Still he didn't come. Another long moment passed. Carrie took a deep breath, filling her lungs with hot, dusty air, trying to slow her heart. She pressed one hand against her breast—as if to hold inside her that heart which seemed on the verge of bursting out of her body altogether—and took some reassurance feeling the solid shape of the locket tucked inside her bodice. It was a reminder of her father's love and—since it contained a tiny picture of herself as a babe—of who she was...and was becoming.

But as always, her mind crowded itself with questions. And too many possible answers. Why didn't Danny come? Perhaps it was a game. She knew so little about courting. What should she do? Probably she should wait there and let him come to her. That's what a proper lady would do.

But it was impossible. She'd already waited forever that morning. She made herself walk slowly down the porch. Shep started to follow her, but she gave him a stern look and the hand signal Papa had taught him for "Stay!" Well-trained, he obeyed but not without a soft, fretful whine of protest.

Carrie gave him the signal again and moved to the end of the porch...then stepped off into the dust at the side of the house. She could see part of the corral from there, full of uneasy mares milling about with the whites of their eyes showing. They certainly seemed excited about Danny's bay stallion. And she could see the privy was empty, so he hadn't stopped there.

Carrie walked toward the far end of the house, wondering what kind of game this was. How was it played and what should she do to not show her ignorance? Before she got to the corner of the building, she'd decided she mustn't reveal her uncertainty or annoyance. She must be pretty and gay and captivating, turn the situation to her own advantage. So she grabbed up her skirts—though they were already short enough to be out of the way of her kidskin shoes—laughed aloud, and rushed around the corner to surprise Danny first.

She stopped short—frozen, staring—unable to draw a breath into her lungs. There were four of them, naked and hard-eyed atop their painted war ponies.

In the long moments that followed, Carrie saw everything in great detail: their wide-boned, unreadable faces marked with slashes of red and black paint, the sweat-shined copper skins of bodies clothed only in loincloths and moccasins with long-trailing fringes. They carried feathered lances and shields, and their ponies' tails were tied up for war.

One of them never took his eyes off the corral full of tempting horseflesh. The other three never took their eyes off her. The one closest to her had the bearing of a leader, despite his apparent youth. He sat easily atop his wild-eyed Appaloosa, a striking black horse speckled with white like a dusting of snowflakes.

The rider watched her coldly. His black hair hung loose past his shoulders, and around his throat Carrie saw a clutter of bright ornaments: glinting beads, a small buckskin bag, a gleam of silver on a leather thong, what must be claws or animal teeth.

Carrie didn't move. Her lungs were empty, and she began to feel lightheaded while her heart beat as wildly as that of any small creature about to be devoured. What could she do, she wondered, desperately searching all her inner resources for an answer. She thought fleetingly of the rifle, loaded and ready inside the door, but she knew she'd never make it. And Shep would stay put on the porch till someone gave him permission to leave. Not that he could help her much in the face of this dilemma, even if he tried.

The black Appaloosa, held only by a leather thong looped around his lower jaw, shifted his hooves and whinnied excitedly to the mares. When he tossed his head, Carrie realized the dangling ornaments on his rein were human scalplocks. One of them was very long and curling and blond.

Carrie found her eyes locked to those of the young Comanche leader, trying to read his soul—and her fate—behind them. Her mind continued to race, but she found no plan except to wait and see what would happen.

A mare whinnied shrilly, but Carrie never moved. *Perhaps they'll be satisfied just to take the horses,* she thought. And she waited.

# CHAPTER TWO: RUNNING

It almost seemed to Carrie that she did what she did without thinking about it at all. One moment she stood, breathless and waiting, without a shred of inspiration, and then the next, she drew in a great lungful of air and acted.

It was all one movement: her arms sweeping upward—close in front of the black Appaloosa—as she expelled the air from her lungs in a piercing shriek and leaped away to her right.

The already-spooky war ponies squealed and reared in fright, and for a moment it was all the warriors could do to stay aboard them and regain control. By that time, Carrie had dashed to the corral and slipped between the rails. Her long skirts snagged on the rough wood, but she ripped free and moved quickly in among the mares, which were by now totally unnerved. They wheeled and plunged wildly, whinnying in terror. With a calm sureness that surprised even herself, Carrie eluded the flying hooves and put out her hands to ward away crowding shoulders and hindquarters.

She was not moving blindly. She knew exactly what she needed, but the precious seconds she'd won with diversion were lost. Without looking, she knew at least one of the warriors had dismounted to follow her into the corral and must be close behind her.

She pushed the grey mare Pearl out of her way and found Brandy, recalling Wes's voice exclaiming, "Damned if this one can't run!" She hoped to God that Wes was right.

"Ho, Brandy," she soothed, quickly grabbing up the hem of her skirt and then grasping the long red mane at the withers. But Brandy was not the same calm creature of two weeks ago. She reared, nostrils wide, yanking Carrie up off the ground so that her arms cracked in their sockets, and she heard her dress rip at the shoulder seams. But she didn't let go.

From the edge of her vision she saw the ruddy-brown body rushing toward her, and she put all her energy into one mighty upward swing. This time the pull in her shoulders wrenched a cry from her, but after a half-second of panicky scrambling, she found herself astride Brandy with her hands tangled securely in the coarse mane.

At that moment—as she saw the outstretched bare arm marked with stripes of red—she drove her heels into Brandy's sides. Snorting, the mare bolted forward across the corral, and the Comanche's hand—grabbing for her ankle—slid down her foot and captured only her kidskin shoe.

The corral seethed with sound and motion: horses squealing and snorting, dust boiling up from under their hooves. Carrie heard the unintelligible voices calling to one another. It seemed the three outside the corral—one on a buckskin pony and two on pintos—were both mocking and encouraging their companion. When he appeared again at Brandy's shoulder—casting aside the useless shoe—Carrie saw it was, indeed, the leader, the one who had ridden the black Appaloosa. He moved very quickly and in an eyeblink, had caught Brandy's left ear with one hand and was reaching for Carrie with the other.

*He's got you!* one part of her cried, convinced that all was lost. It was the other part of her that didn't think at all, but brought her bare foot up sharply, smashing against his chin and nose. He grunted in surprise, and bright blood spattered his face like new paint. His companions hooted from somewhere nearby, and he groped for her again. Carrie gave a war whoop of her own and thundered her heels against Brandy's ribs. The mare leapt away again, dragging the warrior who still tried to hold her by one ear.

He was forced to let go or be crushed among the other horses. Carrie kept Brandy moving quickly about the corral, shifting her weight and using her heels to make the mare weave in and out among the others.

What else could she do? The corral was too high to jump and too sturdy to be pushed down by stampede. But she knew she was only buying time. At any moment, the other three could come into the corral and have her in seconds. Or Brandy could be brought down with a single well-placed arrow.

Yet the black-horse warrior stood in the center of the corral a moment, unconcerned, it seemed, by the horses milling about him. He appeared quite lost in thought, perhaps listening to the suggestions of his friends, or formulating an even more formidable plan of his own.

For a quick moment in passing, Carrie looked full into his face again. It was sweaty and dust-caked, marked with red paint and red blood. It was still unreadable, but where it had seemed cold before, now Carrie saw fire instead.

He barked some words, and the others moved to the corral gate. *Oh, God!* Carrie thought desperately. *Why doesn't someone come help me?*

Where was Danny? *Perhaps they've killed him,* one voice said, but the other part of her refused to believe it. Not Danny. He just hadn't been able to meet her, and Papa and Wesley wouldn't be home for hours. She was on her own.

Without dismounting, the warrior on the buckskin pony leaned down to unlatch the gate. It swung wide, and the four Comanches set up such a terrible noise that the horses fled, straight out of the corral and across the Texas grassland beyond. All ten prize mares. Papa's dream. Brandy galloped in the forefront of the band, with Carrie still aboard.

Glancing back over her shoulder, she saw the leader swing atop his black Appaloosa and quickly catch up to the others, whose speed was no match for the speckled horse.

The warriors fanned out behind her to keep all the mares moving in the same direction despite their wild flight. Carrie clung to the sorrel mare, gripping tightly with her hands in the mane and with her long legs around the horse's body. The hot wind smashed against her face, billowed her calico skirts about her legs, and tangled her long, red hair where it flew like a fiery banner behind her.

It wasn't as difficult as she'd thought it might be—riding bareback at a gallop without bridle or reins or any other way to control her mount. And it was worlds different from the sedate paces she'd ridden sidesaddle in Kentucky before her Aunt Emma put an end to even that. Thank God she'd asked Wes so many questions, listening carefully when he explained how he made riding bareback look so effortless. "If you keep your eyes up and your heels down," he had told her once, "there's a point of balance that makes it easier to keep your body upright and in place. Now, not everyone seems to be able to find it, but somehow it always came easy for me." He hadn't been able to resist pointing out, "Of course, you'll never get to try it, 'cause—if Aunt Emma ever lets you on a horse again—you'll still have to ride a sidesaddle." But here she was now, not only riding astride but also finding that knack for balance within herself as well.

The horses ran flat out for what seemed like forever, and when she noticed the terrain beginning to change—the golden buffalo grass giving way to growths of thorny mesquite—she knew they must have come at least ten miles from her home.

On both sides of her and slightly behind ran the other mares. They were all of racing stock and bred for speed. But this was not a cool Kentucky morning nor a cultured turf beneath their hooves. The ground was becoming steadily more rough and broken, littered with sharp stones and the treacherous openings of prairie dog tunnels.

The horses weaved in and out among the mesquite bushes as best they could at the speed they were traveling. Sometimes Brandy would leap over the bushes directly in her path, and when she did, Carrie thought it felt like flying. Strange, she thought, that while one part of her was filled with terror—and an increasing sense of inevitable doom—there still seemed to be a part of her that felt only the thrill of the ride. It was this same part which noted with pride her ability to maintain her balance and coordination. Despite her growing weariness, every muscle seemed to know exactly what to do to keep her securely poised atop half-a-ton of powerful muscle as it hurtled uncontrolled across uncertain footing.

And she realized, *I'm born to do this! They'll never keep me off horses now. Not Wesley, not Papa, not even Emma.*

It was then she became aware of the stinging pain on her legs. Glancing down, she saw for the first time how the mesquite thorns had caught and torn her skirts until now the barbs reached her bare legs beneath, leaving long red welts and scratches that oozed blood and burned like fire when the sweat reached them or when new scratches were laid on top.

The sun—high and hotter than before—dazzled her eyes, cooked the fair skin of her face. She knew that burning tingle meant pain to come later ...if there was a later. More and more lightheaded, she tried to swallow, but she couldn't; her tongue was like a dusty hunk of leather in her mouth.

Sensing Brandy begin to slow, she dazedly glanced about her, saw the other mares were just as dark with sweat, flecked with lather, their nostrils so distended she could see the blood-red linings. *They're all going to die,* she realized. *They'll run until they fall dead from exhaustion.* And there were sudden tears in her eyes. Not for herself, but for her father's dream.

The hot wind whipped those tears from her eyes, so that her vision was clear when the bay mare called Flyer went down. She'd been running close beside Brandy and when she hit the chuckhole—Carrie heard the legbone snap like a shot—she squealed and lurched against Brandy on her way down. Carrie felt the hot hide crush against her leg for a moment, the sweat stinging in her scratches, felt Brandy falter from the collision. The sorrel instantly regained her footing, galloping on, but the bay mare, Flyer, was down and screaming behind them.

Glancing back, Carrie saw the buckskin rider swing close to Flyer. There was the silver flash of a knifeblade. Carrie faced forward quickly; and when the whistling screams ceased abruptly, she tried desperately to think about something—

anything—else. But it was as if one of her own veins had been opened, and she could feel all her resolve and energy and hope bleeding out of her.

An overwhelming tiredness settled over her, and she closed her eyes against the aching sun. Before she looked back she knew she would still see the Comanches behind her. There was no escaping them. Whatever made her think she could?

She saw the one on the buckskin had stayed far back to collect a few mares that seemed barely able to keep moving, their heads lowered, mouths dripping foam. The two Comanches on the wiry pintos were not far behind her, easily keeping pace with the mares that still followed Brandy.

And where was *he*? Carrie wondered. The leader. The black-horse Comanche. She looked over her other shoulder and saw him, off to the left and—strangely—a bit ahead of them. It was then she realized he was turning the mares in a long slow arc to her right, straight toward what seemed an impenetrable barrier—a rocky escarpment rising like a steep wall from the prairie—and she saw that they had come all the way to the end of the valley. The valley that God protected, where Comanches hadn't raided for thirty years.

Carrie's fingers ached from holding on so tightly, and her legs trembled weakly instead of gripping the way they should. Gasping air into her dry throat was like breathing in lungfuls of fire. Yet she felt strangely detached, as if she were someone else, watching a girl being chased by Indians. She wasn't even sure if she cared anymore. Staring at the wall of rock as it loomed closer and closer, she thought dully, *I can't hold on any longer.* But she did.

*Will they run us right into the cliff?* she wondered, for the three Comanches were actively herding the confused and weary mares toward a particular spot. Then her eyes saw the opening, barely large enough for two horses abreast, and the mares galloped into it, along a narrow, winding passage that ended abruptly up ahead in a tall, leafy thicket. *It's over now,* Carrie thought distantly, almost thankfully. But when the mares tried to slow to a stop, the Comanches pushed their ponies in amongst them, screeched chillingly, and struck at the mares' rumps with their weapons. Brandy squealed and plunged directly into the bushes with the other horses pushing her from behind.

Whiplike young boughs slashed at Carrie's unprotected face and then were gone. She had barely the energy to register surprise when she saw the small canyon opening out before her and the five hobbled ponies that whickered greetings to the arriving horses.

All of the animals slowed to a canter now, wheezing, and some stumbled to a halt, barely able to stand. But she urged Brandy with her heels, hoping to find another opening—and a path to freedom—at the other end of the canyon. The sorrel mare responded, her breath whuffing in and out of her lungs like the sound of a tired steam engine. When they had jumped a steep-banked creek and circled the far end of the valley, Carrie could see for certain that they were trapped: it was a blind canyon with only the one hidden entrance.

When Carrie ceased to urge her forward, Brandy turned back toward the others, her nostrils flared wide. Carrie saw the three Comanches riding back and forth lazily as if cooling their horses, and their voices carried to her words with no meaning. It seemed strange that all the mares —including Brandy—would try to draw near the Indians now. Then staring at the small clump of cottonwood trees and tall bushes ahead, Carrie realized they concealed a largish pond of water where the creek widened into a shallow bowl.

The mares jostled together, whinnying their thirst, but for the time, the three riders kept them away and slowly moving, not letting them drink until they had cooled.

The fourth Comanche, the one on the buckskin, finally appeared through the thicket, herding ahead of him the mares that had tired earliest and straggled behind. He rode directly to the pool and let his horses—which had been moving more slowly and so were already cooled—drink their fill. Three of the warriors slid from their ponies to drink among the horses. The last, still mounted on his black Appaloosa, kept the mares moving, his attention never seeming to leave Carrie.

When the others had finished drinking, they remounted, laughing and chattering together. Their voices sounded proud and satisfied.

At last, the leader slid off his black horse, knelt at the edge of the pool and drank sparingly beside the Appaloosa. Then, scooping up water, he cleaned the paint from his face. By now the three riders had circled around the mares, encouraging them, at last, toward the pond. They moved greedily toward the water, and Brandy went with them. Carrie tugged on the sorrel mane, used her heels to signal a turn, but the mare seemed too tired and thirsty to respond. So Carrie found herself being taken directly to her captors.

The black-horse leader moved quickly to Brandy's side, slipping a rawhide noose behind the sorrel's ears and pulling it snug. Beyond any tiredness she had ever known, Carrie drove her heels into Brandy, hoping she could still bolt free. But the mare was truly exhausted, and all she could manage was some head-tossing and a few half-hearted side steps.

Carrie sat like a block of wood, watching as the Comanche put his hand on Brandy's muzzle, then over her eyes, speaking to her in a low and soothing voice. He seemed to have completely forgotten Carrie, as if the horse were a more important focus for his attention. The little sorrel calmed immediately. The warrior breathed into her nostrils for a moment, then took his hands away completely. Brandy stood as still as if she were tied to the earth by the trailing rope, and her eyes watched him expectantly, as if ready to follow any command he might give.

The black-horse Comanche turned his attention back to Carrie. She sat, avoiding his gaze, aching in every muscle, dizzy and feeling the sting of her scratched legs. He moved toward her, and her eyes were drawn down to his. She saw his face for the first time without its paint—and the blood she had caused to be there. It was a young face and still fierce even without the paint, but she saw more now in the strong features: pride and intelligence, certainly curiosity, and perhaps, a touch of sadness.

And there was more. Something so bold and burning, she was shocked at the quick response it kindled in her. And impossible as it seemed, she sensed something akin to recognition. *But I don't know him—how could I?* She didn't want to know him. *He's a savage,* she reminded herself. *He's going to kill you. If you're lucky.*

Knowing she was too tired to fight anymore or to try to flee again, she wanted more than anything to just give up, let go, slide down from Brandy and melt into a pool on the hot earth, let whatever was going to happen, just happen.

But still a part of her wouldn't allow it. She found herself straightening to her fullest height, her chin lifting in a way that she knew made her green eyes flash. She became aware of the sight of her bare, scratched leg amid the brown tatters of her skirts. A very white leg, fair-skinned to begin with, but—beyond that—a leg always demurely hidden from the view of even close family members. Her fingers trembled as one of her hands untangled itself from Brandy's mane and reached down to clothe this indiscretion.

But his hand was quicker, the black-horse Comanche's, and it closed with finality around her ankle. His touch jolted her like a small bolt of lightning, and she was aware of the warmth and strength of his grip. It seemed a very long moment that they looked at each other. There was no way to communicate except with their eyes, and what she saw in his was as much a mystery as any words he might say. So she sat, waiting again, and it seemed that the only thing she could feel in all the world was the heat of his hand like a shackle of fire on her bare skin.

# CHAPTER THREE: CAMPING

Gazing so intently into his eyes, Carrie saw the subtle shift of expression: a kind of softening...and then genuine surprise, as if he could read her warring thoughts and perhaps even sense the stirrings she felt within herself. Her eyes slipped away from his, and she felt the hot color flood her face.

His hand slid slowly up her bare leg from ankle to knee in a way that made every hair stand on end and brought her eyes instantly back to his. It was *his* eyes, now, that searched hers, and he spoke a few soft syllables with the rise of a question in them.

What had he asked her? *Oh, God!* she prayed. *Help me. Get me away from him before something terrible happens.* She could only sit watching him—full of her own questions—letting the seconds stretch out between them like an overdrawn bowstring.

It was Brandy, at last, who broke the moment. She stamped her feet and whickered longingly, her nostrils flared wide to drink the scent of water. The warrior's attention went immediately to the mare. His hand left Carrie's leg and touched Brandy's sweat-darkened shoulder. Speaking softly, he took up the rawhide rope and led her to the pool. The sorrel mare plunged her muzzle into the water and drank deeply.

Carrie's throat squeezed in on itself at the thought of drinking, but she feared if she slid down off Brandy, her legs wouldn't hold her.

The black-horse Comanche gestured grandly in the air and spoke in a bold way that gained the full attention of his three companions, who drew closer to hear what he had to say. His voice was quietly dramatic, his language very different-sounding than those she had learned in school, punctuated often with breaks and tiny catches of breath like a person saying "Uh-oh." It turned out to be rather a long speech, embellished with hand gestures, facial expressions, and pantomime, undoubtedly to help her understand, but with limited success.

The first part was easier to interpret. He was obviously recounting his exploits of the day, the stealing of the horses and his capture of her. But he seemed also to be telling of *her* brave deeds —how she, unarmed, had wounded him and escaped for a time at least. Josh Ward had spoken often of the esteem Comanches placed on courage, and how there were few deeds honored more than striking an armed enemy while weaponless oneself. Would her bravery make any difference in their treatment of her?

The next part of the warrior's speech was harder to understand, the gestures more ethereal, and Carrie couldn't even guess what most of it might mean, though the thought crossed her mind it might have to do with dreaming. She remembered Josh Ward leaning back in Papa's creaking chair to tell Wes, "The Comanches put a lotta store in their dreams and visions and the messages they get from their spirits. Treat 'em like they're as real as things you can see and touch. Guess you could call it their religion kinda."

At last, the black-horse Comanche turned back to Carrie, reached up to touch her hair where it hung in a tangled mass down her back. His eyes held a sense of wonder, perhaps at the length and red-gold color, perhaps with the notion it might be the source of her power and daring.

He said some words, or maybe a longer word of several syllables, and somehow, it felt as if he were giving her a name. What would he call her in that way that Indians name themselves? Fighting Girl? Girl-Who-Rides-Fast? Or since it was her hair that seemed to fascinate him, perhaps he named her Red Hair or Flaming Hair or Fire-Down-Her-Back.

His speech was not yet finished, and his companions still listened politely. The warrior touched Brandy's shoulder as he talked and then lifted his hand toward Carrie in what might have been a kind of salute. It seemed that there was pride and respect in his voice, and when he was—at last—finished, she felt she had been honored in some way. How to respond? She hadn't the least idea, so she just sat proud and tall on the red mare, lifting her chin and looking at each of the other warriors, one at a time.

Their expressions reminded her of Josh Ward's face when he had come to see Papa's Kentucky mares: that look of admiring something valuable and beautiful that would never be his.

Had that been part of the speech? she wondered. Had this bold young man claimed her as his own personal property? And if so, what was he to do with her?

The question had barely touched Carrie's mind before his hands grasped her around her waist and dragged her down from Brandy's back. It all happened so quickly that she barely had time to begin struggling. One moment she was swept up into his strong arms, kicking and squirming, and the next she'd been dumped unceremoniously into the pool of water. She went all the way under and came up gasping and snorting in a most unladylike manner.

And then, they surprised her. They laughed. All four of them. Their impassive faces split open, and the sound of real amusement spilled out of them. Their dark eyes and white teeth flashed as they looked down at her, but it didn't really feel as if they were laughing *at* her. More as if she had been part of a very funny joke and they were inviting her to share it.

Who ever heard of Comanches laughing? Scalping you heard about. Butchery and theft and rape and burning. But laughter? Never.

Carrie took the opportunity to drink her fill of the murky, sun-tepid water. Then she stood up—losing her other kidskin shoe to the sucking mud at the bottom of the pool. Part of her was surprised to find she felt like smiling. *Why not?* the other part of her asked. *You have to admit there's a droll touch to the whole situation.* After all, she had just been given a new name. Why not a second baptism too?

As she felt some of the tension and anxiety ebb out of her, and sensed the return of at least a bit of her calm assurance, Carrie realized she must hang on to her sense of humor. It had served her well in a life of daily drudgery, and perhaps it could help her in this new and threatening situation.

Sitting in the water, she'd seen the whole pond was set in a rather steep depression, as if it were much larger and deeper at other times of the year and had—only now in the baking heat of July—shrunk to its present size, leaving its clay banks to dry in the sun.

When she tried to flounder up out of the water—slipping where her wet feet touched the clay—the black-horse Comanche reached down to grab her hand and haul her out. She came, barefooted and dripping, aware of how the dress clung to her body. His eyes told her he was aware of it too. She collapsed in the grass under the cottonwood trees, still unbearably tired, but surprised at how refreshed the water had left her. However, the water had awakened another urgent bodily need, and she wondered if she would ever get enough privacy to take care of it.

She watched the four of them talking together as they removed the rest of their warpaint. They seemed no longer concerned with her. *Get up and run!* part of her cried, but exhaustion pressed down on her like a great hand, and she couldn't seem to make her arms or legs move.

As she watched, the youngest of the four—the only one who wore no feathers in his hair—nodded to the others, touching the knife at his belt. He swung aboard his black-and-white pinto and rode out of the little valley.

The black-horse warrior took Carrie's hand and pulled her to her feet. *What now?* She found her legs weak and quivering after the long tension of her ride, and she had difficulty walking. He led her away from the others to where the bushes grew tall and concealing. He turned to face her, and her heart flew up into her throat and caught there, beating wildly. Her pulses seemed to echo the question: *What now? What now?*

He spoke to her and gestured vaguely; then he turned and walked away. Stunned, she watched him go, then gratefully took advantage of a few moments' privacy in the bushes. When the call of nature was satisfied, she thought, *Now I can escape! Run and hide.* How foolish of him to leave her this opportunity.

But perhaps he was wiser than she gave him credit, for she realized it was simply impossible just yet. Her legs felt like jelly, and the dazzling sun made it difficult to think clearly. She was barefooted, without food or a way to carry water. *I'll think about escape a little later,* she decided. *If I cooperate with them, maybe they'll start to trust me enough so that a better chance will present itself.* She slumped down onto the sand amid the bushes and thought, *Just now I won't think about anything. I'll rest and get my strength back.*

But her mind would not empty itself of the images of that nearly naked body—stocky but well-muscled beneath the bare, coppery skin. On the inside of her closed eyelids, like a vivid daguerreotype, she saw his proud face—framed with loose-hanging hair, black and shiny as obsidian—and the way his hard eyes looked softening in surprise. What was his name, she wondered.

She thought about Indian names and the way most white people seemed to view them. She could hear again Aunt Emma's voice asking, "How can you expect to understand or sympathize with someone named Kills-Two-Enemies… or Bloody Knife?"

"Or Stinking Water," Maysie Ward had added. "Or Wolf Droppings. Or Take-a-Lance-and-Stab-Someone." And she'd grimaced her own version of the green-persimmon face, shivering as if the names themselves smacked of savagery.

Secretly, Carrie had always admired and been intrigued by Indian names. Josh had mentioned several more benign and poetic than those the women found offensive: Long Shadows was born in the late afternoon and Like-A-Turtle was the slowest person in camp. Usually whole phrases that brought a picture to mind, they were names that had a real connection with people's experiences and personalities and the world around them. Not like Carrie. The only picture *that* brought to mind was of fetching endless pails of water from the well.

*What would I call him,* she wondered, *knowing nothing of his life?* She only knew that he was young and impressive-looking, a leader who rode a black Appaloosa. He-Rides-a-Black-Horse would be fitting, but it needed to be shorter. Like Blackhorse. Yes, that would do: Blackhorse.

Almost as if thinking this name had been a magic charm, he appeared silently beside her and pulled her to her feet. Without speaking, he led her back to the cottonwood trees by the quiet pool. She saw that all the horses were grazing now: the mares, the ponies the Comanches had ridden, and the five they had left waiting in the canyon. The other two warriors were using handfuls of grass to rub the sweat and dirt from each animal until the coats shone again in the hot sun.

Blackhorse spent only a moment deftly binding Carrie's wrists together with a long strip of rawhide, which he then fastened around one of the cottonwood saplings, leaving Carrie on a fairly generous tether. Then he rejoined the others in grooming the horses.

Carrie tested her bonds and found them more than secure, so she sat—leaning back against one of the larger trees—and told herself wearily, *It would be good to take a little nap now, get any rest you can to build up your strength for escape.* She willed herself to relax and was just beginning to slip into a light dozing sleep when that easing of tension lowered her guard, allowed the terrifying possibilities of her capture to flood into her imagination. A lightning bolt of terror smashed through Carrie's body, left her shivering and covered with cold sweat. She fought the surging panic with all the resources she could muster, but the most effective proved to be her trust that God would protect her as He always had before.

Drawing strength from the fact that—so far—she was unharmed and in no immediate danger, she waited for her body, mind, and spirit to calm themselves. Carrie knew fear was a powerful tool in self-preservation, but it could also be a devastating enemy, so she resolved to do her best to keep her mind free of images of what might happen to her in the hands of Comanches.

Instead, she tried to fill her mind's eye with pictures of her family and visions of a safe and speedy return home. She wanted to hold her locket, squeeze its solid shape in her hand to remind herself of those who loved her, but she feared her captors would take it from her if they saw it. Rubbing one of her bound hands across her chest to ascertain it was still there beneath her clothes, she wondered how the little picture inside had fared in the dunking, but she would have to wait to find out.

Before long, her drenched clothes had dried in the hot air, and the tingling of her skin warned of severe sunburn on her face and scratched legs and where the shoulder seams of her dress had ripped. She again felt uncomfortably warm and thirsty, but no one offered her another trip to the pool, and she wasn't about to ask.

When the horses were well cared for, the Comanches busied themselves making camp. Carrie saw they had equipment hidden in the bushes, and they brought these things out now. Though they appeared to ignore her, she was sure they would be instantly aware of any movements she made. When they seemed satisfied with their preparations—a small amount of wood was gathered, but they lit no fire—they removed and stored away their feathers and some of their other ornaments. Then they stripped off their loincloths and moccasins and dove joyfully into the water.

Carrie was too curious about them to feel very embarrassed, and they obviously didn't care a whit about what she thought. She watched as they laughed and splashed and snorted, calling out to each other in boastful voices. As if, Carrie thought, they were nothing more sinister than schoolboys playing hooky on a spring afternoon.

As she observed their brown bodies, she thought of Danny. Where was he right now? Could he still be unaware of her danger? Or had he already begun to search for her? Were Wes and Papa with him? She thought of the distance she had traveled, and realized they'd come at least fifteen, possibly twenty, miles. The first part of the journey, too, was across buffalo grass that bent easily beneath hooves and then sprang back as if no one had ever passed that way. How hard would it be for Danny to find her trail?

She wondered about the little blind canyon. Did any of her own people even know of its existence? Judging from the lush grass and untrodden look of it, she thought not; otherwise some rancher or homesteader surely would have taken advantage of it long ago.

Finding these thoughts depressing, she told herself, *It may be difficult for them to find my trail at first, but they will before long, and I'll be rescued. Or I'll manage to escape before that, if I can.* Tired and thirsty and very sore, she found it more difficult to hang on to a hopeful outlook, so she quickly decided to think of something more cheery or distracting.

Again, her eyes drifted back to the mysterious people—barely older than her brother—who held her destiny in their young hands. Blackhorse and his companions. She thought, *I should give the others names too.* The one who rode the buckskin pony—the one who always seemed to think about the horses first—she would call Buckskin. But what of the two pinto-riders? The one who had left earlier, as yet unadorned with feathers to mark his acts of prowess as a warrior and raider, could be No Feathers.

And the fourth? She'd seen the long line of red paint across his belly—with wavy lines drawn down from it like flowing blood—and thought it only a decoration like the patterns on the others' bodies. But when he had rubbed the paint away, she saw it had been applied over a long and terrible scar.

How many times had Josh Ward talked about the importance of warfare in the life of Comanche men? How they took pride in boasting about wounds they had survived—the deadlier the better. Scar seemed a very fitting name for him.

Seeing they paid her no mind, Carrie turned her body to shelter her actions. It was a slow and difficult task with her wrists bound, but after a bit, she managed to undo two buttons and work the silver locket out where she could grasp and open it. A credit to its maker, it was surprisingly dry inside, and there smiled the little painting of herself at five years of age. The image brought tears to her eyes: a secure and happy child who could never guess that one day she would be motherless or that on the brink of a romantic new life, she would be kidnapped by Comanches!

A sudden flurry of splashing drew Carrie's attention, and her heart leaped when she saw the three warriors abruptly leave the water. They were quick to clothe themselves and take up their weapons. She hastily tucked the locket away and buttoned her dress while their attention was riveted on the thicket hiding the canyon entrance.

Barely breathing, she squinted in the same direction, hoping to see Danny—or Wesley and Papa—ride into view with their rifles, and perhaps, an armed search party. But it was No Feathers on his pinto, lugging a great bundle wrapped in dark brown hide. The other young men seemed well pleased. Scar brought out a bag of buffalo chips—Carrie recognized them immediately, for dried animal droppings were the main fuel for all residents of the nearly treeless Plains—and helped No Feathers make a small, almost smokeless fire.

When they opened the hide bundle, Carrie saw great chunks of raw meat. With a wry smile, she thought, *It's probably Wiley Todd's milk cow that's always slipping her tether.* The sight in the bundle wasn't appetizing—she'd never had a very strong stomach for such things—but when the meat had begun to roast, the odor wafted to her with delicious promise. She realized she was very hungry. Would they feed her?

They sat to eat, and Carrie noticed how each—before ever taking a bite—pulled free a small bit of meat, offered it up to the blue sky, and then buried it in the soil near him. The three ate with great gusto—roasted meat and something from their stores that looked like cakes of dried fruit. Carrie watched with saliva pooling in her mouth, and she waited. Hunger felt like a small animal in her belly, trying to gnaw its way out.

At last, Blackhorse rose from the fire and brought a piece of meat to her. He loosened her bonds somewhat, but it still was difficult to eat with her hands tied. The meat was delicious—a little too raw perhaps, but smoky-tasting and slightly sweet in flavor. The juices ran down her hands and arms and chin and spotted her dress. The warm food restored enough of Carrie's sense of humor that she could smile while considering what her Aunt Emma would say if she could see her in such unladylike dishevelment.

By the time they had all finished eating, it was dusk. They let the fire die out and made ready to sleep. Blackhorse came and freed her from the tree, pushed her down toward the pool. She knelt gratefully to wash and then drink from the cup she made of her hands.

When she turned around and moved back up the steep bank, she saw No Feathers working at some new task near what was left of the hide bundle. He was twining a rope from what seemed to be a pile of black horsehair in front of him. She stared at it as if there should be some message in what she was seeing, and then a dull sense of horror seeped into her.

Black horsehair; a rich brown hide. The image was clear at last, and she knew No Feathers had gone back to butcher the bay mare where she had fallen. Flyer! Papa's favorite, who would nuzzle his pockets for a taste of tobacco. Then No Feathers had brought the choice cuts of meat and the hide and a few other useful parts, like the horsehair. Carrie's mind went on with the pictures: They'd cooked the meat and then they'd all ...including her...eaten it.

The quick lurch of her stomach made Carrie fear she would lose her dinner then and there. But one of the voices spoke right up, scolding, *Don't be silly! Flyer was dead. You needed food. You need your strength to be ready to escape.*

*Yes, escape! Think of escape.* The nausea passed, but still she felt weak and feverish, her skin on fire where the sun had cooked it. She sank down on the bank, pulling her knees up to her chest and burying her face on her arms. *I want to go home!* she thought like a small child too long at church. *I want to sleep in my own bed with Aunt Emma snoring in hers across the room.*

She started as if shot when something cold and wet touched the back of her shoulder where the sun had burned her through the torn dress seams. Blackhorse had appeared silently, knelt beside her and was applying a salve of some kind. When his fingers touched her face, smoothed the preparation on gently, like a caress, Carrie found she couldn't meet his eyes. What would she do, she wondered, when he began to anoint her legs? And what would happen later, when it was time to lie down for the night?

Buckskin called out, and Blackhorse grunted a reply. He rose, setting a small dish beside her, and moved away toward the horses. Carrie found she could reach the dish—a piece of cut buffalo horn—and she peered at the contents, dabbled one finger in it. Most probably it was some kind of cactus pulp, she decided. She spread it on her legs as best she could with her hands bound. Already her face and shoulders felt cooler. She applied more salve on her forehead, cheekbones and nose where the damaged skin had already drunk in the healing cactus juices.

Dimly, she could see the Comanches moving about, hobbling all the horses, even though the animals seemed much more interested in filling their bellies with the rich grass than in wandering.

Carrie waited tensely, her mind filled with questions of what would happen when Blackhorse returned to her. But when he did, he almost seemed to ignore her, binding her wrists more tightly, then her ankles. Lastly, he looped a length of rope about her neck. All without looking once into her face. *Like tethering a horse,* Carrie thought. But he probably would have spoken to a horse or touched its shoulder gently.

He attached her neckrope to his wrist, and then his eyes met hers as he tugged the line taut, showing how it could take her air supply with little effort. In the tug and in his eyes she read a stern warning. He lay down very near her and seemed to fall into deep sleep almost immediately.

Carrie was not so lucky. She lay, feeling the gentle pressure of the neckrope, her body aching and bruised and gritty with dirt. She tried to sleep, but her mind kept recalling the vivid images of the day while she tried to sort through the impossible tangle of her emotions and fears. Trying to find answers for any of the thousands of questions that pressed in on her.

What was going to happen to her? By next sunset would she be dead and scalped or sitting home by the cookstove mending Wesley's shirts while she dreamed of Danny's laughing eyes? Or would she be somewhere in between doing God-knows-what?

Was she Blackhorse's property now? And if she was, why hadn't he taken advantage of that? She thought again of Josh Ward and all the things he had said about what made Comanches act the way they did. Somehow her mind kept coming back to dreams and visions...powerful messages from the Spirit World.

"Sometimes they'll do something right unexpected," Josh had said. "Kill a favorite horse or not go into battle or decide to pull up stakes and move a hundred miles—just because a spirit guide in a dream told 'em to do it. And everyone else in the band will respect that and go along with it... unless of course, their own spirits tell 'em to do somethin' else."

But even considering all that, it still didn't make sense to Carrie. How could he have dreamed about *her* or anything to do with her? They'd never even seen each other before. So what else could possibly explain this day's bewildering surprises?

*Questions!* Carrie thought. *How do you make them stop crowding your brain?*

*I must sleep!* she told herself desperately. *I need to be rested and well so I'll be ready for anything that happens tomorrow. Anything.*

Carrie began to shiver. The night—very black and thick around her—was still warm as a fine spring day, and yet she shook. Perhaps because of the shock the sunburn had caused her system. Perhaps because of her thoughts. She curled herself into a ball and tried to still the chattering of her teeth.

Blackhorse rose as suddenly as if he had never been sleeping. Carrie's heart jolted painfully in her chest. He stood towering over her, and she lay frozen to immobility like a mouse hoping the snake won't see it. He studied her a long moment ...then untied the neckrope from his wrist and walked away. She lay unmoving in her surprise, and moments later, he reappeared out of the black night, spread a blanket over her, tugging it down to cover her bare feet. He bound her to his wrist again and returned to his sleeping place.

Carrie lay astonished, warming under the blanket, which smelled of smoke and grease and horse sweat. She tried not to think of how she'd wanted to thank him for his almost-tender gesture.

*I **must** escape!* she thought frantically. *I must get away from him. Should I make myself try now?*

But she was more than weary, and there wasn't a shred of light to aid her. She gazed at the night above her. No moon at all yet, but a sky full of stars like a blanket of crushed and glittering glass—more stars than the once-uncountable buffalo that had roamed these very plains. But those stars were no help to her, failing to provide the light she needed, and they seemed so cold and distant—as far away as Danny.

The night was soft and deep around her, filled with the sounds of horses' teeth tearing long grasses and of frogs serenading one another by the pond.

*Tomorrow I'll escape,* Carrie told herself. And then she fell quickly—like a small stone—all the way to the bottom of a black well of sleep.

# CHAPTER FOUR: RESTING

Dawn had barely pinkened the eastern sky when Carrie woke, trembling, from the dream. She saw the Comanches moving about, and it looked to her as if they were packing up to travel. One of the voices inside her said, *Maybe they'll leave me behind.* But even that part of her couldn't quite believe it would happen.

She huddled under the blanket, pretending to sleep. She heard Blackhorse's voice going on and on as if he were issuing a great number of instructions. They didn't make a fire, but they ate. Knowing it had to be cold meat left from the night before, Carrie decided she could miss breakfast. Perhaps by dinnertime she would already be safely home, for surely Danny would find her soon.

Thinking of Danny brought back the dream, though she'd tried to hold its memory away from her. The first part was good—a very vivid image of herself moving into Danny's warm arms, lifting her mouth for his kiss. Again, the wild eagerness flared in her until she felt like a prairie swept by wildfire. But when she had opened her eyes, it was Blackhorse's face she saw, not Danny's.

In the dream, she had stumbled back away from him, staring at his fiercely handsome face, shocked at her own feelings. That made her think of how she'd felt when he touched her yesterday, sliding his hand up her bare leg.

*I was exhausted!* she told herself. *Barely alive, I was so terrified and weak and affected by the sun…all my defenses were down. I don't really feel that way about him. He's a cruel, Godless murderer, and I hate him. I'll never feel that way about him again. I won't!*

The blanket was stripped suddenly from her, and she saw him looming above her. He tugged on the neckrope—not gently, but not harshly either—until she sat up. A small groan escaped Carrie. Never in her life had she hurt as much as she hurt in that moment. Every muscle in her hands and arms, back and legs had been stretched beyond endurance the day before and was rebelling now. He signaled for her to stand up, but she found it almost impossible, what with the pain and stiffness and her feet still bound. She floundered a moment, most ungracefully, and then he reached down, grabbed her arm, and hoisted her to her feet.

As she tottered there, Blackhorse studied her intently…her face and clothes and hair. The sight must be appalling, she thought: her best calico workdress shredded and stained; legs and face sunburned and marked by thorns and branches; her hair—her pride—tangled by the wind, then soaked in muddy water and left to dry.

Still trying to hang on to her sense of humor, Carrie told herself, *If Aunt Emma could see me now, she probably wouldn't even want me back.* But then her mind turned a small, dark corner, and that thought held no humor at all. She thought of Aunt Emma saying—on more occasions than Carrie could count—"You must at all times behave as a proper lady, so that your reputation remains above reproach. Only then will you be able to marry well and better yourself."

*How will she treat me when I get back today?* Carrie wondered. *Will she believe me when I tell her my reputation is still above reproach?* And another dark thought as she looked into Blackhorse's eyes: ***Will** it still be?*

He grunted, stalked away, leaving her to stand wondering, but he returned almost immediately with a strange object in his hands. He had instructions for her too, and he poured them out to her as if she understood his language completely. She stood listening but without the least idea of what was being said. Part of her thought that if she really wanted to, she could have understood at least some of it, for several of the words already sounded familiar to her ears. But why should she want to? She'd soon be away from them, and their language would be as unnecessary to her as the Greek she had once mastered.

At last, Blackhorse held out the strange object to her. It appeared to be a mass of porcupine quills attached to a stick. *Whatever is it?* she wondered, staring mutely, afraid to touch it.

Blackhorse grunted in an exasperated way and dragged the thing through his own shiny-black hair so that she understood it was a hairbrush. She took it then, and he finished with his instructions.

Glancing over at Scar and No Feathers—who were mounted on fresh horses and obviously impatient to be on their way—it occurred to Carrie that Blackhorse was a very talkative young man, given to long, eloquent speeches, and as leader of the group, was probably prone to be rather bossy when he gave instructions.

Yet there seemed a kind of good-humored tolerance in the others. Scar sat on his pony, gnawing the last bits of flesh from what must be one of Flyer's bones. No Feathers waited a little less patiently on his brown pony, holding the rein of a spirited black gelding.

Blackhorse picked up his lance and shield and moved toward them. *He's leaving me here!* Carrie realized, surging with wild hope. And indeed, he swung atop the black gelding and then looked back at her to give a last unintelligible command. Then they pushed the ponies into a canter, heading for the thicketed passage, leaving her there in the box canyon. Leaving her!

Carrie's heart sang. Then ceased altogether, it seemed. Only three had ridden away. Where was Buckskin? She whirled about so quickly, she almost fell over her bound ankles. He sat nearby, smoking a small bone pipe, watching her.

She considered her situation. Buckskin had been left behind to guard her and watch the stolen mares. They—and the four horses the Comanches rode yesterday and one of the fresh ponies that had been waiting in the canyon—were now unhobbled so they could range wider in their grazing. There was still a look of weariness about the mares, and good horsemen would recommend another day's rest and feeding before they were forced to travel.

Only the last of the fresh horses was hobbled, grazing nearby with a rope looped about his shoulders, close at hand should his owner need to run or fight.

Carrie wondered if—given the opportunity—she could catch and control a Comanche warhorse. It seemed unlikely, but it was certainly worth a try. Being only guarded by one warrior, possibly for most of the day, might offer many opportunities for escape. She vowed to be watchful and ready.

Buckskin regarded her as if she were of little interest to him—as indeed, it had seemed all along. Perhaps because the horses really *were* more important to him. But Carrie was beginning to be very sure that she was considered Blackhorse's woman, even if all he chose to do with her was dump her into ponds or lecture her about God-knows-what.

Carrie gazed longingly toward the tall bushes, back at Buckskin, then at the bushes again. He must have understood her meaning, for he put his pipe away, rose and came toward her. He untied her ankles, giving her more slack at her wrists, but kept a careful hold on the noose about her neck. He walked with her to the bushes, but did not give her quite the privacy she had had the day before. Keeping the neckrope taut in his hand, he merely looked away for a very few moments and glanced back to check on her almost before she had finished rearranging her clothing.

When she made a cup of her hands and pretended to drink, he led her to the pool. Her thirst satisfied and feeling encouraged by his cooperation, she motioned that she wanted to go into the water and bathe. He seemed to consider, probed her eyes as if for intent to escape, then took the rope from her neck, releasing her. More surprisingly, he also untied her hands.

She cast her eyes down so he couldn't read the surge of exultation in her. She was free! And now escape would be possible.

But somehow, at the moment, bathing seemed more important. She felt an overpowering need to "put herself right"—as Emma would say—before attempting any action. Besides, Buckskin was sure to be more on-guard at first, and she could think about a plan while she enjoyed the pond's refreshment.

She eased herself into the water with a little gasp at its cool shock, trying not to stir up the mud that had settled to the bottom since yesterday's dunking. It felt so good, she lay back on the water, gazing up at the sky, and it was like floating in the bottom of a bowl with another bowl of bright blue inverted over her.

She bathed as well as she could with no soap and without removing her clothes—mindful of her tucked-away locket and keeping her back to Buckskin so she wouldn't know whether he was watching or not. She cleaned her hair, lamenting its sad condition. Well past the time she was finished, Carrie lingered in the pool. It was pleasant in the growing morning heat, and Carrie found it not so easy to decide on a suitable escape plan.

Buckskin seemed not to mind that she stayed. He sat on the bank, repairing some arrows, having only to be peripherally aware of her since—as she now realized—a quick or stealthy escape from the mud-slippery pool would be quite impossible.

At last, though, with the fair skin of her fingers and toes shriveled into pale raisins, she scrambled out of the pool and stood on the bank, squeezing water from her skirts. Buckskin dropped the porcupine tail hairbrush beside her and tied her ankles together once again.

So Carrie sat and pulled the brush through her hair again and again and again until at last it fell straight and clean down her spine. Buckskin watched all this with uncustomary interest, forgetting his repairs to stare fascinated at the fall of red-gold that was not only long enough to touch the ground where she sat, but to curl about in the grass like eddies beneath a waterfall.

*Perhaps he's just thinking how it would look flying from his lance,* Carrie thought, and she shivered.

What to do with that hair? Left loose, it would soon be unkempt again, and it might even hamper her escape in some way. So she divided it into two huge masses and wove each into a fat braid that hung past her waist. When she was almost finished with the first, Buckskin tossed her two strips of softened hide, which she used to tie the ends.

Finished at last, Carrie eyed the sun high above them and thought it would be good to nap for a time in the dappled shade of the cottonwood trees, drawing back to her the energies she had depleted yesterday.

But Buckskin's repair work was done, and he had other plans. The mended arrows joined others in a quiver, which he slung over his shoulder. After stringing his hunting bow, he grabbed up a soft-leather bag and walked over to her.

He tied her hands with nearly two feet of slack, and her ankles with only enough to allow small steps but certainly not running. With shooing motions, he guided her to the far side of the pool where there were bushes heavy with plums. Buckskin tossed the leather bag to her and gave an order that was perfectly clear. She began to pick the ripest-looking fruit. The third and fourth she ate, for she was feeling quite hungry now. She watched Buckskin as she did so, to see if he had any objection, but his face didn't change. When she had fallen to a steady rhythm of picking—stopping to eat every so often—Buckskin moved stealthily away from her. He didn't go far.

The swiftness with which he was able to pull an arrow from the quiver, nock, aim and release it took Carrie's breath in a little gust of surprise. He sprinted a short distance, stooped, hefted the still-kicking rabbit by the ears, and glanced back at her. As if he were not only checking on her, but also giving her some subtle warning.

She went quickly back to her picking, and it was not hard to pretend to be intimidated by what she had just seen. He fastened the dead rabbit's back leg to his belt and began to move about as if searching for signs of another. By the time she had half-filled the bag with plums, he seemed to have almost forgotten her, and she knew her opportunity for escape had come at last.

Immobile and intent, he seemed to be watching the opening of a burrow and hadn't turned to check on her for several minutes. Heart pounding, still pretending to be interested only in choosing the best fruit, she moved cautiously away from him, taking the largest steps the hobble would allow. She watched him over her shoulder so she could freeze and play innocent should he turn to look.

Inside her head, she kept up a soothing monologue to him: *That's it, Buckskin, watch for rabbits. Have you checked the horses lately? Aren't they wandering a bit? Don't bother about me. I'm doing just fine picking these plums for dinner. Don't you have more important things to think about?*

Just when she began to believe she'd get away with it—while her eyes searched the cliff face for the possibility of caves the Comanches might not know about; while part of her calculated how quickly she could find a sharp-enough stone and saw through her bonds—just then Buckskin appeared menacingly before her. Two rabbits swung from his belt, and he held his bow, arrow nocked and half-drawn. It was definitely a threat, and quickly—before they could betray anything else—she filled her eyes with surprised and terrified innocence. The surprise and terror were not difficult at all.

She felt his eyes burning into her, trying to read her true intentions, and she did her best to keep them hidden. At last, he pushed her roughly back to the camp, and she shuffled along on bare feet that were now quite sore from the hot, stony ground.

In the shade, he hobbled her ankles tightly again. He brought out a large, squarish envelope made of rawhide...Josh Ward had one at his house

house and called it a parfleche. Inside this one there was jerky: thin strips of buffalo meat sun-dried until they seemed like bits of leather, almost black in color. It was tastier than the jerky she and Maysie and Emma had made last fall after Josh helped Papa and Wesley bring down three buffalo to help them get through the winter. When Carrie had finished slicing all that raw meat and nursing it through the drying process and especially after eating it so often over the next months, she had thought she'd never want to see another piece of jerky as long as she lived. But she found it welcome now.

Before she finished eating, Buckskin tossed the dead rabbits down beside her and then—to her surprise—a knife! She could slash through her ankle ropes and run for it. Could she outrun him? Possibly. Comanches were horse Indians, not foot Indians. Of course, his pony stood close by. Could she—if she had to—drive the knife into his body with enough force to make it matter? She thought she could, if it meant saving her own life.

She glanced up at him, trying to keep her expression free of her hopeful thoughts. But then she saw he held his lance, and she knew that any Comanche entitled to carry such a weapon would easily be able to strike her down before she could free herself. *Wait,* she thought. *The time will come.*

Misinterpreting her blank look, Buckskin made a disgusted noise and knelt beside her. Carefully laying his lance within his reach, but out of hers, he took the knife and demonstrated the most efficient way to relieve a rabbit of its skin.

A strange, wild scent wafted up from the carcass—not unpleasant but warm and sweet, unlike anything Carrie had ever smelled. She watched Buckskin's actions with her stomach churning. Though she had managed to hide her squeamishness from Papa and Wesley, she made sure they always handled any initial butchering chores. Slicing up a chunk of meat was worlds different from hacking apart something that still looked like an animal.

But it occurred to her now the more useful she appeared, the greater might be her chances to survive until she escaped or was rescued. So when Buckskin handed her the bloodied knife, she took it and steeled herself to do her best. After a few moments watching her awkwardness, he leaned over and unbound her hands so that the work went much faster. Her performance was certainly no match for his deftness, but she actually felt proud of how well she did. Buckskin grunted, said words Carrie interpreted to mean, "It will do." He rolled together the rabbit pelts and stored them in a leather bag.

While Carrie was washing her hands and drinking from the pond, Buckskin rose suddenly, lance in hand, and went quickly to slip the hobbles from his waiting pony. His eyes flicked briefly back to hers, and she thought, *Now's the time! Escape!* But he had taken the knife, and though her hands were still free, her ankles were too tightly bound to run.

Then she heard the hoofbeats coming. Many more than the three sets that had left, and her heart leaped wildly with the thought, *Danny!* Horses burst through the thicket, twenty or more of them in a multitude of coat colors and markings. Then behind them came Blackhorse and Scar and No Feathers.

No Feathers rode a new horse. It was a rich blue-grey color—what the Spaniards called grullo and what some Plains Indians simply called Blue. They were highly prized, and there was no mistaking the look of pride on the boy's face. Carrie could tell he was the youngest of them all —possibly seventeen to the others' early twenties.

She was sure he had come along on the raid as a kind of apprentice: he alone carried neither lance nor shield, and he had been given most of the camp-keeping chores.

Now that he had captured the blue horse—didn't Hank Davis buy a grullo last May?—he would deserve to wear a feather or two. So already the name she had given him was probably obsolete, but she decided in her own mind, no matter how long or short she knew him, she would think of him as No Feathers.

These new horses weren't as fine as Papa's mares, but better suited to the Texas prairie. Her heart jerked when she thought she saw Danny's bay stallion among them, but when she noted the markings on its face, she realized it was Wiley Todd's buggy horse. That also led to disquieting thoughts, but she had hardly time to begin them, for she noticed the galloping horses were heading straight toward her. They hadn't been run as hard as Papa's mares yesterday, and they were allowed to go directly to the water to drink. Carrie found herself, ankle-bound, directly in their path.

Just then the fleet black gelding swerved across in front of them, and Blackhorse leaned down to pluck her up as if she were no more than dandelion fluff. Something in the way he did it made it seem like a move in a game—like a continuation of the hunting/raiding game they had been playing—and she found she almost felt more annoyed than relieved to be rescued from the horses. She thought defiantly, *I could've made them swerve aside!*

She had only a moment to think about how it felt to be held tight against him with an arm like a band of steel. Then he pulled his pony to a plunging halt and set her down on her still-hobbled feet. He had several items tied about him, and he began to loosen them, toss them down to her: trousers, a shirt, a dusty old hat.

*I hope these were stolen off a clothesline,* she thought. They did look clean, anyway. She was glad to get them; they would make escape and riding easier. Why were there no boots? And where had they gotten the hat? Her eyes went quickly to their lances and reins, but she saw no fresh-looking scalps. That was a relief anyway.

Blackhorse gazed down at her, noting, no doubt, her braided hair and tidied condition. He spoke to her, and when his pony sidestepped and he turned a bit to keep watching her, she saw something flash silver among the ornaments at his throat. Could it be what she first thought?

*No!* her heart cried out, but as she moved closer, she could see it was, indeed, a silver ring. Blackhorse's face filled with surprise as she stepped forward—forgetting to be cautious—and reached for the ring. Perhaps intrigued by her boldness, he leaned down and let her take the metal circlet in her fingers.

*It can't be! God, it can't be!* one voice insisted, but she could see the proof with her own eyes: the arc with wavy lines falling; the darkened half-circle. Danny's ring. And his words echoed in her ears, "Can't take it off anymore. Been on there so long and I've grown so much since then, I guess."

Yet here it was now, removed from his hand. Did they come across him as he searched for her today and murder him? Was it quick and brutal? Or was he even now staked somewhere under the scorching sun, scarcely alive and the victim of unspeakable acts?

She blotted out the images with a kind of numbness, drew it around her like a cocoon of fog. The ring slipped from her fingers and swung back against Blackhorse's throat on the leather thong. His eyes studied her curiously, but she hardly noticed.

She sank down on the earth, scouring her memory, trying to make a clear enough image. Hadn't Blackhorse been wearing the ring yesterday, there among the clutter of blue and silver beads and buckskin bag and elk's teeth? Hadn't she seen it, but just not noticed it? Allowed herself to depend on Danny being alive and searching for her? Did it matter when? Yesterday or today, Danny was dead. That was what mattered. She had been fooled by not seeing his curly black hair flying from their lances—had they been in such a hurry they hadn't taken time to collect so worthy a prize? Nor had she seen Pirate among the stolen horses. Had they been forced to kill that brave and beautiful bay stallion as well?

A blackness grew around her, though sunset was hours away. She drew into herself as she never had before—not even when Mama died—and sat unmoving, totally unaware for a time of Blackhorse's response to her or anything that happened around her. *Why can't I feel something?* she wondered. *Where's the pain? Danny's dead,* she kept reminding herself. *Papa and Wes will never find me now. I'm well and truly lost.*

Her mind filled with images of Danny's sun-dark, wide-boned face. The quick smile that always touched his eyes first. His lithe young body swinging into the bay's saddle. The way he tugged his hatbrim and winked at her when no one was looking. She saw his throat move as he drank from the dipper, and the sun flashed on his precious silver ring.

She lived the next hours in a kind of trance. When she was to look back on it later, she realized she had eaten roasted rabbit and wild plums; she'd been made to clean up the camp and wash the utensils.

Blackhorse seemed to accept her withdrawal with only a mild curiosity—as long as she completed the tasks he ordered. And he seemed much more interested in a spirited gambling game he played with his companions than he did in her sudden shift of mood.

Later he applied more cactus pulp to her sunburn, which had worsened after a second day's exposure, and bound her for the night, covered with the blanket. But she was hardly aware of any of it. She lay curled in on herself in a tight and aching ball, grieving for what had been lost before it was ever possessed.

Hours later, when the others' breathing confirmed their deep sleep, secretly clutching the locket in her hand, she allowed herself—at long last and almost silently—to cry.

# CHAPTER FIVE: TRAVELING

When she woke in the half-light of morning, Carrie found she was once more aware of her surroundings. She felt as if she hadn't slept at all; as if, while she lay there, some part of her had been opened and all her energies drained out. The only feeling that seemed to remain was the aching in her muscles.

Last night's fog of numbness had receded to one small pocket that held her memories of Danny. She remembered she had dreamed about him: She had held him in her hands—a tiny, fragile figurine—and taken a last, long look at his features, frozen forever-smiling and young. Then she had carefully wrapped the precious object in layer after layer of cotton wool and tucked it away in her cedar chest at home. So, too, it seemed had she isolated and enshrouded all her feelings for him, hiding them away in a secret corner of her heart. She thought it strange that one night's sleep could provide so much acceptance and resignation, but she was grateful for it. There was nothing she could do to help him now, and she needed every shred of her strength and determination to get herself away from the savages who held her prisoner.

The blanket was pulled roughly away from her. Blackhorse knelt, removed her bonds, tossed down the clothes he had found for her yesterday. She saw he was still watching her curiously after her withdrawn behavior of the night before. Though she tried her best not to look there, her eyes searched his throat for the silver ring. But it was hidden again behind his other ornaments and amulets.

"Did you have to kill him?" Carrie heard her own voice say aloud, the first words she'd ever spoken to Blackhorse. He looked surprised but uncomprehending, merely pointed to the clothes and made motions of dressing.

*It won't do any good to think about Danny,* she told herself. *You have to think about* ***you****. You're truly on your own now, you know.*

Part of her wanted to believe Papa had been able to organize a search party—perhaps it was even camped somewhere nearby—but another part of her was probably more realistic when it said, *What does Papa—or Wesley—know about tracking Indians?* And who could he get? Ancient-seeming Josh Ward on that thirty-year-old horse he rides? Who else? The neighbors? The Todds, the Calvins, the Grants? How long will they leave their homes and families unprotected to search for one unfortunate girl? One silly girl who insisted on staying home alone, despite the dangers.

While these thoughts ran through her, Carrie removed her tattered dress and pulled the pants and shirt on over her undergarments, making sure the locket was safely tucked into her camisole. Blackhorse did not stand watching her, but attended to some chores that took him only far enough away that he could quickly reach her should she try to run.

The clothes were too large, but not extremely. She rolled up the sleeves of the shirt, and tried to do the same with the pants, which fit well in the hips but were loose in the waist and seemed miles too long. Blackhorse came then, handed her a length of black horsehair rope to use as a belt. Carrie threaded it through the belt loops, thinking of Flyer's black mane in the wind.

Blackhorse drew his knife suddenly, and Carrie shrank back in surprise, but he grabbed her, speaking rough words, and gave her a little shake as if to say, "Stand still!"

She steeled herself, feeling as if her heart would run away without her, wondering what would happen now. Blackhorse stooped and slashed with the knife, cutting away the too-long bottoms of the pant legs. Something in the way he handled the sharp blade—and the sound of it ripping through the sturdy cloth—made Carrie feel cold and breathless.

He stood up, still grasping the knife, and stared at her with chill warning in his eyes. Then he pointed to the old hat he had brought and said a word to her. She quickly bent, grabbed up the shapeless piece of felt and pulled it on atop her still-braided hair.

Seemingly satisfied, Blackhorse grunted and pushed her toward the pool. The tender soles of her feet—accustomed to going barefoot mainly on carpets and wooden planks—reminded her she was still without shoes, and if she was going to escape, she'd best do so on horseback. From here—wherever they were—surely Brandy could find her way home if given a free rein.

*Today,* she told herself, thinking of the knife. *Today I'll escape for sure.*

She drank at the pool and was given jerky and plums to eat. She then was urged to help No Feathers with the packing. He had caught the last of the fresh ponies—a stocky dun with black ears —and outfitted it with a kind of pouched rawhide saddle he brought from the bushes. Carrie was amazed at how many implements and supplies could be tucked away in it. Several times No Feathers stopped her work to demonstrate a more efficient way of placing a certain item. The horn and cantle of the packsaddle were tall and very similar in shape. They, and a few knobs on the wooden frame, provided hooks on which to hang other bags, containers, and two freshly-filled canteens, which had obviously been stolen from the U.S. Cavalry. The three warriors who possessed shields pulled rawhide covers over the painted designs and tied all three in easy reach on top of everything else.

Meanwhile, Scar had left the valley alone, probably to scout the area for danger. The other two warriors had spent the time unhobbling all the horses and collecting them together into a small herd ready to drive.

When everything was packed, Blackhorse came toward Carrie leading Brandy and his own Appaloosa. There was a saddle of sorts on the speckled stallion, just a pad of thick buffalo hide. Around his muscular shoulders was looped a rawhide rope to which was attached the leadline of Brandy's new makeshift hackamore.

The little sorrel looked well and rested, and she whuffed in recognition when Carrie touched her white-blazed face. Blackhorse boosted her on top of the mare, leaving her hands and ankles free.

It seemed to Carrie that her muscles were even more painful than they had been the day before, especially since they were now required to do the same tasks that had so strained them: grasp the mane, grip around Brandy's curving sides. At first Carrie thought, *Oh, God. I'll never be able to endure this. I won't last a mile.*

But she did. In fact, within three miles her muscles had loosened and relaxed themselves to the horse's rhythm, causing her only a dull sense of discomfort.

The Comanche band left the shelter of the canyon before the sun had edged above the horizon, traveling at a quick, mile-eating canter that was only slowed to negotiate particularly rough ground. They stopped not once in the first five hours, though occasionally, Scar or Buckskin dropped behind the party to confuse their trail before catching up again.

Carrie couldn't believe horses could sustain such a pace—and in fact, two animals did drop of exhaustion and were left behind to an unknown fate. *I guess in a way it's a test,* Carrie thought. If a horse couldn't keep up this pace, it would be of little use to a Comanche. *Am I being tested too?*

She was again impressed by how simply she was prevented from escaping. With Brandy tied to the Appaloosa, Carrie was almost within an arm's length of Blackhorse at all times, yet his hands were free to attend to his own rein and lance. It was the only weapon he carried. His others were tied to the packsaddle where he could reach them in a moment if they were needed but where they were well out of her reach. She knew, even with her hands free, she had no hope of capturing his lance, and he could use it very effectively against her should she try.

Still she must wait, Carrie decided, but she could meanwhile add to what seemed a growing trust in her. Hadn't she been without bonds so far this day while dressing, packing, and riding? *Even Comanches can get careless,* she reminded herself.

There was not much Carrie could do except to try to memorize the country around her so she could find her way home when she escaped. But this simple-seeming task proved quite difficult, because each hill and dry streambed looked identical to the last one—and the next. The area was alive with game, but she couldn't use antelope or rabbits as landmarks. So in the end, she gave up and tried to content herself with the sun's information that they were moving north.

Her mind was free now to think. Mostly she tried to remember everything Josh Ward—or anyone else—had ever said about Comanche captives. She knew they had long been carrying off women and children from Mexican settlements, and as the Anglos moved into the territory they, too, fell victim. Sometimes they were used as slaves: either put to work for the captor or sold to other Indians. Some captives were ransomed back to their own families as Josh himself had been. But what was it he'd told Papa and Wes that day as he sat smoking his pipe on the porch?

"Mostly they want the kids, and girls are best. They get 'em young enough, adopt 'em right into their families, raise 'em up as their own, the kids don't seem t'know the difference."

"You'd think they had enough young 'uns," Papa had said.

"They lose a lot. Most before they're born. The Comanche are getting smaller and smaller in number. First there was smallpox, and then cholera wiped out a mess of 'em back in '48-'49, and they've never been able to make it up. The Mexican and white girls usually grow up to make strong wives and good child-bearers."

Carrie remembered Wesley's voice interrupting. Sweet, protective Wes. Had he, even then, considered the danger to her? He had asked, "But what about the women they capture—and the older girls?"

There'd been a long pause. Inside the sod house Carrie had likewise hesitated—holding the cup of milk over the bowl of dry corn meal mixture—waiting to hear Josh's answer. Perhaps he was listening too. From the small back bedroom that Carrie shared with her aunt came the voices of Maysie and Emma nattering away as they hung the new curtains they'd just finished. Perhaps Josh thought Carrie, too, was out of hearing distance at the back of the house. Still, he lowered his voice so it hardly carried from the porch through the open door to where she stood by the cookstove.

"Depends," he said, "on how they behave themselves. One time when I was with them, a raiding party brought home three white women."

Carrie swallowed, carefully poured the milk into the bowl, added a little more.

"They'd captured four, but one of 'em raised such a ruckus—screaming and crying—they just smashed her head in, took her hair, and left her where she lay."

Carrie's hand trembled as she measured the bacon drippings. Josh Ward said quickly, "They had to, of course, for their own safety. Can't have all that noise when you're traveling and raiding. Anyway, the other three were smart enough not to make trouble. Got some more tobacco, Wes?" The silence drew out while Josh refilled his pipe and got it lit. Carrie added the drippings to the bowl, wondered how to crack the eggs without making a sound.

In the quiet Carrie could hear Josh sucking on his pipe to get it going. Then his voice started up again. "Captives are usually treated pretty rough at the beginning to show them their place and test their bravery. See if they're good enough to be one of The People. That's what Comanches call themselves in their own lingo: Nuhmuhnuh...The People.

"Well, it was a bad thing that there'd been several deaths in the war party—and most of the village was already mourning other losses to the whites—so at the scalp dance that night, the beating of captives got a little out of hand. One of the women died. The oldest one tried to escape four or five times, so they sold her to another band. The third one, she did okay. She was brave, but she knew when not to talk back. She got used to it, got to be the chief's third wife, had a coupla young 'uns. She was still there when I got ransomed. She could've come back with us, but she decided to stay."

Remembering now, Carrie closed her eyes against the hot Texas sun and prayed, *Let me do the right thing, God, so I can stay alive and get back home.* Then she wondered, *Aren't we ever going to stop? What about water?* She ran her dry tongue over cracked lips, and feeling Brandy swerve a bit from her straight line of travel, Carrie opened her eyes.

Blackhorse had moved his Appaloosa over next to the black-eared dun carrying the packsaddle. Without stopping or slowing, he reached down to take one of the canteens. He did not drink from it but passed it to her. She took it with one hand and managed to open and drink from it while atop the cantering mare. The water was blood-warm, but it felt so good in her parched mouth that she could have cried—if there'd been enough moisture in her body to make tears.

She returned the canteen to him, so that he, too, could drink, but he merely slung the strap around his shoulder, let it bump against his back as he rode. Later, she wouldn't let herself ask him for more water, but when he offered it to her for the second time in the long five-hour ride, she took it gratefully.

None of the Comanches or horses drank until they came to the river. It could be seen from quite a distance, and as soon as it came into sight, they slowed the pace so the horses were cooled by the time they got there. It was a wide river and appeared a forbidding obstacle but proved to be quite shallow where they urged the thirsty horses across to the other side and toward a small stand of willows offering a bit of shade.

The horses shouldered each other irritably, though there was plenty of room to drink. The warriors, too, drank and then began to unsaddle their ponies. Shifting uncomfortably on Brandy's bare back, Carrie eyed with envy those traveling saddles the warriors used—thick pads of buffalo hide whose mat of curling brown hair provided, no doubt, a kind of springy cushion between a person's body and a horse's backbone. There didn't seem to be an extra for her.

She was allowed down to drink among the horses. Then, despite her own modesty and whatever Aunt Emma might say, she removed the stolen shirt and dunked it into the lazy current, pretending not to care who enjoyed the view of her white-lace camisole. The wet shirt, when donned again, helped to cool her for a quarter hour, the time it took for the sun to draw every hint of moisture from it. As soon as they'd had their fill of water, the horses moved quickly to the grass along the riverbank. Carrie headed for the willows' shade, wanting more than anything to collapse and sleep.

But Blackhorse called the words she recognized as her name, pointed sternly to No Feathers and told her, Carrie was sure, to go help him. The youngest raider had pulled the packsaddle from the exhausted horse and was rummaging in it. Carrie thought, *I hope he's finding food, at least.*

It was, indeed, food inside the large rawhide envelope he brought out and handed her. When she had served the others, she was allowed to eat. She realized the strange compound must be what Josh Ward had called pemmican: buffalo jerky and dried fruit and sometimes nuts, pounded into a fine meal and mixed with animal fat. Carrie wasn't sure if it tasted so good just because she was ravenous, but in that moment, it seemed the most delicious thing she had ever eaten.

They rested for more than an hour, letting the horses feed, and when they made ready to leave, they picked fresh mounts. Carrie watched Blackhorse catch up another of Papa's mares—the sturdy dappled grey they'd called Pearl—and his own black gelding. He looped the rope around the gelding's shoulders as he had with the Appaloosa, and showed her how to twist and loop the rope around Pearl's head to form a hackamore like the one Brandy had worn.

When Pearl was tied to the black gelding's shoulder rope, Carrie was helped to mount and they began to travel north again. Carrie found the grey easy enough to ride, but not as smooth in her gaits as Brandy.

Now they moved at a slightly slower pace, stopping occasionally to water, if not to rest. Carrie never would have found the waterholes on her own, for mainly they were unexpected springs bubbling up out of the earth, concealed by thick bushes or back in small arroyos. But the Comanches went to them as if there were street signs; as if, Carrie thought to amuse herself, these people knew the exact location of any bit of water bigger than a dewdrop.

She was very grateful for the hat she wore. It helped to shade her face and reduced the ever-present glare that made her feel as if she'd never get her eyes unsquinted.

They changed horses once again in late afternoon, and Carrie found herself on a bald-faced brown gelding she was sure she had seen Luke Calvin ride to church last Sunday. Had all her neighbors been raided? Were any of them still alive?

Well after sunset they made camp in a grassy draw that would keep the hobbled horses from straying far. Carrie was once again expected to help unpack, provide the meal—they made no fires—and clean up afterward.

When she was finally allowed to crawl under her blanket, she fell immediately asleep, too tired to think of escape or anything else.

# CHAPTER SIX: ESCAPING

The next two days passed almost exactly as the first. They traveled at a quick and efficient jog-trot from waterhole to waterhole, changing horses frequently, camping and eating without making fires. Carrie cooperated fully with her captors: did the tasks she was set, showed she could learn quickly, repeated and remembered the words and phrases they tried to teach her—telling herself, *I'll forget every bit of it as soon as I'm safe at home.*

She ate and drank what she was given. Many times the only food they took was a pale-yellow, almost-tasteless powder, mixed in water. Carrie was quite surprised to find it sustained them all as well as any hearty portion of meat.

She thought frequently of escape, but could find no opportunities, so bided her time and tried to increase the Comanches' trust in her. She began to observe them as individuals with separate personalities, watching for weaknesses that might benefit her attempt to gain her freedom.

Blackhorse, indeed, was bossy and overly talkative, but could also listen well when it was someone else's turn. He seemed to have a good sense of humor, was quick to laugh when amused, and appeared especially fond of young No Feathers, who himself was quite a prankster and always ready to gamble, probably because he often won from the older men.

Scar wore a subtle air of ruthless power about him, and Carrie guessed he saw Blackhorse as a rival as well as a friend. Scar was also the most vain about his appearance, taking even greater pains than the others with his hair and ornaments. But it was he who had patiently worked at removing each and every one of the cactus spines she'd managed to walk onto barefooted. Blackhorse had started out at the task, but had given up halfway on her first foot—there were hundreds of the almost-invisible needles, and she flinched and jerked her foot so often that he abandoned her with a grunt of disgust, telling her, she was sure, to do it herself.

Then Scar had showed her the bone tweezers he used to pluck his facial hair; he seemed to be the only one of the four who had found it necessary to bring such an item on a raiding expedition. At first, she almost refused him. He frightened her more than the others; there was such a fierceness in his eyes, and his mouth looked to her more like a hatchet wound than a place for smiles to visit.

But she knew it would be extremely hard for her to find and remove all the spines herself, even if he let her use the tweezers, and it was much too painful to walk until they were extracted. So she had nodded to Scar, and he sat down and spent the next whole hour gently plucking one after another—never seeming annoyed when she lost her steely calm and yelped or flinched—while his friends gambled nearby, laughing or groaning according to their luck.

After watching Blackhorse and Buckskin together and studying their facial features more closely, Carrie felt convinced they were brothers.

Buckskin appeared to be the oldest of the four raiders and a bit more staid and dignified. He spoke little and tended to smile rather than laugh aloud. The horses and their care always seemed his first priority.

Carrie had come to realize that they'd divided up those horses in some way unknown to her, for the same men always hobbled and groomed the same horses, except as ownership changed among them. It seemed No Feathers had added several horses to his original share through his skill and good fortune while gambling.

He was most proud, of course, of the grullo. Daily he rubbed the smoky-blue coat with grass and combed at the long black mane and tail. He never passed the horse without touching its white-marked face and speaking as if to a lover.

Carrie found she was expected to care for Brandy—as if the mare were her horse alone—and she was careful to make sure the sorrel's feet were always free of stones and her coat was as gleaming as any of the others. She'd had the opportunity to ride several of the animals that now belonged to Blackhorse: Pearl and Kyota and Belle had been her father's and there was Luke Calvin's brown gelding, Baldy, and a skittish piebald that had almost thrown her when he was frightened by the sudden whisper of a rattlesnake's warning.

But there were others he never let her ride: his black Appaloosa, of course, and his swift black gelding, a surly-looking palomino, and a fine steeldust grey she was sure had come—like the grullo—from Hank Davis's Slash D Ranch.

Carrie's muscles had finally grown used to riding, and she hardly noticed when the soreness was completely gone. She still enjoyed being on horseback, but was bored with the monotony of the long ride. About the most exciting thing that happened was swimming the rivers that seemed to have no shallows for crossing.

At noon of the fourth day's travel, almost-dozing aboard the bay mare Belle, Carrie was shocked fully awake by the realization that she couldn't quite remember what Danny's face had looked like. The browned skin and curly hair she remembered, the prominent cheekbones and the eyes that laughed. But around those features there seemed a wavering mist. That little depression—almost a dimple—was it on the right side of his mouth or the left? And how did his lips look when they weren't smiling?

Carrie pushed away her feelings of shocked guilt. *It doesn't matter now, anyway,* she told herself. *He's past having his feelings hurt. Remembering him can't bring him back; it only uncovers the pain in your own heart, and pain can weaken you, make you vulnerable. It's best just to forget him.*

Better to think of Wesley and Papa and Emma, she decided. The sense of shock deepened when she realized that even those faces were touched with a sense of unreality. Almost as if they themselves—and her life with them—had only been part of a long dream. As if the only place she had ever been—and ever would be—was on the back of a horse jogging through a vast trackless wilderness in the company of savages who knew not a word of her language.

The thoughts left her shaken. *The sun must be addling my mind!* she thought. Of course she remembered her family! Of course they were real!

"I *must* escape!" she whispered aloud, and prayed silently, *Please, God. Deliver me an opportunity today. I promise I'll use it. Just give me a chance.*

That opportunity came after the midday stop. Carrie found herself back on Brandy and realized that Blackhorse had tied his lance on the packsaddle with his bow and arrows, so he was only armed with the short knife in his belt. He swung up on the mean-eyed palomino he had stolen after her capture. It was a rather heavy-legged and lazy gelding, and Carrie was sure Brandy could outrun it easily.

Just as her heart began to pound excitedly at her good fortune, she further realized the hackamore rope was still hanging to the ground, not attached to Blackhorse's palomino at all. She quickly leaned forward and captured the line, coiling all the extra length to tuck under her belt so it would be safely out of the way of Brandy's hooves when she began to run.

Blackhorse seemed to take an extra-long time to gaze about the area, checking that they left few, if any, traces of their camp and direction of departure. By the time he finally urged his palomino into motion, the band of horses and other riders were all well ahead of them. Carrie sat unmoving atop Brandy, giving her no cue to go, but the red mare readily followed the palomino, never considering her path should lie in the opposite direction from the others.

Carrie didn't stop her. Let them all fall into the lulling rhythm of their travel, she thought. Let them relax and allow their minds to wander, the captured horses ranging a little wider, making a less noticeable trail while they snatched bits of brush to munch on the move.

Carrie rode to Blackhorse's right and slightly behind, almost as close as if the horses were still tied together. She must be careful not to arouse his suspicions. It took every bit of her inner strength to make herself ride there beside him when she could be free. She clamped her teeth together until her jaws ached, and she felt damp and sticky under her arms, though she had long since become accustomed to traveling in the heat.

After an hour that seemed like three, Carrie slowly began to draw back on Brandy's rein, so that very gradually—perhaps a half-step every six—the sorrel mare began to fall behind.

Blackhorse seemed not to notice. In fact, could he possibly be dozing? His body was a bit slumped on the palomino, and his head seemed to be nodding with the rhythm.

Still Carrie did nothing rash. She merely continued to pull Brandy back. The mare didn't like it, protested a little by shaking her head and whuffing through her nostrils. She didn't seem eager to be left behind by her companions.

*Ho, Brandy,* Carrie thought, speaking to the mare inside her mind, as if Brandy could hear and understand. *Ho-o-o, now. Easy, girl. Oh, please don't whinny. It's all right. We're going home. Ho, now.*

The red mare continued to show her unease in the way she moved her body and kept her ears flicking forward, then back. But she'd been well-trained and so responded to Carrie's demand until at last she was not moving at all. The others, including Blackhorse, went on ahead, not seeming to notice her absence at all.

*Turn Brandy and run!* part of Carrie cried, but something held her back. She looked over her shoulder at the way they had come. She could barely find the tracks the horses had just made on the hard and rocky earth. Behind her stretched the miles of unmarked prairie. Four days' ride of it. How far back was the last waterhole? And could she find it? She had no canteen, no food. Wouldn't they know she would head for water?

And if she managed to find that one, what about the others? It had been a day and a half since they'd crossed a river. Could she really hope to find her way home? Since she left her homestead, she had not seen one sign of human life or habitation, not a landmark that wasn't a meandering creek or an almost-hidden pool of water.

Carrie sat on the impatient sorrel mare, weighing her chances. How long could she keep the two of them alive? How long before she found her way back home or died of thirst, lost and utterly alone? And there was another thought too, almost amusing: What about Indians? Kiowas and Cheyennes and Apaches and other bands of fierce Comanches? How would she fare with them? For whatever mysterious reason, she seemed to have some favored status with Blackhorse's band.

Carrie glanced ahead at the herd of horses and riders drawing farther and farther away. Before she could stop herself, the thought was there in her mind: *At least with them I'll have food and water and protection.*

Part of her found the thought cowardly but another voice assured her, *Being smart is worlds better than being brave. Being brave against long odds can get you dead. Right now being alive is more important than anything else, isn't it?* The last words echoed over and over in her mind: *Isn't it? Isn't it?*

"Yes," she said out loud and touched Brandy with her heels, pinning her eyes on Blackhorse's distant back instead of the endless miles of freedom behind her. The mare needed no more encouragement but broke gladly into a canter, taking Carrie moment by moment, closer to her captors.

*Turn and run!* her heart cried again, and her hands twitched on the hackamore rein, but she did nothing to stop or turn the mare.

Blackhorse, too, had fallen back from the others, but he didn't turn if he heard her quick approach. Could he really be that deeply asleep that he had neither noticed her absence nor heard her returning?

When Brandy fell in beside the palomino, Blackhorse sat suddenly upright, fully awake, his eyes searching out Carrie's. In his warm gaze, she read it all: there had been no carelessness on his part; it had been a test. But of what she wasn't quite sure.

*Perhaps,* she thought, *to see if I can tell the difference between smart and brave. To see if I could really understand how much I must depend on him.*

Blackhorse seemed well pleased. He spoke to her in a quiet way, swerved the palomino so that he was close enough to capture one of her braids in his hand. He held it a moment as they rode, tugged the woven red-gold and said something else to her. And smiled, warmly and honestly, as if she were a friend who had given him a gift.

*Don't be too kind to me,* she wanted to say, but he wouldn't understand her if she did speak aloud. *I don't want to like you. I want to hate you for the rest of my life. You killed Danny, and I'll never forgive you for that.* So many conflicting emotions rose up in her, threatening to tear her soul apart, that it took all her power to put them aside as she had her grief for Danny. Armed with her new steely calm, she stared at Blackhorse and thought, *Don't ever believe that you can trust me. If I ever see a chance to get away, I will.*

Carrie wondered if he could read all that in her eyes. Or perhaps he knew it without even looking, for he nodded to her, still smiling, then released her braid. He lifted his rein, and the palomino moved into a canter, eager himself to catch up to the other horses. Brandy followed as closely as if she were still tied.

Carrie, unbound and with the rein in her own hands, went with them.

# CHAPTER SEVEN: ARRIVING

Shortly before noon on the fifth day of traveling, they moved into a chain of hills higher than any Carrie had yet seen on her journey. An hour later, she noticed strange vertical clouds marking the blue sky ahead of them and decided they must be columns of smoke.

The four Comanches had been speaking together excitedly, and now they allowed the band to slow and stop. Scar kicked his pony into a run and disappeared in the direction of the smoke. He returned after a bit with obviously good news.

Could it be they had finally reached their destination? Carrie wondered hopefully. But instead of riding on as she expected, the four dismounted and told her to do the same. It certainly didn't make sense to her, but she had learned to do as she was told and wonder silently.

Chattering happily, the four transferred their buffalo pad saddles to their favorite mounts: the black Appaloosa, the buckskin, the grullo, and Scar's black-and-white pinto. Then Blackhorse caught Brandy and brought her to Carrie, telling her to change mares. Carrie took the hackamore from Pearl's head, shook the loops out until it was only a rope again, then deftly refashioned it into a hackamore around Brandy's white-blazed face.

Blackhorse nodded at her newfound skill, and moving close to her, took the dusty hat from her head and tugged loose the rawhide thongs that held her braids. She understood a few of his words, and certainly his meaning, and began to unbraid her hair. He went to the packhorse, returned with a canteen and the porcupine hairbrush. She drank first, then used some of the water to bathe her face. She traded the canteen for the hairbrush and began to work on her long, red hair.

Blackhorse watched her admiringly. It seemed he never tired of observing this task. But when she began to rebraid her hair, his hand came out to stop her, and he said "No" in the Comanche tongue. She reached for the hat, but he shook his head and tossed it aside. So she left her hair as it was, a fall of red-gold fire down her back, rippled with waves from being crimped into braids for so long. He inspected her closely from all sides and up and down, then grunted with satisfaction and walked away.

Carrie took the opportunity to sit down and rest herself in a position that wasn't on top of a horse, trying to figure out what they were up to. She watched the four of them comb out their straight black hair, adorn themselves with feathers, and finally, begin to paint themselves as if going into battle. Was she wrong? Was it not their home beyond the hills, but some hapless, isolated homestead about to be relieved of its livestock and, perhaps, its scalps?

As she sat watching them absorb themselves with their appearances, Carrie realized it wouldn't be so hard to escape right now, slip around them with Brandy, and if that were actually a white habitation….

Blackhorse pushed her shoulder—rather sharply, as if he had spoken to her before and not being answered, had become impatient. He looked quite fearsome once again decked out for the wartrail. His rawhide shield—painted with hoofprints and a design that looked like flames—was fastened at his left elbow, its lower edge aflutter with feathers and scalps. Above the red slashes of paint across his cheekbones, his eyes tried to pierce her secret thoughts.

Carrie leaped up obediently and swung herself—almost effortlessly now, after days of practice—onto Brandy's back. She reached down to take the hackamore rein from his hand. But he ignored the action, kept tight hold of the rein as he mounted his Appaloosa and nudged him into a run. Carrie grabbed quickly at Brandy's mane, steadied herself, and gave up wondering what was about to happen.

All four Comanches had transformed themselves while she had been lost in thought. They were painted now even more flamboyantly than when she'd first seen them, their bodies and their horses marked brightly with red and blue, black and yellow and white. Feathers bristled in their hair, and scalps fluttered from their reins and lances. Whooping and brandishing their weapons, they galloped their ponies straight toward the band of stolen horses, stampeding them the way Scar had gone, toward the smoke.

Carrie hung on to Brandy's mane as the horses ran, winding between the hills, and then poured out onto a flat, brushy plain sliced by a wide river and dotted with more than thirty tipis.

The sights and sounds and odors all seemed to hit Carrie at once in a hail of fragments, like a mirror shattering in her face: Smoke lifting lazily from cookfires. A large herd of horses on the riverbank, raising heads from grazing to whicker greetings and challenges. Bright symbols painted on the smoke-darkened tipi covers. Dogs racing close to yap at the new horses' heels. People of all ages running toward them—yelling, laughing, singing. Pole racks laden with strips of drying meat. Tautly stretched hides, pegged around the edges, like flesh-colored pools on the ground. The smells of smoke and sweat, cooking and animals, ripening hides and sun-baked earth.

Buckskin and Scar showed considerable skill in their handling of the stolen horses, managing to stampede them in two complete circles around the entire encampment before allowing them to slow and stop among the herd animals by the river, where they plunged chest-deep into the water, gulping down great quantities before turning hungrily upon the rich grasses.

Blackhorse—and so, Carrie too—pulled to a halt before the centermost tipi where stood an old man with the bearing of a chieftain. He was wrapped about in a blanket of brown fur so soft and sleek it must be made of otter pelts. His hair, liberally shot with iron-grey, hung in two braids also wrapped in otter fur. His old eyes were still very sharp and gave his sober face the regal bearing of a king surveying subjects who greatly depended upon him. With a solemn nod and welcoming gesture, he accepted the honor Blackhorse seemed to pay him.

The others—Buckskin, Scar and No Feathers—had joined them, and it seemed every person in the tribe must be crowding around them.

As the upturned faces pushed closer and brown hands reached out toward her legs and feet, Carrie felt suddenly terrified—hearing again Josh Ward's words: "Captives are usually treated pretty rough at the beginning." Remembering other tales she had heard of prisoners beaten, humiliated, tortured, seeing the hot eyes on all sides of her, reading their pain and outrage and frustration, she wanted to scream, "It wasn't me! I never harmed you!"

One in particular—a narrow-faced woman with a terrible scar across her left cheekbone—bared her teeth, snarling incomprehensible words as she stretched past the others to grab the calf of Carrie's leg and pinch savagely. Carrie yelped and twisted free of the biting fingers, readied herself to kick back in response to the assault, but Blackhorse's voice interrupted her action and the sudden roar of voices.

*"Kee!"* he declared—a word she knew well by now; it meant *No*—but she didn't recognize what he said next: *"Ketaka!"*

But the hands stopped reaching for her, faces turned toward him to hear his words. The cheekbone woman glared at Carrie before turning her attention to Blackhorse.

It was one of his shorter speeches and quietly told, but commanded the attention of all those listening. Even while her heart still beat wildly in her throat, Carrie saw the hostility begin to ebb in most of the faces around her, slowly replaced by curiosity and other emotions more difficult to read. The cheekbone woman snorted in disgust and moved to the edge of the crowd, where she continued to glare menacingly. But it was easier for Carrie to ignore her there, turning her attention to the crowd in general. There were many more women than men, and Carrie wondered if any of these were wives of Blackhorse. Which of these naked, curious children might be his?

At first the Comanche people seemed much alike to her—most of only medium height and somewhat stocky. The men wore little more than moccasins and breechcloths—though some had fringed buckskin leggings, like pant legs tied to their belts at the hips—so it was easy to see that most of them were rather bandy-legged. Hadn't Josh Ward said Comanche children began a life on horseback before they could walk? She herself had noticed over the past few days how her captors seemed almost two different beings when mounted and when afoot. Once on horseback, they attained a sense of grace and power even beyond what Indians must have seen when they first viewed the Spanish conquistadors and thought them like gods—half man, half horse.

The women and older girls were clothed in deeply fringed buckskin dresses with leggings on underneath, some attached to the moccasins, like tall boots. Most of these clothes were decorated with pretty patterns of beads whose bright colors glittered in the sunlight. After observing the attention her captors paid their appearance, it was surprising to find some of the women rather grubby and disheveled. Nearly all had painted decorations on their faces; some wore red paint behind or in front of their ears. Few wore their hair past their shoulders; mainly it was cropped and let hang undecorated but for red paint along the parting. The men tended to be tidier and cleaner-looking, with hair worn long and beautifully groomed.

Carrie sat tall and proud on Brandy, trying not to let anxiety show as she met the gazes focused on her. What was Blackhorse telling them? she wondered. Was he saying she belonged to him? Was he saying she was to be his wife?

Perhaps. Some of the women seemed to gaze at her with a new curiosity and, maybe, a bit of envy. Wouldn't a youth as brave and attractive as Blackhorse be a coveted prize for any young woman? Even if he already had a wife or two, might not his newly stolen horse-wealth allow him to take another? Perhaps some of these women—especially those who'd obviously taken pains with their appearance—had been awaiting his return with hopeful expectation. Carrie let her gaze touch the cheekbone woman, wondering if this might underlie her particular venom.

Then Carrie noticed there was one maiden, at least, not interested in her or Blackhorse. This slender, soft-eyed girl with red crescent moons painted on her cheeks, gazed fixedly at someone or something behind and to one side of Carrie. Curious herself now, Carrie glanced over her shoulder to see No Feathers there, sitting straight and proud on the new grullo he had stolen, returning the girl's gaze as if they were alone in all the world.

Just as a painting can sometimes tell a whole story in one frozen scene, Carrie found an impression in her mind: A young warrior without wealth or honors—and so unable to marry the girl of his choosing—returned now from a successful raid with ponies and honors and promises in his eyes.

It was a pleasingly romantic thought, but quickly interrupted by the crowd's exuberant response to Blackhorse's story. Before she could even wonder what would happen next, Blackhorse had slid from the Appaloosa and was pulling her down off Brandy's back.

Her bare feet—still tender from their encounter with the cactus spines—cringed on the hot, hard earth, but she was forced to walk a few steps before Blackhorse stopped in front of a young woman standing beside the girl with red moons on her cheeks. His wife? Carrie wondered. But when he spoke, it sounded very formal, not like a man to his spouse.

The woman nodded, taking Carrie's elbow, and led her gently toward one of the tipis. Carrie saw this woman was a little taller than most of the others and her facial features not so broad, as if she might be of blood not entirely Comanche.

She stooped and motioned Carrie under the tipi flap and into the dimness beyond. Carrie sat as she was instructed, waiting for her eyes to adjust after days in the glaring sunlight and to the slight smokiness of the air. Slowly the room came into focus for her. The first impression was surprise at how large the circular space was—nearly fifteen feet across, Carrie guessed. The floor seemed to be clean river sand, swept smooth and carpeted most everywhere with well-worn animal skins and a scattering of fragrant plants. In the center a small pit was dug quite deeply into the earth, and from it rose a tiny curl of smoke, showing the fire was carefully banked and smoldering.

Though most of the objects around her were unknown and unidentifiable, the whole room seemed to have an air of tidy efficiency. She noted the careful stack of firewood, the trunk-like storage containers of decorated rawhide. Certainly those must be beds—those two elevated areas covered with buffalo robes and smaller, softer-looking animal skins.

The whole room smelled pleasantly of woodsmoke and herbs. Carrie saw more drying plants pinned about on the supporting lodgepoles amid hanging utensils made of wood and horn, bone and turtle shells. A sort of inner drape—also attached to each pole—encircled the room and was brightly painted with what looked like picture stories.

The woman went to one of the rawhide trunks and searched for a moment, gathered some items and brought them to Carrie: a buckskin dress and leggings, a long rectangle of blue cloth, a length of cord, a pair of moccasins. Despite the lush fringes and beading, the dress appeared rather worn, though still serviceable. The almost-new moccasins were brightly beaded in the same dark blue, light blue and white design that ran in a narrow but exquisite strip both across the upper chest and shoulders and around the skirt a little below the knees. Like others she had seen in the crowd, the dress's bottommost part was dyed yellow.

The other woman knelt near the door, sat back on her heels waiting for Carrie to change clothes. Carrie hated to give up the trousers for a dress again. Riding was so much easier in pants, and she hoped soon to be riding away from this place—wherever it might be.

Since no undergarments had been provided, Carrie removed her borrowed shirt and pulled the buckskin dress on over her camisole. Then it dawned on her that the blue material must be a breechcloth, but she wasn't sure how to put it on even if the thought appealed to her—which it didn't. She slipped out of the trousers from underneath the skirt and left the breechcloth where it lay, keeping the underwear she was used to and hoping that action wouldn't be seen as defiance.

But all this seemed to quite amuse the Comanche woman—though she took great pains to hide it, as if she didn't wish to be considered rude. Remembering the momentary fierceness she had seen in the faces around her—and remembering other tales from Josh Ward—Carrie thanked God she had been, at least temporarily, entrusted into the care of such a gentle-seeming spirit. What if she had been given to the cheekbone woman? Carrie shivered.

When she held up the leggings—which were strangely short, like the bottom halves of pant legs—and looked bewildered, the woman showed her how to tie them just above her knees with leather thongs. Picking up the moccasins, Carrie decided the design, though geometric, reminded her of stars. *Shoes at last!* she thought, brushing the last grains of sand from her bare and sensitive feet. When she slipped into the moccasins, she found they fit as if made for her, and were even more comfortable than she'd hoped they would be.

Carrie smiled, and the woman—who had risen to stand beside her—warmly returned the smile, then reached tentatively and shyly to touch Carrie's long red hair. The woman spoke softly and with wonder in her voice. Carrie understood many of the words, but did not know how to answer, so could only continue to smile at her.

The woman stooped again to the floor, traced a small design in the swept sand, glanced back up at her. Carrie bent to see it better: very clearly a long-legged bird up to its knees in wavy lines of water—a wading bird.

Touching her chest, the woman spoke her name. Carrie nodded, repeating the Comanche syllables while thinking, Wading Bird.

"Car-rie," she said slowly, pointing to her own chest, "Mc-Eee-dan."

But Wading Bird shook her head, repeated the syllables Blackhorse had said the first day by the pool—"*Wehanaibi*"—what she had come to recognize as her name. Perhaps the woman could read some of Carrie's uncertainty, for she quickly drew another figure in the sand. A person with a triangle to symbolize a skirt, it was obviously female. Then, instead of hair, waving flame shapes rose from the head and out from the body. Like, Carrie mused, a woman burning or a girl on fire.

Wading Bird once again repeated those syllables, her tone encouraging Carrie to say them too. She did. Pronounced, for the first time, her Comanche name: "*WAY-hah-nye-vee.*" The other woman smiled and led the way from the tipi.

Outside, the sun assaulted Carrie's eyes, and she stood blinking. Blackhorse and the other three were nowhere to be seen, but all around the camp, people bustled about as if great preparations of some kind were underway.

Buckskin walked over to them, carrying some things Carrie recognized from the packsaddle, and handed them to Wading Bird. Watching them closely, hearing their tones as they spoke together, Carrie realized they must be husband and wife—though they seemed to be taking great pains to avoid any open display of affection. But it was clear they were pleased to see each other.

So, Carrie mused, if she was right about it all and Buckskin *was* Blackhorse's brother, then Wading Bird must be his sister-in-law. Josh Ward said Comanche brothers often shared their wives. That set Carrie's mind to wondering about Wading Bird and Blackhorse. She couldn't help it.

Buckskin ducked inside his tipi, appeared again after a brief moment, hands full of new arrows, which he added to the quiver slung with his hunting bow across his back. He walked quickly away toward the horse herd where a few other men—Blackhorse among them—were catching up fresh horses. They rode east, splashing across the river shallows in a cloud of spray, disappearing into a small canyon some distance away.

Wading Bird led Carrie to another tipi very near her own. This second lodge was decorated with bold paintings of running horses. One of them, a black Appaloosa, bore a rider who seemed to be driving the others ahead of him. Because of this—and painted hoofprints like those on Blackhorse's shield—Carrie was certain it was his tipi, and it appeared he had already gained great honor as a horse thief.

Carrie lingered, gazing up at the figures painted on the weathered buffalo hide. They were carefully done, colored mostly with red and black between a slanted black area at the top and a wide red border at the bottom, but there were touches of other colors too: green and yellow, blue and brown. Wading Bird waited beside Carrie, watching her with both patience and curiosity.

What held Carrie's attention were the symbols above the head of the Appaloosa rider. She was sure they must be a pictograph of the tipi owner's name—Blackhorse's real Comanche name. Carrie gazed at them a long moment, trying to read their meaning: the head of a reclining man—eyes closed—with a wavy line rising out of the forehead and ending in marks like those on his shield which she thought were flames. What could it mean?

Wading Bird touched her arm, and Carrie bent to enter the tipi. Inside, it looked much like the other lodge. In fact, the same air of tidiness and orderly arrangement seemed to prove that Wading Bird had been caring for this home as well.

There were fewer possessions here: only one narrow bed, it seemed. Had he no wife? Had he never? Carrie very much wanted to ask Wading Bird, but she couldn't think of any way to make herself understood. Anyway, the other woman seemed to have forgotten her, busying herself with making sure everything was placed as it should be.

Carrie thought the air seemed stuffy—as if the place had not been used for a long while—and even the once-fragrant plants hanging here and there smelled dead and dry.

Wading Bird signaled for her to wait there and slipped back out of the doorway, leaving Carrie, as usual, with many questions in her mind. Only a short moment later, she could feel the air begin to stir and new light crept into the room. Quite curious now, Carrie went closer to the down-slanting wall. She saw the lower five foot section was, as in the other tipi, an inner drape attached along its top edge to each of the lodge poles. It, too, was lavishly illustrated and, in Carrie's mind at least, by a more skillful and artistic hand than the other. The bottom edge of this curtain tucked neatly under the animal skins scattered on the floor. Peering over the top of the drape, Carrie could watch Wading Bird raise and prop the bottom edge of the outer tipi skin so that moving air flowed upward and inside the room in a way that wouldn't cause a draft on anyone sitting or sleeping near the ground.

When Wading Bird returned, she carried a thick wooden bowl with hot coals in it and a handful of buffalo chips. She smiled at Carrie, signaled for her to come close and watch. Carrie did, saw how to nurture the coals into small flames in the central firepit. Then the other woman stripped the walls of the dry plants, which she fed to the flames, releasing a new perfume in the round room.

Carrie continued to glance around, wondering about the man who lived there. Wading Bird watched her and, catching her eye, cocked her head to one side, as if questioning. Carrie searched back through the long hours of Josh Ward's recollections. He was very proud of his ability to communicate with almost any Plains Indian through sign language. Wesley had been especially interested in that, and Josh had demonstrated several signs on different occasions. Had "wife" been one of them?

Carrie couldn't recall if it had, but she did remember the sign for "woman," and she made that gesture now by curving her open hands and pulling them from the top of her head to her shoulders, like combing hair.

Wading Bird's face lit up with both recognition and amusement. *"Ikuse,"* she said, pointing to Carrie with her right thumb.

*Me?* Carrie thought. *So I am Blackhorse's woman.* She remembered Josh saying there was no real marriage ceremony among the Comanches. When the union was agreed upon by the families involved and gifts had been given, the two simply moved into the same tipi, and that was that. There might be dress-up clothing and a feast or celebration, but it was not the romantic picture she had envisioned with Danny: leaving the little wooden church in her mama's white-lace dress with her arms full of flowers and the bell ringing.

So was tonight to be her wedding night? Would Blackhorse try to make her his wife here in this room, on those buffalo robes in the herb-scented darkness?

Carrie tried to still the panic rising up in her. What would he do when she resisted? How could she get away? *Perhaps,* she thought, *I should try to escape tonight after all. Even if I don't have the slightest idea where I am or which direction to go. As soon as it gets dark, I'll find a way.*

She became aware that Wading Bird was speaking to her, using both Comanche words and sign language. Much was lost to Carrie, but she truly felt she understood some of it and tried to fill the gaps in between.

That sign was "woman" and surely that could only be "baby." Perhaps Blackhorse *did* have a wife and a small child, but where? That sign—a finger drawn across the forehead like a hatbrim—meant "white man," and the next gestures were so graphic that they unmistakably meant violent death.

Seeing the pain and anger in Wading Bird's dark eyes, Carrie wondered if people of her own supposedly civilized race really *had* murdered Blackhorse's wife and infant with such brutality? Or had she misinterpreted certain details—or the whole story entirely?

Tears sprang into her eyes. Perhaps because of the story she'd just been told. Perhaps because she'd begun to wonder again, *How am I to survive this? I can't even talk to them. I could say or do the wrong thing at any moment and pay my life for it.*

Whatever they were for, Carrie's tears brought a softening to Wading Bird's face, and she motioned for Carrie to come and help her. Together they took the robes from the bed—under them Carrie saw a kind of mat made of painted willow slats supported on a low pole structure—and took them outside to shake and air. When they finally left the tipi a little later, the fire was well-banked and the bedding returned to its place, ready for whomever would sleep there that night.

The hunters returned with good luck and bad. They'd killed two deer and an antelope, but Buckskin was injured, and his chestnut horse was limping. Scar had to help Wading Bird's husband into the tipi, and she looked very worried as she followed. Someone must have called for the medicine man, as he arrived a few moments later—wearing a buffalo horn headdress—and disappeared inside.

Carrie was forgotten, it seemed, standing uncertainly outside the lodge, wondering if the horse had fallen on Buckskin and how serious his injuries might be.

Then she became aware that Blackhorse was staring at her, sitting on a trim roan pony with a dead antelope lying across his thighs. Watching his eyes on her as they noted the buckskin clothes, lingered on the starry pattern of beading across her shoulders, around her skirt, and on the new moccasins, she suddenly felt sure these things had belonged to his wife. She tried to read his eyes, but she couldn't.

He spoke then and hefted the antelope carcass so that it slid from the horse and dropped at her feet. Then she realized he wasn't speaking to her but to someone behind her. Glancing back, she saw the girl with the red moons on her cheeks. The girl's eyes were cast down, and her voice respectful when she answered Blackhorse.

He took a last, long look at Carrie—perhaps he, too, was wondering what would happen that night—then he turned his roan and cantered it away toward the pony herd.

# CHAPTER EIGHT: CELEBRATING

As Carrie watched, Red Moon Girl pulled a knife from her belt, held it up, and told Carrie, *"Nahuu."* When Carrie had repeated, *"Nahuu"* —carefully drawing out the last vowel—Red Moon Girl pointed to the antelope and said, *"Kwahare."* Even before Carrie finished saying that word, the other girl had begun to work on the animal with the knife. It was a bloody business —worse than the rabbits—but, steeling herself, Carrie watched how it was done and helped when Red Moon Girl showed her what to do.

As they worked, a few camp dogs crowded around hopefully, wet-mouthed and grinning. And all the while, Carrie could hear the sounds of the medicine man at work: singing, gourd-rattling, muffled footfalls that might be dancing. Carrie realized suddenly that she, too, was praying for Buckskin, saying inside herself, *Please, God, let his injuries be minor and easily mended.*

*Praying for an Indian?* one voice cried.

*Why not?* another part of her countered. He had never harmed her—not even when he'd suspected she was trying to escape. And besides, Carrie didn't want to see that terrible sadness return to Wading Bird's eyes.

When they had finished cutting up the antelope meat, Red Moon Girl cleaned and sheathed her knife and gathered a few items, including the freshly removed antelope hide. A few paces to one side of the tipi, she began to stake the skin out on the ground—hair-side down—stretching it and pounding pegs around the edges with a stone hammer. Then she showed Carrie how to use a stone-and-bone tool—shaped something like an elbow—to remove the bits of meat still clinging to the skin.

Using another of the elbow-shaped hide scrapers—Red Moon Girl called it a *toʔtsimuhpe*—Carrie copied what the other young woman did, feeling the pull of new muscles in her own arms and back. Carrie worked well, but even so, when she finished, Red Moon Girl showed her several spots that needed more attention. As they were unpegging the finished hide, they heard the tipi flap open and turned to see Wading Bird step from the opening. Even before the woman spoke, Carrie began to breathe again, seeing the smiling relief on Wading Bird's face.

Red Moon Girl sprang up happily, as if to embrace the other woman, but only spoke warmly instead. Surely they were sisters, Carrie thought. Didn't Comanches often take sisters as wives? Hadn't there been two beds in Buckskin's tipi? Was Red Moon Girl—who seemed no older than Carrie—also his wife? And if she was, why was she so obviously in love with No Feathers? Carrie sighed in frustration, thinking how she had always taken for granted the opportunity to ask questions and get answers.

She helped the two women—yes, they must be sisters, she decided—carry the freshly cut meat to an area on one side of the camp where other women were already working. Thankfully, the cheekbone woman was not among them.

The sun had set behind the tipis when the women began to roast the meat. Each great chunk and section of ribs was skewered on the end of a long stick, then that pointed end was suspended by a leather thong from the top of a pole tripod over a hot fire. The butt of the stick trailed in the dirt, providing a ready handle to help in turning the meat and in keeping the thong damp so it didn't dry out, burn through, and dump the sizzling meat into the fire.

The women chattered together companionably as they attended to these tasks, and Carrie felt that she was being included in the conversations, though she could understand little of what was said, much less participate. They were pleasant to her, but she was well aware they watched her every move. They needed to make sure she tended the meat correctly, and it was quite natural that they would be intrigued by the look of her fair skin and fiery hair. But beyond all that, she was watched too closely to even contemplate escape.

Dusk drew around the camp like a heavy buffalo robe, and Blackhorse's people gathered together at a large flat area near the fires. The cheekbone woman arrived with another woman and an older man, but she now took great pains to ignore Carrie. Drums began and singing. It seemed wild and alien in Carrie's ears, and yet it was exciting too, caused her heart to beat faster, pulsing her blood through her veins. For the steady underlying drumbeat was like nothing more than the beating of a massive heart.

Then the dances began; first men only—the firelight glinting on paint and feathers and other ornaments—and then the women, the two lines forming separate circles, dancing and singing apart yet together. Some of the sounds were so eerie they lifted the hairs on Carrie's arms.

In the center of the dance area stood a cottonwood pole, and Carrie tried not to dwell on the knowledge that the decorations fluttering from it were the scalps her captors took on this last bold raid. But when Blackhorse pulled her to the center of the circle, pushed her to a sitting position and bound her to the pole, she remembered all Josh Ward had said about that scalp dance, where "the beating of captives got a little out of hand" and one of the women died. Would Blackhorse let her be beaten now? Had he only been saving her for this ceremony? Had all those friendly women been simply lulling her with a last kindness, like a condemned man's last meal or fattening a prize calf before the slaughter?

Carrie watched breathlessly as, one by one, her captors came into the open area to dance alone. As the leader, Blackhorse danced first—and well. In fact, Carrie found his movements quite beautiful to watch—almost mystical, as if the spirit of all Dance moved through him. She had never seen a man—or anyone—dance with such energy and grace and joy. She sat enthralled...until she suddenly realized he was acting out his exploits on the raiding expedition. The scalps flickered like black flames in a sudden gust of breeze, and the long, blond hair Blackhorse had taken seemed to glow softly in the shifting firelight as he pantomimed how he had acquired it. She could recognize, too, the parts of the story about her capture and how she had wounded him with her foot. When he finished, he stared at her a long moment and then went to sit at the edge of the circle.

Scar danced next, garishly painted and with heavy silver ornaments swinging from his earlobes. His face and body showed in every line how he had enjoyed taking revenge on his enemies, and Carrie had to look away before he finished. It was then that a young woman with a weasel tail tied in her hair—perhaps his wife?—rose from the crowd and sang alone, as if adding further praise of her brave husband.

Buckskin, Carrie saw, was propped up against a backrest of willow slats. Though apparently well enough to attend the celebration, he was unable to dance his exploits, so Blackhorse did it for him. And when he was finished, Wading Bird's high, sweet voice added further praise.

At last it was time for No Feathers—though now he wore three painted feathers in his hair. He seemed so young and exuberant as he acted out the shooting of a settler and later, the theft of the smoke-blue horse. At first, when he finished, no voice lifted to say more—perhaps he had no one in the camp to praise him further. But then Red Moon Girl rose like a flower unfolding and began to sing. Her voice was not as lovely nor as true as Wading Bird's, but it moved Carrie more, the sound was so full of love and pride.

Feeling eyes on her, she turned to see Blackhorse watching her, his eyes unreadable; but Carrie thought perhaps he was thinking that there had been no one to sing for him. When the dancing was finished, Wading Bird came and released Carrie, smiling easily as if to show that her being bound again as a captive had only been for the sake of ritual. At least Carrie hoped that was what it meant.

The feast began. When the men had been served, the women and children ate, and Carrie was given some of the delicious antelope meat, roasted venison, fresh blackberries, and some cooked roots very like potatoes.

The feasting and noise lasted all night. Carrie sat, past exhaustion, almost past caring what would happen when it was time for her to go home with the man that she belonged to.

There had been no possibility of escape at any time. Always, it seemed, one of them was near her and watchful. When she left to go to what she thought of as the "privy place"—wondering how quickly she could run to the horse herd and catch Brandy—she found Wading Bird walking beside her, relaxed and smiling. Carrie couldn't quite believe it was coincidence.

Just before dawn the celebration ended, and the Comanche people began to scatter to their lodges, calling farewells, tossing scraps to the lurking dogs, carrying children who had long since fallen asleep.

A shadow fell across Carrie, and she glanced up to see Blackhorse standing over her, tall and dark and menacing as a column of smoke rising above a burnt-out cabin. The dying firelight rippled across the flesh of his bare torso as he reached down to take her arm. She avoided his eyes and stared instead at his throat where Danny's ring lay among the bits of bone and claw and bright beads.

Her heart beat wildly in her own throat, and she had to will herself to breathe, felt herself being lifted to her feet by one arm. All around them, people were laughing and talking, moving toward their homes and waiting beds. But Carrie could only gaze into Blackhorse's hot eyes and pray silently, *Please, God—*

A sudden voice called out—apparently for silence, for it seemed every noise in the camp ceased—and then Carrie, too, could hear the sound of horses whickering down by the river and the small thunder of galloping hooves, the camp dogs barking.

When the horse and rider slid to a plunging halt not far from her, Carrie realized the old chief in the brown otter robe hadn't left the area, and it was he whom the rider was seeking. Blackhorse moved quickly toward them, pulling Carrie along by one arm, almost as if he had forgotten he was holding her.

The young rider was wounded, but not seriously; his bay horse was so marked with lather it might've been mistaken for a pinto. The rider's words were too quick and excited for Carrie to catch any but one. That word, repeated more than once, sounded like *Kwana,* and Carrie thought immediately of the church picnic conversations about Quanah, half-white warchief, son of captive Cynthia Ann Parker. Chiding herself for what was probably only a wild leap of intuition, Carrie still wondered, *What about this Quanah?*

Blackhorse spoke to the old chief and was answered. People seemed to be hurrying now, spreading some news, and men who had already retired to their tipis were coming back out, moving toward the chief's lodge in the center of the camp. Someone took the rider's horse, and the youth was given a huge portion of leftover venison by one of the women extinguishing the fires.

Blackhorse fairly dragged Carrie to Buckskin's tipi, entrusting her once again to Wading Bird and Red Moon Girl. It seemed that every man in camp was on his way to the chief's tipi, including Buckskin, who had to be carried by two of his friends.

The three women sat waiting—untalking and almost unmoving—in the tipi. Carrie was so tired that several times she dozed off and woke with a start to find the others staring at her reproachfully, though she wasn't quite sure why they did so.

It seemed a very long time before they heard the men's voices calling out. The two Comanche women stared at each other a moment as if saying many things without speaking. Then Red Moon Girl rose silently and left the tipi. Shortly after that, two men brought Buckskin inside and put him on his bed. He was excited and angry, and he talked quite a lot to Wading Bird, but still Carrie understood little more than "Quanah."

But she thought Wading Bird's eyes and manner seemed relieved as she fussed with Buckskin's robes and with the fire. Not so Red Moon Girl when she returned, looking somehow disappointed and sad. She left again shortly, after saying a few brief words to her sister and grabbing up a buffalo robe, which she wrapped about herself as if the new summer morning weren't warm enough for her.

Already exhausted, Carrie felt a stab of irritation that she didn't understand the apparently important situation she was in. What was going on and how would it affect her?

And what was the meaning of *mahimiʔarʉ* and *nabitʉkʉrʉ* and *taibooʔnʉʉ*—words she'd heard more than once. She wondered especially about the latter, since Buckskin's eyes had often touched on her when he spoke those syllables. But it hardly seemed the time to assert herself and try to find out more.

Blackhorse did not return to the tipi for her, and Wading Bird allowed her to sleep for a few hours before sending her to Blackhorse's lodge with what seemed food enough for a dozen men.

She entered nervously, wondering what would happen now. Inside there were several men, including Scar and No Feathers, and Blackhorse sat cross-legged and proud with a long, elaborately carved pipe in his hands. His eyes on her were stony and cold, and he told her almost immediately to go back: "*Pitsa mia!*"

She set the bowls of food on the ground and fled, almost bumping into a warrior just entering the tipi. She returned to Wading Bird, who set her to work shelling pecans. She knelt outside Buckskin's lodge, using a rock to break the shells, and she kept a curious watch on the nearby tipi of

Blackhorse. She could hear little from within, but did smile to herself once as she could hear his voice going on and on and on in the way that he sometimes did, and she imagined those other men waiting politely for him to finally finish.

After a time, all the visitors left and went in separate directions. Blackhorse remained inside and for a while, his lodge was silent. Then drumming began, and Carrie heard Blackhorse's voice lift in what might be warsongs. The singing and drumming went on all afternoon. During that time, the other men returned—painted and ornamented for battle—and joined Blackhorse in his medicine-making.

When she'd separated all the pecan meats from their shells, Carrie was put to work helping Wading Bird prepare a great stew. Buckskin's wife had no real kettle but hung a buffalo paunch from a structure of four poles tied together at the top —much like the tripods used for roasting. Into this gut kettle, Carrie poured bags and bags of water she had to tote from one of the springs flowing into the river. Meanwhile, Wading Bird had heated smooth, fist-sized stones in a very hot fire. When she told Carrie the pot was full enough, they used forked sticks to pull the stones from the fire and lift them into the water. It was soon boiling and they dropped in chunks of raw meat, the potato-like roots called *sʉhʉtsina,* and many *kʉʉkanʉʉ*...wild onions. Wading Bird seasoned the stew with pinches of this and that from small buckskin bags, and Carrie stirred it with a buffalo rib bone.

Carrie thought the stew was the best she'd ever tasted—better even than Maysie Ward's—and she ate quite a lot of it, sitting in silence with Wading Bird, who had, of course, served Buckskin first.

As the sun was lowering itself toward the edge of the world, Carrie took the dishes they had used to the river to rub them with sand and rinse them. Since Wading Bird had stayed with Buckskin, Carrie hoped she would be able to just slip away. But there were other women on the riverbank attending to the same chore. Pretending to be even clumsier than she felt at this new task, she was still scouring when the other women bade her farewell and headed back to their homes. Elated, Carrie thought, *As soon as they're far enough away, I'll ford the river here and....*

Then she saw Blackhorse and the others coming toward her, and her breath caught at the terrible fierceness she saw in them. But it was the horse herd, not her, that they were after. They each caught up several horses and led them back to camp, though Scar seemed to be lagging to make sure she returned. Curious and excited—and unable to slip away from Scar's scrutiny anyway—Carrie hurried back to see what was going on in the camp.

The men quickly painted their favorite horses and hobbled the others near their tipis. It was the Appaloosa that Blackhorse marked with red lightning marks on its legs and a circle of red around one eye. The other horses he had chosen stood quiet beside his lodge: a claybank dun and a dark chestnut with a flaxen mane and tail.

When the black Appaloosa was fully decorated, his owner mounted and rode through the village. Soon the other men rode single-file behind him, singing warsongs and apparently encouraging others to join them. They went four times through the camp, and it seemed all the other people—men, women, children—came out to watch them, joining in the singing.

When it was fully dark, the people once again gathered for a night of singing and dancing round a fire. They did not make a complete circle but left a part open toward the southwest.

Occasionally, the drums stopped and older warriors would rise and talk at length—apparently recounting past deeds of their own—and were applauded with whoops and stomping, and rattling of gourds. Then the dancing and singing would begin again.

Carrie sat, exhausted and mesmerized. In some ways it seemed strange for people to be celebrating warfare in such a joyous, festive, spiritual manner. But if she had learned only one thing from Josh Ward, it would have been that warring and raiding were the most important part of Comanche men's lives, and the whole society revolved around that. Josh had been one of the earliest white captives, taken even before Cynthia Ann Parker, and his master had been a great one for telling tales of glorious days long past, so Josh knew more than most whites about how things had been before there was a Texas.

Wesley was always pestering Josh for stories, and like most any young man, he was enthralled by tales of fighting and brave deeds. "Used to be," Josh had explained to Wes one day, "war was really more a game than anything else. And the rules were different. For one thing, most Indians don't take personal property very seriously. Like horses for example. You have a lot of 'em, that shows the world you're a brave and clever warrior, and if you wanta marry some woman, you can give her family a bunch to prove what a good catch you are. But horses're really more like a way of keepin' score than what we'd call property.

"Say you've got a bunch of ponies. Some Apaches come raidin' and steal them. Well, those ponies just belong to the Apaches then, and—unless there was some personal injury to avenge or some 'specially prized horse you really wanted back—you'd probably just as likely replace those ponies by raidin' someone else. And then *those* would be your ponies...till someone took 'em from you. And when that happened, they wouldn't be committing a crime; they'd just be beating you at the game. See?"

Wes had laughed. "We Texans don't quite see it that way." They were out on the porch, and Josh was supposed to be showing Wes how to repair some broken leather harness. Inside the soddy, in a chair situated to catch the light and breeze coming through the door, Carrie had smiled down at her mending as Wes distracted Josh into something more interesting than leatherwork. Always fascinated by glimpses into other cultures and other times, Carrie waited eagerly to hear more.

"I know," Josh continued. "It never works when the players in a game are usin' different rules. You can see that even more clearly when it comes to war itself. For Comanche men, war used to be a combination of fun and what you could call religious ritual, I guess."

He had his audience, and he was never one to pass up such an opportunity. "Long, *long* ago—before the horse, when they had to hunt on foot—they probably got their fill of danger just tryin' to keep their families fed and protected. But they took to the horse so quick and so expertly that pretty soon huntin' was just too easy to be challengin'. An' they could also move farther and faster, so different bands started rubbin' up against each other—vyin' for the best hunting grounds. Like I say, it all worked while it was just Indians. They knew and respected the rules. So what you had was bunches of young men testin' and demonstratin' the power of their own personal medicine. The greater the risk that you take and survive, the greater your power must be, and each time you face death, that power's increased."

Wes interrupted him. "Wait a minute. You make it sound like just a sport. Like no one got hurt."

"No, not exactly. Sometimes things got personal—like if a warrior was after revenge for a lost friend or relative—and it could get brutal. But otherwise they weren't tryin' very hard to kill each other, and there was no real prestige in dyin' —hell, if you died in a battle, it just showed that your medicine had failed you. Warriors wanted to show off...risk their lives in spectacular ways, tryin' to step as close to death as possible but live to tell the tale." He gave a short bark of laughter. "And they'd tell it over and over and over, believe me! So anyway, what you had was a kind of warfare where plenty of horses and *things* changed hands frequently—and there were lotsa wounds and scars to brag about—but not many people died."

"It's different now," Wes said grimly.

The old porch chair creaked as Josh leaned back. "White men don't know how to play the game. They don't understand the concept that while you're usin' land—huntin' or campin' on it —it can be yours, but it isn't property that can be owned. It belongs to itself—like animals do—and it provides the necessities to live day-to-day. Everyone just takes what's needed, and it all balances out in the end." After a rueful chuckle he said, "Whites don't understand that, and they sure don't understand about their livestock. When they own something, they think it belongs to 'em until *they* dispose of it. Anyone who takes it is a thief and a criminal needin' to be punished. And of course, the more personal the loss—like scalps and captives—the more outrageous the crime."

The captive Carrie, watching now Blackhorse's preparations to go to war against her people, remembered the rest of Josh's words. How matter-of-factly he had summed up the bitter escalation as Texans sent their Rangers and later, federal soldiers, to punish what they saw as depredations.

Usually, since the real culprits were long-gone, these actions were carried out upon bands who were blameless—for at least those particular raids—and often against the very ones who'd tried to make some kind of peaceful settlement and—trusting the word of the treaties they'd signed—were completely vulnerable. Such injustices precipitated Comanche vengeance upon the handiest and least protected whites, who were probably as innocent as those whose deaths were being avenged. The savagery, too, had escalated on both sides—though usually one only heard about Comanche atrocities. Eventually even the whites who had earlier sought resolution saw peace as hopeless and only wanted the Comanches removed in any way necessary. And the U.S. government was ready to oblige, its forces prepared to kill anyone who dared resist them.

*They can't win,* Carrie thought of Quanah and Blackhorse and the others they were leading. *Not if they insist on fighting in the old ways.* To deliberately face soldiers' weaponry and deadly intent with tests of their personal bravery seemed clearly and foolishly suicidal. Perhaps this particular raiding expedition would succeed...and even the next. But eventually the warriors would be overrun by the sheer numbers and firepower of the whites. Like a lone buffalo bull on the railroad tracks, defiantly standing his ground while a huge locomotive hurtled toward him.

Yet, unaware of destiny hurtling toward it, the Comanche camp continued its preparations with joy and hope. Perhaps two hours after midnight, Blackhorse made a great, long speech which was enthusiastically followed by more dancing. A few moments later, Carrie realized Blackhorse had disappeared. Then she saw other warriors—one by one—slipping away. She became even more curious when she saw Red Moon Girl slide away into the night only a few moments after No Feathers left the crowd.

Carrie, too, moved away from the dance; she was very tired of it after two whole nights, and she felt jangled by the constant noise and hours of sleep she had missed.

So it was that she saw Red Moon Girl go into the tipi where the grullo was tied beside a cream-colored gelding and a roan. Smiling to herself, Carrie turned toward Blackhorse's lodge and saw him emerge, carrying several things. She watched as he cinched the buffalo pad saddle on the back of the claybank dun and looped a rein around its lower jaw. Even with his shield, bow, quiver of arrows and other articles slung about his body, even with the feathered lance in one hand, he seemed to swing effortlessly aboard the dun. As he turned away from the tipi, taking the now-unhobbled chestnut and the black Appaloosa, his gaze fell on Carrie.

They looked a long moment at each other across the distance between them. The moonlight gleamed on the silver at his throat as the claybank shifted restlessly. Blackhorse did not speak to her —perhaps he would have if he'd been nearer— but after a moment, he merely nudged the dun and rode away without looking back.

*When will he return?* Carrie wondered, watching him until he was swallowed by the darkness. *Is his medicine strong enough to protect him and bring him back? Will I still be here? Or is this the last I'll ever see of the black-horse Comanche?*

She was still standing, wondering, when a small sound made her turn, and she saw No Feathers come from his tipi and mount the cream-colored horse. Then Red Moon Girl emerged and went to him, taking something from around her neck and handing it up to him. In the moonlight, the silver of tearstreaks glistened on her face, and with a reassuring smile, he reached down to touch her cheek. Then he rode away straight and proud on his pony, eager to add to his new battle honors.

Carrie slipped back to the dance before she was seen, and she noticed that several other of the painted warriors had left. By the time the dance ended, a few hours before dawn, all of the members of the war party had ridden quietly out of camp, and Carrie felt sure they must have some appointed place to rendezvous and begin their travel together. Who could predict where they would go, with whom they would fight, and which of them might return?

*And what,* Carrie wondered tiredly, *lies ahead for me?*

# CHAPTER NINE: WORKING

It seemed to Carrie that she spent the next long weeks doing little more than constant work. No wonder, she thought, Comanche women welcomed—even urged—the addition of other wives to their marriages. There never seemed enough hands for all the tasks.

At the beginning she was given chores that kept her near Buckskin's household, which made it easy for someone to keep a close eye on her at all times. But it also allowed her to observe the rhythms of the Comanche community from its edges first, rather than being immediately immersed in an alien culture and language. As she cooked and cleaned and gathered, though, Carrie found she was picking up quite a lot of the Comanche tongue.

Mostly, of course, it was the names of things she could see or do, the terms most central to the life around her: *sokoobi*...earth and *tomoobi*...sky, *paa*...water and *sonipʉ*...grass. She came to know the names of body parts, colors, numbers, countless plants, animals and birds, as well as the chores that filled her days: *tʉkʉ ahwerʉ*...dig up food roots, *tai konookʉ*...bring firewood, *tai tuukʉkwa* ...fetch water, *tai pomakʉkwa*...pick fruit. She soon referred to the river as *hunubi,* to their tipi as *nʉmʉ kahni* and a parfleche envelope as *wosa.*

And though much of this learning was by necessity prosaic, she sometimes found and appreciated poetry or humor in the translated meanings: what she knew as a redbud tree, they called "red-bursting tree"; the name for tarantula meant "big, fuzzy brother-in-law"; a river bend was, quite literally, the "water's elbow."

Using repetition, pointed fingers, *moʔatekwapʉ*...hand talk and an occasional drawing, Wading Bird proved a patient and inventive teacher, but there were many things she could not explain. So there were times when the question *"Hakaniyu tʉ̲?* Why?" hung between them, and in the end, they both could only shrug in frustration and go on with their work.

Carrie found another benefit to staying close to Buckskin's household: it was easier to avoid the still-hostile cheekbone woman who had attacked her upon her arrival. Carrie learned she—like Carrie herself—was not *nʉmʉ ruaitʉ*...Comanche born, but of some enemy tribe, and her name proved Carrie was not the only object of her disapproval. The name meant Glares At but the words translated literally to Bone Look, and that's the way Carrie thought of her, rather than as Glares At. While making it clear the woman was now a respected part of the community, Wading Bird seemed to take pains that Carrie wouldn't have to work anywhere near Bone Look, and she kept Carrie so busy she hardly had time to wonder why the woman might be so disagreeable.

Sometimes Carrie felt amused, thinking back to how she had dreamed of adventure while she attended to the chores of homestead life. Now, here she was, caught in the greatest adventure imaginable, and how did she spend her time? Attending to the chores of Comanche life!

Much like her former life, gathering and preparation of food were the most constant and important responsibilities. Carrie had always preferred cooking to other tasks, and she was proud to find that she soon could match Wading Bird's talent in this area, remembering to call boiled meat *saapʉ* and jerked meat *inapʉ*, roasted meat *tʉkwʉsʉkʉpʉ* and summer-dried meat *tahmai napʉ*. And now she knew to call the pemmican *tʉrayapʉ*.

She quickly learned to combine honey, tallow, and water to make a sauce for roasted meat, and Wading Bird declared that Carrie's stews were better than her own once she'd learned the flavor possibilities of the different available plant foods and the spice bags her teacher treasured—which included dried herbs, hardwood ashes, and even *onaabi*, a coarse, greyish salt.

Carrie was amazed how many *ahwepʉ*—foods dug from the soil—they used. Not only wild potatoes, onions and radishes, but also sego lily bulbs and tubers of the sunflowers Maysie called Jerusalem artichoke. The trick was in finding which tasted best combined with the different spices and types of game.

Those rich stews seemed to be the very thing Buckskin needed to strengthen his body and begin to heal. He soon was so well, he became an annoyance, constantly underfoot and in the way of chores that needed to be done. At the same time, he seemed always in a state of irritation, chafing at life itself because he had been prevented from joining the war party.

A number of other men had not ridden off to raid with Quanah, and at first Carrie felt very annoyed at just how idle they could be while the women were constantly at work. True, the men went off hunting and brought back fresh meat, repaired their weapons, and one or two spent time painting picture stories on hides using porous pieces of bone instead of brushes. But they spent a greater amount of time lounging and talking together, smoking and gambling and being waited upon.

When Carrie felt vexed enough to ask about this inequity, Wading Bird looked surprised and made Carrie understand that women's work was different from men's work. After all, men and women were different. Wading Bird held up her hands, one symbolizing male, the other, female.

"He is what comes and goes," Wading Bird told her, moving one of the hands. "The wind, the leaves, the arrowhead." Then, moving the other, "She is what stays, what continues: the earth, the trunk of the tree, the stone from which the arrowhead is made." She put her two hands together to show how men and women made the two halves of a complete whole, and Carrie remembered the first night's dancing, the men and women separate, yet together. She could understand the concept, but she wasn't sure she agreed with where it went from there.

Perhaps this showed on her face, because Wading Bird stooped and drew a circle in the dirt and said the syllables Carrie had come to interpret as "community" and—when Carrie nodded her understanding—poked several dimples in the earth at the circle's center, then said, "Women." When Carrie nodded again, Wading Bird added some smaller dots and glanced up at Carrie, who guessed, "Children?" With a quick smile at this continuing success, Wading Bird made larger dots around the edge of the circle and said, "Men." It reminded Carrie of what Josh Ward had once said about how bands of some grazing animals protected themselves from predators by forming circles with the young at the center. Here, on the human level, Carrie saw a community with men protecting and providing for the heart of that society, the women and the continuing generations.

Wading Bird spoke further, confirming the concept: It was the man's job to be a good hunter and defender. These responsibilities and raiding —which seemed to be considered just another form of "hunting"—might take men away from home for weeks or months. Someone had to keep the camp running smoothly and efficiently. The life of a man—often traveling great distances to provide the community its raw materials for survival—was uncomfortable, exhausting, and risky. While he was home, it was his time to rest; women were grateful for these efforts and happy to make him comfortable in a pleasant environment. There was a sense, too, that—while men owned most of the horses, their own clothing, weapons, and medicine objects—the household goods belonged to the women, who gladly accepted all responsibility for their care and replacement.

Though she could see the practicality and harmony of such a system—which probably had been more equitable in the harsher times before the horse—Carrie experienced a familiar pinch of irritation at the idea of "women's work" which, within her own culture, had prevented her from doing much she wished to. She felt her chin tilt up as she struggled with the words to frame her next question.

Yes, Wading Bird told her, there were among the Comanches women hunters and warriors and medicine doctors, though usually this only happened after they were too old for child-bearing. But if spirits spoke to a young woman and told her to walk a certain path, she was free to do so... she was *expected* to do so. Just as men were free to choose against ever taking the wartrail if they were so guided.

Carrie had wondered about the men who had stayed behind. Some were obviously injured or ill or too old, but there were others young and strong and certainly fierce-looking. It was good to have them to hunt for the camp and to know they were ready to fight if the Tonkawas came raiding, but why had they not gone too?

Wading Bird assured her no man was required to go raiding or on the wartrail. It was always a choice he made after consulting his spirit guardian, and he would never be expected to go if he dreamed of death or if his guide advised against it. Would it not be foolish to ignore such warnings?

*Dreams and visions,* Carrie thought. Never had she known people to believe so much in these things, let their lives be shaped and changed by them, unquestioningly. And to have those dreams accepted and respected by the surrounding community was an equally novel idea. In her old life, she had often wondered with both amusement and trepidation what response she'd get if she shared her dreams with anyone. And who could she tell—Wes? Papa? Emma? Not likely!

Now her dreams were full of images from her new life and of unsuccessful attempts at escape. She saw in clear detail plants and birds and animals from the prairie—living things she'd hardly noticed in her sod house life but now saw all around her. More than once the same grey bird visited her dreams, and she wondered if there might be some significance. She thought to ask Wading Bird, but she was too used to keeping her dreamworld a private place. Perhaps someday she might tell someone her own visions....

For the Comanche, Josh Ward had once said, the greatest dream experience of all was the vision quest of each young man moving into manhood. On the fifth day after the war party left, a boy of about fourteen—called Pony Colt—met with the medicine man and then walked out of camp toward the hills. He was gone four days, fasting and praying to the Spirit World, waiting for a vision to reveal his own personal power to him.

He returned exhausted and weak but exultant. When he had eaten and rested for a day, he went again to the *puhakatʉ*...medicine man. Late that afternoon, the camp was alive with the news: Pony Colt was now to be called Buffalo Bird, named for his spirit guardian, the small birds that follow and groom the roaming bison. The proud young man assured them all that he would soon have a message from his spirit guide, telling where to move the camp to find good hunting.

This news was met with great excitement throughout the camp. Within her own family group, she heard Buckskin anticipating the taste of roasted buffalo tongue, Red Moon Girl reserving a hide for a special dress she wanted to make, and Wading Bird's enthusiasm about having a new paunch kettle for her stews.

Carrie had been too busy to think about it before, but now she realized that at no time since her capture had she seen a single *tasiwoo*...buffalo. She knew that the bison had been called the "commissary" of the Plains Indians because they harvested food, clothing, shelter, tools and utensils, all from this one animal.

And Josh Ward said Comanches preferred the taste of that meat above all others. She remembered the conversations at church about the destruction caused by the buffalo hidehunters. Still, she had heard there were once tens of millions of the great creatures roaming across the Plains. Surely they couldn't *all* be gone?

Remembering something else Josh Ward had said, she asked Wading Bird, who confirmed that yes, even in days long past there had been times when the buffalo were scarce and life was hard. Carrie wasn't sure she understood exactly what the other woman said, but the belief seemed to be that sometimes the buffalo went into a hole in the ground and no prayers or dancing could convince them to come out.

But Buckskin, who'd been listening to them, had more to say about it. "What is happening now is different from those times." The herds, he said, were getting smaller and smaller, and they were harder to find. It was good that Buffalo Bird would locate some for them. And it was clear the restless Buckskin was ready for a move and the excitement of a hunt.

Carrie, too, looked forward to a move, hoping it would bring her in contact with some person or place that would help her understand where exactly she was and how to escape.

Of course, she still thought of going home, but not quite as often. She assured herself that was only because she was so busy all day and so tired when she lay down at night. She was given her own willow-slat bed in Buckskin's tipi, and she slept near Red Moon Girl. Usually Carrie was too tired to have trouble sleeping, but there were nights when she had to pull the buffalo robes over her head to shut out the sounds of Buckskin and Wading Bird's lovemaking. On those nights she lay hot and trembling under the animal skins, thinking about the return of Blackhorse and wondering which she wished more: that he would stay away forever or that he would return soon to protect her.

For she found she had a suitor. He was much older—perhaps forty—and rather gaunt for a Comanche, with a perpetually hungry look about his eyes and mouth. Carrie thought his name fit him aptly: Wolf-At-Dawn. She found him lurking near her tipi often, and as she worked, she could feel his eyes devouring her.

Wading Bird noticed too, told Carrie he already had two wives—Sageblossom and Bone Look—but was horse-wealthy enough to afford another. Maybe that explained why Bone Look seemed so mad at her? Carrie wondered aloud.

*"Nahkia,"* Wading Bird mused, "perhaps." But, she explained, that one was once herself a captive and had had a difficult time finding her place among the People. She had been treated roughly —including the disfiguring wound to her face— but eventually Wolf-At-Dawn took her as his second wife, affording her a secure position in this camp. But now, according to Wading Bird, she was the most likely to be harsh with new captives.

Carrie thought this attitude might be even stronger toward her, given how well she was being treated, how easy she had it. Further, with the possibility of Wolf-At-Dawn bringing Carrie into the very household Bone Look had attained, mightn't she feel her hard-won status threatened? And, Carrie wondered, just how much of a possibility might that be?

Though not yet married in the eyes of the community, Carrie had learned she was, indeed— as his captive—Blackhorse's property, but he had entrusted her to his brother while he was absent. Should he not return from the battle trail, it would be Buckskin's place to dispose of her. As captive property, he could sell her or marry her off to anyone he chose. Wading Bird said in that case, Wolf-At-Dawn was sure to ask for her to be his third wife. That prospect made even the uncertainties of escape seem less daunting, and she looked forward to the move and the opportunities it might provide.

Then one dawn, the *tekwu̲niwapi̲*, the camp crier, spread the word: Buffalo Bird's spirit guide had spoken. A small herd grazed three days' journey to the southeast, and preparations should be made immediately.

Carrie worked as quickly as she could, but she had never felt so clumsy. Wading Bird and Red Moon Girl were very patient, but it must have been frustrating for them to have to repeat things so many times and redo what Carrie had done inexpertly. She felt like a child...until she glanced around her and saw children of other households doing the same work with speed and grace. Girl children, of course. The boys and men helped only by readying their own possessions and the horse herd. Carrie noticed Buckskin waiting nearby, carefully groomed and lounging idly aboard a mud-colored gelding he had won only yesterday gambling with Wolf-At-Dawn.

Perhaps she made a face, because Wading Bird reminded her whose property they were packing. Then she laughed and whispered what Carrie translated as, "I don't want him packing *my* household! Half of everything would be under the horses' bellies before we get to the hills!" More seriously, Red Moon Girl added that the men must always have their hands free to take up weapons and protect the camp, especially when everyone was this vulnerable.

Even without the men's help, it was surprising how rapidly the lodges could be dismantled and pulled down. The gigantic tipi covers were folded just so and strapped onto the horses' packsaddles. The lodgepoles, lashed together at one end, were then fastened to the packsaddle so that the large ends dragged behind, scratching lines in the earth. Hide platforms attached between the poles were loaded with rawhide trunks and hide bundles holding all a household's belongings. In some families, small children or the elderly or sick rode on one of these A-shaped drags. Carrie knew the

French had called the device a *travois;* in Comanche it was *wʉtaràa.*

Soon Carrie found herself mounted on Brandy, who seemed rather nervous in her first contact with an Indian saddle and the poles that scraped along behind her. It was Blackhorse's household goods packed on Carrie's *wʉtaràa* and in the rawhide saddlebags hung about her. She held the rein of Pearl, who was likewise loaded with Blackhorse's belongings, her packsaddle filled with the lodgecover Wading Bird and Red Moon Girl had helped Carrie fold.

Within an hour the camp was packed and on the move, a noisy and excited procession of armed warriors mounted on their favorite traveling ponies, women chattering and laughing together as they walked or rode pack animals, loose horses galloping about chased by young boys showing off their horsemanship, yapping dogs, and children too energetic to ride a bumping *wʉtaràa* running noisily back and forth instead. The youngest members of the community could observe it all, riding comfortably in *waakohno,* the padded daytime cradleboards strapped to their mothers' backs or hung from saddlehorns where they were lulled by the familiar rhythms of a horse in motion.

Carrie wondered what would happen when the war party returned and found them gone, but learned signs would be left to guide the warriors to their new location.

By dusk of the third day, the camp had been re-created on the bank of another river, though this one was narrower and muddier than the last. But the grass was good and showed many signs of buffalo passage, which also meant a new supply of droppings to dry and save for fuel.

Carrie helped Wading Bird and Red Moon Girl erect their lodge, and then they helped her with Blackhorse's. Just as they had done in dismantling, they stood on each other's shoulders to be tall enough to fasten the tipi cover together down its front, pushing the lodgepins through holes in the smoky hide. It was Carrie—still feeling awkward but sensing some improvement—who did all the rest of the preparations in Blackhorse's tipi: hanging the inner drape, covering the floor with clean sand and sweeping it smooth before carpeting it with skins and herbs, stacking firewood, arranging the rawhide trunks, hanging utensils and fragrant plants about the walls.

She set up the bed then. Her fingers stroked the willow slats held together with sinews. Had his wife made that bed? Painted the wood strips with those bright colors? Carrie's hands lingered on the soft skins she spread on top, wondering if she would ever share that bed with Blackhorse, lie beside him here beneath the smoke-scented robes, no longer hearing the night sounds of Buckskin and Wading Bird.

*Where is he now?* she wondered. *Is he scalping and stealing from my own people or is he lying dead in some rock crevice—facing east—with stones piled on top to keep away the wolves?*

*Keep away the wolves!* The last words echoed in her mind and brought the question, *If he doesn't return, how can I keep myself from Wolf-At-Dawn until I can escape?*

For freedom, returning home, were still in Carrie's mind though their journey had provided none of the hoped-for clues to her location. She must wait longer. The waiting didn't seem so hard anymore. She was usually too busy.

And with the buffalo hunt, life got even busier. The night they arrived was marked by a ritual of dancing and praying sure to bring success in the hunt. The men left at dawn the next morning, moving silently on their best buffalo horses.

Carrie, following the lead of Wading Bird, Red Moon Girl and many of the other women, fashioned a *wʉtaràa* behind her horse and rode away from camp—following the direction the men had taken—with the as-yet-empty poles and platform bumping along behind.

They rode very quietly for several miles before they came upon the first dead buffalo, a huge black mound with a single arrow piercing its right flank. Sageblossom and Bone Look—Wolf-At-Dawn's wives—crowed triumphantly as they recognized their husband's markings on the arrow, proof he had made the first kill. As Carrie and her companions rode past, Sageblossom set to work with the butchering, and Bone Look—brandishing her knife—glared up at Carrie, who glanced quickly away. Up ahead, she saw Wading Bird find Buckskin's yellow-striped arrow in the next black mound.

Before long, the men rode back to share the skinning and butchering work; Buckskin had killed four, and he left the women to his first kill and went off to locate his next.

It was a sight that would long stay with Carrie. By now she was used to skinning and cutting up animals and rarely got queasy anymore, but she had never in her life seen so much blood and bone. And when Wading Bird sliced the still-warm liver, spread it liberally with the green juices of the gall bladder, and offered it to her —urging, *"Kʉhpuni.* Taste...try it"—Carrie could only shake her head mutely. At first the sisters were greatly amused and pressed her further to eat, saying that the flavor would soon change and not taste so good. As she continued to refuse, they seemed disappointed and perhaps a bit exasperated, but they ate the liver themselves, sharing it with Weaseltail and Cricket Song, the wife and widowed mother of Scar, who had no one to hunt for them while he was away on the wartrail. It was a treat obviously savored by them all.

Carrie swallowed repeatedly and gripped the handle of the knife she'd been given until her knuckles were white. Then she fixed her eyes on the work at hand, watching carefully what should be done and how. Weaseltail and Cricket Song, too, worked alongside Wading Bird and Red Moon Girl on Buckskin's kills. They moved quickly and expertly, and it was obvious that there was a pattern to the work—strictly followed—so that the hides remained in huge pieces, and the precious sinew bundles along the spine were not severed or damaged.

Accustomed as she was now to Comanche efficiency, Carrie was still amazed at how swiftly all those curly black mountains of hair and flesh were reduced to hide-wrapped bundles of meat, bones, and organs loaded on *wʉtaràa* platforms and packsaddles. They left only the massive spines in the bloodied grass—and the hearts, to appease the great Buffalo Spirit and coax the return of once-mighty herds that had dwindled to small bands of fifty or fewer.

Amid great good cheer, the women led the horses back to camp, where Weaseltail and Cricket Song went on to their lodge. No matter that Carrie felt weary to the center of her bones and much in need of bathing. She was put immediately to the work of pegging the hides hair-down to the earth and scraping the flesh away. Red Moon Girl helped her with a cheerfulness Carrie found annoying.

Meanwhile, Wading Bird began cooking up a stew of herbs, buffalo brains, liver and fat that made Carrie hope to God she wouldn't be expected to eat any for dinner.

Then she was outraged to find that—having finished scraping one side of the hides—she was expected to turn one over and begin rubbing off the hair on the other side! Carrie almost threw down her hide-scraper and refused. Ever since she had been captured, she'd been ordered around and expected to do an endless series of tiresome chores. *Someone's always telling me what to do and how to do it better,* she thought, *and I'm sick of it!*

*What would happen if I just refused?* she wondered. As compliant as she'd always been with Aunt Emma, she remembered a few times when she'd simply said no, she was too tired, and nothing terrible had happened. Where was that sometimes-outspoken old Carrie, she wondered. Where was the plucky girl who had fought for her freedom and bloodied the nose of a Comanche warrior in her efforts to escape?

*She's alive,* she told herself now. *Alive and healthy enough to feel peeved about the burden of her duties.* Many other captives hadn't been so fortunate. And who was there to rebel against? The one who had forced her imprisonment wasn't here. His brother Buckskin never gave her any orders, leaving her care and guidance to the women. And how could she refuse Wading Bird or Red Moon Girl, who never asked her to do more than they did and always treated her with utmost respect and kindness? And after all, she was being well fed and clothed and protected. Was it not simply fair for her to do her share? Neither Mama nor Aunt Emma had raised her to be an ungrateful guest.

So Carrie clenched her teeth against the frustration, sighed tiredly and, sinking to her knees, got to work on the buffalo skin, trying to match the brisk strokes of her Comanche companions. By the time the three women had prepared the hide, the stew was ready, and Wading Bird mashed the mixture into a paste and brought it over to Carrie and Red Moon Girl in a large turtle shell.

*I will not eat it,* Carrie thought with frantic determination, her lips pressing together to keep her stomach from revolting. *Even if they're offended, I won't!*

She saw puzzlement and then, again, amusement in the two sisters' faces. Their dark eyes laughed as they handed her a smooth, flat stone and showed her how to rub the paste—which turned out to be a tanning solution—into the hide. The three women worked together, and because speed seemed to be important to the others, Carrie worked quickly too. When Wading Bird was satisfied with this step, they sprinkled the whole surface with warm water, rolled the hide and placed it in a shady spot among some low tree boughs. Wading Bird said, since there would be more new hides tomorrow, the others from today could remain untanned, sun-drying into rawhide. Relieved, Carrie thought they would rest now, but found it was merely time to go cook the buffalo feast.

At the great celebration that night, the proud hunters were presented with roasted buffalo tongues to honor their bravery and prowess. And every member of the tribe was able to gorge on fresh roasted meat...when they weren't singing and dancing.

The following day was very similar, except Buckskin killed five buffalo and gave two away to the household of Cricket Song and Weaseltail. A third day of hunting was planned, but next dawn, the scouts found the herd had vanished in the night, leaving only a churned-earth path leading to the west. All over the village, the pole racks called *inawatanʉʉ* were heavy with long, red-black ribbons of drying meat, and women were busy transforming the hides and other gifts of the buffalo into household goods. The grey-haired chief—Old Otter—proclaimed it a good hunt and decided the village would stay in this agreeable place a while longer.

It was during these days of the buffalo hunt that Carrie found herself moving closer into the heart of the community. Perhaps Wading Bird felt Carrie now understood enough of the life and language to allow more exposure, for their work seemed to take them among the other women more than ever before. Carrie reflected that Josh Ward had unknowingly prepared her for much of what she encountered in Comanche life, but she was totally unprepared for what she found in the women's community as it opened to her.

She knew Josh had had little contact with the women of his own camp. Had he been stolen at a younger age, he might have been adopted into a family structure and had totally different experiences. But he had been taken captive by an older warrior who needed someone to care for his household because he'd lost his wives and children to smallpox. As the man's slave, Josh was treated well enough, but found himself a true outsider, doing women's work without the familial warmth and sisterhood Carrie was discovering. Josh's stories, like all the other reports of contact with Plains Indians, had given Carrie the impression that the women were secondary, had little voice in the workings of the camp, and endured a life of drudgery serving the men. She had even perceived life that way herself at first.

But now she saw expanded the concept of women at the center of the circle, learning that the internal matters of the camp—all that was part of maintaining the solidarity and continuity of the community—were the province of the women. Men handled all the external affairs, which included not only hunting but also what could be called "foreign relations": any contact with outside forces, whether hostile or amicable, once again taking the risks to protect the center. No wonder white people—who often equate visibility with importance—assumed women's place was unimportant because they were seen serving the men instead of representing their people in peace councils or other such visible roles.

There were many times when Carrie felt irked watching the way the women seemed to humble themselves serving the men, but gradually she realized the women saw it differently: they believed those who were truly aware of their importance to the community—like elders or medicine doctors—were the most self-effacing.

"Women have no need to prove their power by showing off," Wading Bird told her. "Which is more important—which can survive without the other: the leaves without the treetrunk or the tree without its leaves?" Smiling contentedly, she shrugged and said, "My husband takes great risks to kill a buffalo. I am happy to make it into food and tools and handsome clothing for us."

It took about a week before the hides from the buffalo hunt were ready to be made into clothing. They were left rolled in the shade for several days; then there was a long, laborious time of working the hides by hand.

They took them to the tipi of Star Blanket, where most of the other women of the camp congregated with hides they had tanned. As they sat laughing and gossiping, they pulled and tugged and stretched the skins with their hands. They had to work at it all day and could not stop for long or the hides would begin to stiffen. Sometimes they sang, and Carrie found the songs easy enough to follow and join in. Star Blanket's oldest daughter brought them *tʉrayapʉ* to eat and water to drink, so that none of them would have to stop working to cook.

Carrie was surprised at the new strength in her hands and at how much of the laughing conversations she was able to understand. She learned that Red Moon Girl was so enthusiastic about her work because she would use her hide to make a bridal dress, which she would wear when No Feathers returned and they began their life together as husband and wife.

"Deerskin is better for bridal dress," Cricket Song, Scar's mother, pointed out with laughter lurking in her voice. "Are you so eager to be ready?"

Red Moon Girl blushed, smiling, and said, "He may return soon."

Some of the other women hooted with laughter and continued the teasing, especially the married women, who speculated about No Feathers's abilities as a husband and lover. They called him by his true Comanche name: Laughing Fox. By now, Carrie had also learned the others' real names: Buckskin's meant The-Water-Is-Very-Still—or more simply Still Water. Living in his tipi, she heard this name so often, she began to think of him as Still Water instead of Buckskin. When Carrie first heard Scar's true name—which *did* have to do with that terrible battle wound—she was sure she must be misunderstanding the translation, it was so horribly gruesome. But Wading Bird assured her it was correct, and no one seemed the least offended, including his wife or mother. Somehow, though, Carrie couldn't bear to think the other name, and when she heard it, she still translated it as simply Scar.

She knew now, too, the meaning of the symbols on Blackhorse's tipi cover, his true name: He-Dreams-About-Fire. This name she did not use except with other people, and inside herself she still thought of him first as Blackhorse instead of Fire Dreamer.

The women called him Fire Dreamer, though, when they spoke of him. For they also teased Carrie, knowing—somehow—that her union had not yet been consummated. The women always seemed to know everything that went on in every household. Most of them appeared quite friendly and accepting of her, but a few—those who might like to have Blackhorse for themselves and Wolf-At-Dawn's wives, who seemed uneasy about his interest in her—appeared to relish poking fun at her. While Bone Look was not as overtly hostile, she still seemed bent on embarrassing Carrie.

But Wading Bird adroitly turned the conversation away from Carrie and toward speculations about when the war party would return and with what honors. While they chattered on, Carrie sank into her own thoughts about what a peculiar role she presently filled—caught somewhere between captive slave and adopted family member, Comanche wife and marriageable maiden. And wasn't it ironic, she thought, that *kwʉhʉpʉ*, the word for captive, was so similar to the word for wife: *kwʉhʉ*? How long would she teeter there before being pushed one way or the other, and where was she most likely to end up?

That evening Carrie felt the need to be alone, went to sit on the floor of Blackhorse's empty tipi. She thought about her new life and what might happen in the days ahead of her. Would she ever be able to escape? Of course! Sooner or later the right opportunity would present itself.

Until then, she was comfortable enough with the life of the Comanche. She was used to the continual nature of any household's work, and she was beginning to adjust to the more primitive, bloody aspects of her new tasks. Once again she found herself envying young men's activities. She certainly wasn't interested in the wartrail, and—even though she could proudly say she had just about overcome her old squeamishness—she still was glad she didn't have to kill the animals herself. But she would enjoy riding the horses, painting picture stories, learning to craft arrows and bows and shields.

All around her in the camp she had seen evidence of the women's creative arts in beadwork and painted rawhide objects, but when was there ever time to work on these things? She hadn't seen any of the women so occupied, even in the evenings. There were times when Carrie wished for more modern tools or equipment to speed and ease their labors, but she also began to sense the difference in working with implements that came from the earth and returned to it.

Though a couple of women in camp had copper or iron pots—which were certainly more convenient in some ways—Carrie preferred the taste of stews cooked in Wading Bird's buffalo paunch. Such a kettle was also much easier to transport, and when Wading Bird got a new one after the hunt, the old one was used as a water bag until it developed a leak and was then left with other refuse at the edge of the camp, where in a matter of months it would fall apart naturally and be reclaimed by the earth.

If Carrie found her work no more inspiring than she had inside the sod house, she did find one great difference. Though she was still in many ways an outsider, she could appreciate and share the sense of joyful satisfaction in communal work. The women's laughter, gossip, teasing and singing all made the work go faster and more pleasantly. There were even moments when she caught herself having fun—something she would have thought impossible in the realm of "women's work." The closest parallel in her own experience was a quilting bee, and she saw many similarities. But here the pleasant blend of industry and social sharing didn't end with the completion of the task at hand; the women sought to do their work communally whenever they could. And though Carrie was well aware there were disagreements and personality conflicts within the women's circle—not only her situation with Bone Look but among others—she had begun to sense the subtle ways these energies were kept from becoming disruptive to the sisterhood itself and the community at large. She remembered how that very day, Wading Bird had deflected the teasing from her and how others had helped steer the conversation in a new direction.

With a little shock, Carrie thought, *Why, I have more friends here than I ever had in my life before!* Musing on this irony, she sat in the dark of Blackhorse's lodge, listening to the night and realizing how much she liked the feel of a tipi. There was something intimately warm and friendly about it. She struggled with her feelings, trying to pin them down. There was a snugness and efficiency to the tipi home, but more than that, a kind of...roundness...a feeling of circles completed, like the cycles of the seasons, of birth and growing and death.

Even the *ʉnʉʉ* didn't bother her much. These bugs—fleas and ticks, lice, gnats and mosquitoes—had been more of a nuisance in the sod house. Wherever you lived so close to the soil, you had to share it with the creatures who first inhabited it, but these people who lived in closer relation to the earth had also found some strategies. Carrie learned there were good reasons to dress her hair with bear fat, and the constant slight smokiness inside a tipi might irritate the eyes occasionally but it also discouraged mosquitoes. Crushed mescal beans mixed with water also helped keep mosquitoes—and buffalo gnats—off the body. And both fleas and ticks, she discovered, avoided a floor scattered with crushed sage and mint leaves.

She rubbed her hands on the soft furs around her, drank in the scents of drying herbs, felt the tipi hold her in its warm circle like a child in a womb. *Yes, I will miss this feeling when I return to my square home built of square sod bricks. And I will miss my new sisters.*

As if the thought of sisterhood—or perhaps escape—had called her, Wading Bird came into the tipi, silent as the shadow of smoke. It made Carrie wonder, *Do they really trust me? Is it just coincidence that every time I am away for very long, someone from Still Water's lodge comes to check on me?*

There was no light in the room except from the moonbeams falling through the smokehole at the top of the tipi cone. In the dimness Carrie saw that the other woman held something folded in her arms—held it out to her.

When she took the weight, felt the soft, soft texture, Carrie realized it was the hide that she herself had been working that day. Wading Bird's hands moved and her voice spoke, both telling Carrie the gift was for a bridal dress.

Carrie felt tears prickle in her eyes, touched by such a generosity. She well knew the worth of —and work involved in—a properly tanned hide. Her voice sounded thick as she pronounced the Comanche syllables, "*Ʉrako.* Thank you very much."

Wading Bird rose, said something more about the dress and tomorrow, but Carrie didn't understand it. Then the other woman motioned about the room, referred to its owner when she said reassuringly, "That one will return."

Carrie nodded, wishing that she could be so confident. She put the precious hide in one of Blackhorse's rawhide trunks and followed Wading Bird back to Still Water's tipi.

Carrie slept restlessly that night with the robes pulled over her head. She dreamed of sod houses and silver rings, of dying foxes and a great black horse with fiery eyes and three bullet wounds in his side.

# CHAPTER TEN: DREAMING

Wading Bird helped both Red Moon Girl and Carrie as they worked together on the bridal dresses. Most of the other women who had tanned hides were now hanging them over small-flamed fires that gave off large quantities of fragrant smoke. They had to tend them carefully to prevent drying and burning, but the smoking resulted in skins that were very soft, golden-brown in color, and waterproof. The unsmoked—or soft-tanned—hides for the bridal dresses were a mellow creamy-white, but—as Wading Bird showed Carrie on a small scrap—not at all waterproofed. If touched by water, the hide quickly became as stiff as it had been before the tanning.

Carrie still had her own *nahuu*—the knife she'd been given the day of the buffalo hunt. No one had asked her to return it, and she kept it in a leather sheath that hung on the left side of her rawhide belt. She had thought a great deal about that knife, but she knew she couldn't use it against anyone in Still Water's tipi—not even to escape.

She used the knife to follow the pattern Wading Bird drew with charcoal on the soft white skin, and Carrie found it cut as easily as cloth.

Then Wading Bird made her another present: a sewing kit. In the beaded pouches with cone-shaped metal pendants, she found an awl, sharp bone needles and threads of sinew. These fine, strong strands had been painstakingly separated from the bundles of sinew removed with such care from the buffalos' backs. Carrie wondered briefly if the sewing tools had also belonged to Blackhorse's wife. What had been her name and what had she been like?

Carrie quickly learned the knack of piercing holes in the material with the sharp awl, and then threading the sinew—slightly dampened in her mouth—through the holes. She was surprised to find how well this worked, even though it took a little longer than needle and thread. Later she found that moistening the sinew released a natural glue in the fibers so that, when dry, the seams were not only sewed but also glued together.

It took them many days to make the dresses, fitting the work in between their regular daily tasks, which at this time of year involved finding and drying fresh foods to last through the long winter. Everyone in camp seemed to agree that all the plant and animal signs indicated a hard winter ahead. Carrie joined the women's expeditions to gather a variety of plantlife. Though these forays were the usual enjoyable social events—and certainly more fun than hoeing and weeding a garden—she sensed that all was not as relaxed as it might have been in other years. There were long, serious discussions, sometimes heated, and though consensus was reached and harmony preserved, she knew few were completely satisfied and some women were still uneasy.

Questioning Wading Bird provided some answers. Because the buffalo were disappearing, the women must gather more plants than usual to ensure their families would be fed all winter. And most everyone agreed that more filling foods like roots and tubers should take precedence. But that wasn't a happy decision, because digging them up was harder work and less fun than searching out greens and flavoring herbs.

Further, it had been an extremely dry summer with too many hungry locusts, so vegetation was scarcer and less lush. Where normally plants were gathered in a way that thinned the wild crops while leaving plenty to maintain the natural balance and provide for generations to come, now there was pressure to harvest less sparingly, and many women worried about what would be available in the future.

On several occasions, Carrie noticed Bone Look make offerings to the plants as she worked. In private Wading Bird explained, "That is a practice of her birth people...to offer songs and the herb tobacco to feed the spirits of the plants, make them strong enough to return in abundance. It is not the Comanche way, but what can it hurt to let her follow the ways of her elders?"

Red Moon Girl pointed out that Bone Look's similar offerings weren't bringing back the buffalo, and she'd heard the woman worry: "Will the plants be angry at us for taking more than we should? There is so much less to harvest this year. What if the plant spirits desert us too and refuse to return like the buffalo?"

Still, Carrie was surprised at just how many different kinds of food plants could be found in the region and how they were preserved to keep well and be easily transported. Many kinds of fruit and berries were mashed to pulp and usually formed into cakes before drying. Much of the buffalo jerky—dried and then pulverized—became *tʉrayapʉ,* mixed with marrow fat and dried fruit or nuts, then sealed with tallow in rawhide *wosa.* She wore out her arms pounding tough mesquite beans into the pale-yellow powder she remembered from her captive journey.

A few women grumbled because so much of the winter's burden had fallen on them while the men often came home from the hunt with little for the pot. And the joke the women shared—that only meat was considered "real food" by men when in actuality the women's gathering was an essential portion of the camp's stores and dietary balance—seemed to hold less humor.

Even the uncomplaining Red Moon Girl once worried that with all the extra work they wouldn't be able to finish—much less decorate—their bridal dresses before the return of the war party. Now Carrie understood why she hadn't seen women spending their time with artwork.

At last, though, the dresses were sewn together, plain except for long, lush fringes. Then Wading Bird brought out her special treasures and offered them to the brides-to-be: glinting glass beads of yellow and blue and red. There were silver beads too—like those Blackhorse wore among his neck ornaments—made by a Mexican silversmith Still Water's father had taken captive. The silver beads were given to Wading Bird by her mother-in-law. Also, there were porcupine quills that had been flattened between the teeth and stained with colors. Wading Bird explained that her mother—who was not Comanche—had prepared these quills, but few had been used because Comanche women didn't decorate with them as often as other tribes. Carrie had noticed that their tipi alone seemed to have utensils ornamented with plaited porcupine quills.

Carrie was once again touched by the woman's generosity—offering precious gifts from her dead mothers to a captive white she'd known only weeks—but she had learned that unselfish giving was a fundamental virtue of the Comanche way of life. In fact, even the greeting *"Mʉmʉ tʉʉkan"* translated "Have you eaten?"

Wading Bird and her younger sister began to draw patterns in the sand—circles, zigzags, triangles making diamonds and hourglass shapes—trying to decide how to decorate Red Moon Girl's dress. For the first time, it occurred to Carrie that, though the men painted elaborate pictures of real objects—animals, tipis, people—the women used only geometric shapes on the items they decorated. Wondering why and how she might ask, she remembered what Wading Bird had told her weeks before: "He is what comes and goes. She is what stays, what continues."

Suddenly Carrie could see the rhythms of Indian life echoed even in their artwork: The men—whose lives alternated periods of intense excitement, effort, and danger with those of restless inactivity—depicted individuals and specific, transitory events. But the women—whose more steady, even, gentle life rhythm was the very heart of the community—manifested that spirit in the more abstract patterns of continuity.

For her own dress Carrie chose yellow and blue glass beads and some of the silver ones she thought might please Blackhorse since they had come from the woman who was *his* mother as well as Still Water's. At Wading Bird's insistence, she took twelve of the cherished blue-stained quills to complete her design.

The beads and quills were also sewn on with sinew, only a tracery of decoration compared to what could have been added if time permitted, but she also fastened an assortment of the beads amid the fringes. When, finally, her bridal dress was finished, Carrie felt not only proud of her work but as if her soul had been nurtured by creating something both useful and beautiful. As she carefully folded it around sweet-smelling herbs and packed it away in one of the rawhide trunks, part of her reminded, *Of course, I'll never wear it. I've only been making the dress so they won't know I still plan to escape as soon as I can.* She touched the beaded fringes, assured herself, *I'll never wear it.*

But another part of her wasn't so sure. As yet, there had been not a single opportunity for successful escape, and she realized she had just about given up hope of being rescued or ransomed. Had *they* given up hope, her family? Surely they still wanted her back, prayed for her, hoped for her return. Didn't they? Carrie sighed. Would there ever be a time when she didn't confound herself with questions she couldn't answer?

The days passed without word from the war party. Part of her wished for Blackhorse to stay away, postponing the use of her bridal dress. Another part was beginning to feel alarmed at the number of times she found Wolf-At-Dawn lounging about near her tipi. Twice he tried to detain her when she left the lodge at night. Though he stopped just short of touching her, the nearness of him repelled her, made the thought of lying beside Blackhorse seem less frightening.

The evening after another small band of buffalo provided more meat and hides for the women to process, Red Moon Girl came into her time-of-the-moon. She left Still Water's lodge and went into isolation in another tipi not too far away. Only the next morning Carrie also came to that part of her monthly cycle, and she was told she must go there too so her condition would not interfere with Still Water's medicine power. Feeling piqued by what she could only interpret as banishment, Carrie found not only Red Moon Girl but also Scar's wife, Weaseltail, in the lodge. They greeted her with great good humor and a huge bowl of *natsamukwe*...wild grapes.

Too vexed to appreciate that she wasn't expected to scrape any of those hides on a day that was turning into a scorcher, Carrie sat on the cushion of soft mosses and sulked while the other two chattered and laughed together. When they offered the grapes to her again, Carrie asked if they couldn't have some of the fresh meat from the recent hunt. She could think of few things that tasted better than freshly roasted buffalo meat glazed with a honey sauce. She watched the other two women glance at each other and laugh as if she were intentionally making a joke. Carrie was all too used to being the outsider, feeling like a clumsy, ignorant child, but she was in no mood for that at the moment. She looked away from them with tears prickling her eyes and started to remove the bits of thong binding her long braids. *At least I can use the time to tidy myself up a little,* she thought.

But Red Moon Girl reached out and stayed her hands, gently told her, "No." While she was in the Moon Lodge, she could eat no meat. She must not touch or wash her hair or she would be prematurely grey; nor could she wash her face or she would surely get wrinkles early in life. Carrie was reminded of Aunt Emma, who wouldn't talk about "woman's trouble" but was scandalized that Carrie insisted on bathing and washing her hair even during that time of the month, courting illness and God-knows-what.

Though she listened carefully, Red Moon Girl's instructions didn't make any more sense to her than what Aunt Emma had said. But, Carrie decided, it would do her no harm to respect her friends' customs. Still, there was a larger question in her mind, and she asked, "But why do we have to be here?"

It was at that moment Cricket Song, Scar's mother, entered the tipi with a steaming bowl of mesquite bean mush. Red Moon Girl seemed relieved and said some words Carrie didn't recognize while gesturing toward her. Cricket Song nodded and smiled at Carrie, and when she had handed the bowl to Weaseltail, went to sit beside Carrie. "You have questions. That is why I have come. I am *pueтupu*...my body is no longer influenced by the phases of the moon, but I know this is your first visit to the Moon Lodge. It is important to have an elder with you at such a time...to teach you about the mysteries of women's power. If a girl is sent to the Moon Lodge and has not been taught about these things, she thinks she is just being sent away for a bad reason."

Carrie looked away from those bright old eyes, feeling sudden heat rise in her face. The older woman gave her shoulder an affectionate squeeze and said, "Do not be embarrassed. How were you to know if you have never been told? Among your people, was there no elder to teach you?"

Thinking of Aunt Emma, Carrie couldn't help smiling as she shook her head *no*. She'd learned a little from her schoolmates but most from the dreams. In these, her mother had come to tell her more and reassure her, giving her a very different perspective on womanhood than Emma's. And now she listened carefully to what Scar's mother had to say.

Cricket Song tried very hard to explain it to Carrie, but concepts are more difficult to communicate and translate than concrete instructions such as "Scrape this hide" or "Don't pick that plant." There was no way Carrie could be absolutely sure she understood what she was being told, but she, too, tried very hard.

It had to do with *puha*—power. During moontime, Cricket Song explained, women were filled with a very strong and special power that could interfere with, even nullify, a warrior's medicine. If she stayed in Still Water's lodge or—even worse—touched his shield, she could totally strip him of his power, and he would be unable to defend his family in the face of danger. Women had a responsibility to the entire camp to control this power by removing it to a special place that was isolated from the men and consecrated to the moontime power itself. Like the men's Sweat Lodge, the Moon Lodge was a place for the body to cleanse and purify itself.

At Cricket Song's invitation to contribute, Red Moon Girl and Weaseltail pointed out it was a time for women to set aside their chores and appreciate themselves. To relax with and enjoy the company of any sisters who might share the lodge at the same time.

And according to Cricket Song, it was not only a time to celebrate the importance of being a woman—holding the power to bring forth, nourish, and teach the new generations—but also an opportunity to look inward, to meditate and listen to one's personal spirits, to experience powerful dreams.

Carrie tried. More than once while she was in the Moon Lodge, she searched her inner self for these qualities the Indian women found, but she could not say that she ever truly felt that special power. She felt tired and a little crampy and wonderfully thankful for respite from the work and the sun, but nothing she could relate to spirits or *puha*.

Unless she could count the dreams. Perhaps hers *were* even more vivid than usual, sometimes as if she were seeing through someone else's eyes. The familiar grey bird of her earlier dreams appeared several times, but now it came closer, and she could see very clearly the white and black markings on its wings and tail. It was always in flight, never landing for a moment's rest but circling endlessly with a plaintive cry as its bright eyes searched the earth below.

Much more than any introspection, though, Carrie enjoyed her social time with Red Moon Girl, who relaxed more than ever once Weaseltail left the lodge the next day, leaving them alone. Full-to-bursting with her dreams for a happy future, Red Moon Girl chattered about her love for the young man called Laughing Fox. She confided to Carrie that she had suggested they elope, but he insisted they wait until he could show proper respect with his gift of ponies.

She laughed affectionately and observed that he was sometimes too influenced by tradition, adding, "It is hard to wait for us to be together. Whenever I am near him, a strange magic makes my heart go fast, and it is hard to breathe." She said the words almost defiantly, as if convinced Carrie wouldn't understand and might even tease her.

But remembering how she had felt when just thinking about Danny, much less when he was near, Carrie assured her companion, "*Ʉ nakis̱pana*ʔ*itʉ nʉ*. I understand."

Red Moon Girl stared at her in surprise. "You do?" She reached out to touch the yoke of Carrie's dress, over the heart. "You have felt this strange magic too?"

Carrie nodded and looked quickly away, fighting the sudden sadness that welled up in her.

Misunderstanding, Red Moon Girl exclaimed, "Don't be shy...this is wonderful! My other sisters do not understand...but I can see you do." And she launched into a long, animated monologue of words and signs and laughter, which Carrie followed as best she could, feeling somewhat as she had that first wild ride clinging to Brandy.

In the end, she came to realize Red Moon Girl's feelings must be unusual among her people. Most marriages, it seemed—including Wading Bird's—were based on practical rather than romantic considerations. Women looked forward to a warm, respectful partnership instead of some irresistible and impassioned affinity.

Perhaps, Carrie reflected, that was why a multiwife system worked so well here. Not only was there companionship while sharing work and child-rearing—especially when men could be absent for long durations—but it explained how little jealousy or competitiveness Carrie had seen among wives.

She listened carefully to Red Moon Girl's story, learning that Wading Bird had been disappointed when her younger sister fell in love with Laughing Fox. Because of their closeness as sisters, Wading Bird had naturally hoped to have her as a co-wife. Red Moon Girl laughed and told Carrie, "My sister has never felt this way. At first she thought I had a strange sickness. She reminds me often how much more work a single wife must do. She thinks my kind of love makes a person..." Carrie interpreted the next phrase as "forget reason" or "behave illogically." Then Red Moon Girl giggled and said, "Perhaps she is right. Laughing Fox and I share such a strong love we may never take another wife." She paused, then added, "Unless, of course, Wading Bird is widowed. My sister will always be welcome in my marriage."

This gave Carrie quite a lot to think about. Even certain as she was she would never actually become Blackhorse's wife, she couldn't help wondering how she'd feel about sharing him and her home with a co-wife. Startled by the thoughts and feelings she discovered, she quickly pushed them away and concentrated on Red Moon Girl's future marriage instead of her own.

They spent the next few days in an easy blend of silences and conversations, seriousness and mirth, which gave Carrie more opportunities than usual to practice and enhance her use of the Comanche tongue.

Before they could return to the community, Carrie found, they were required to bathe in a running spring. She did so gratefully, glad to wash her hair with the yucca-root soap. Red Moon Girl helped her to oil and braid it again to keep it tidier and out of the way of her work. Though Carrie could appreciate that cropping it to her shoulders like the other women's would make her hair easier to care for, she was glad no one had tried to make her cut it.

Red Moon Girl gazed at it with admiration and asked her would she not like to borrow some red paint to decorate the parting. The girl was sure Wading Bird would give Carrie the face paints that had once belonged to Blackhorse's wife —Carrie had never learned her name, because it was generally taboo to speak the names of the dead. Red Moon Girl offered to show Carrie some attractive patterns for her face. Carrie politely refused but watched the other girl apply her favorite cheek designs, thought about the thin, wavy lines—like water—that Wading Bird drew just below her eyes and wondered what it would be like to paint her face as they did. Would it be possible to mix some red and yellow, get the orange colors of flames and—

*Stop it!* A horrified voice inside her cried. *You're not a savage! You're Carrie McEdan, and you'll be going home soon—without heathen paint on your face, you can be sure!*

As they walked back to the camp, they found that Old Otter had decided it was time to move the camp to another place. Already this area was nearly grazed out by the horses, and Carrie guessed his wife—one of the elder women most concerned about depleting the wild plant resources—had convinced him a move would ease some of the disagreements among the women.

So it was that four days later, Carrie found herself settled in a new location, still without a sight or sign of human life or habitation other than those of Old Otter's band. Sometimes it seemed to her that there were no other humans anywhere else on the earth. Perhaps not even the war party whose return she half hoped for and half wished never to see.

*Some things never change though,* she thought. *We can move sixty, ninety miles from where we were, but the tipis always go up again. Their doorways always face east to drink the light of the rising sun; Old Otter's is always in the center of the crescent of lodges, and somewhere near it will be the old men's Smoking Lodge and the medicine man's tipi with its painting of a tree split by lightning. There's always a river and grass for the horses; and there's always, always work for the women.*

Carrie took her place among those women as they gathered and prepared the winter's stores, a little more sure of herself after that time in the Moon Lodge. Always before she had felt closest to Wading Bird, who filled the role of motherly teacher. But now she shared a new sisterhood with the younger Red Moon Girl.

Once, as a large group of them sat together—pounding mesquite beans in the shade of the *puhi hʉʉki*...brush arbor—and the conversation drifted around them, extolling the virtues of various husbands but never once touching on anything resembling romantic love, Red Moon Girl had given Carrie a secret, knowing smile, and Carrie realized—in this matter at least—Red Moon Girl felt closer to her and better understood than by her own blood sister.

Perhaps it was this that helped give Carrie the courage to deal with Bone Look a few days later. It had been a frustrating morning for Carrie. Almost all the women of the camp had gone together gathering plants, a number of which were new to Carrie. She'd made several mistakes, and Bone Look was quick to ridicule her each time. It was all Carrie could do to hold on to her temper. She spent most of the morning with her jaws clenched so tightly, her whole face ached.

Wading Bird and Red Moon Girl, Weaseltail, Cricket Song and Star Blanket all tried to ease the situation, but Bone Look was oblivious, and Carrie knew no one was likely to be rude enough to try to correct Bone Look in public. And perhaps she was more brash than usual because her co-wife Sageblossom was absent in the Moon Lodge, leaving her to "rule the roost"—as Papa would say—in Wolf-At-Dawn's home.

At midday, the women retreated to the shade of the arbor to spread out their morning's harvest on several blankets and divvy up the wealth. The nearest tipi was Wolf-At-Dawn's; and as they arrived, he was just going off to socialize in the Smoking Lodge, but he called to Bone Look, reminding her she'd promised him a stew. She set to work at it, but she seemed especially disgruntled.

The other women took a break to eat and feed the babies, and then they went back to grouping and separating the various plants. Carrie tried her best, but some of the plants, especially as they wilted in the heat, became harder and harder to tell apart. Often one of her friends would reach over and gently correct her sorting, and Carrie couldn't help feeling embarrassed and frustrated.

Perhaps an hour passed before Grey Pebble, the young son of Star Blanket, came running over to report that Still Water was yelling in his tipi. As best as Carrie could translate, apparently he'd brought in a piece of wood to carve, not realizing there was a nest of wasps inside, and now they were loose in the tipi and stinging mad.

Wading Bird and Red Moon Girl laughed and said they'd better go help him or he might damage household goods trying to deal with those wasps. Carrie started to get up to follow them, but they said, "Stay! It will be crowded in the tipi with everyone trying to catch the *otʉ peenanʉʉ*. You will want to be out of the way of Still Water's big feet!" They hurried off, trying to finish their giggles, Carrie guessed, before they reached home.

She puzzled over a certain sprig of leaves she picked up and put it where she thought it should go. *"Keta!"* she heard Bone Look shout from beside the kettle. "Don't! Ignorant girl! Don't you know anything?"

Carrie glanced up, saw the other woman come barreling toward her, still holding the buffalo rib bone she used to stir the food. Carrie leaped to her feet and faced Bone Look, who went on chastising her for her poor work with the plants.

"Here!" Bone Look shoved the rib bone into Carrie's hand. "Go stir my stew. Do something useful and easy. I'll finish this work."

Her face flaming with embarrassment, Carrie found the other women looking away. It was not their place to interfere. Carrie's "kin" weren't there to help her.

Seeing her cowed, Bone Look pushed her advantage. "And be careful of that stirrer! My father carved that."

Carrie's gaze fell to the bone in her hands and found more than half its length elaborately etched into a true work of art. But there was no time to study it. "Hurry!" Bone Look insisted. "Don't let my stew burn!"

Carrie went to the pot—a real copper kettle—and stirred its contents for a few minutes, keeping her back to everyone else while she tried to regain her composure. Well, if this was her assigned task, she may as well do it to her best ability. Surreptitiously, she took a taste and found the thick soup far more bland than she was used to. Why, this could use some of that herb she'd collected earlier in the day—she couldn't remember its name, but it was a favorite in her household.

She considered. Maybe if she improved the meal—and Bone Look got credit—perhaps the woman would look on her more gently in the future. Carrie felt the need to prove she *was* a valuable member of this community, and she'd had more success with cooking than any other tasks.

With her back still turned, Carrie reached into one of the pouches at her belt and brought out some of the precious leaves. She shredded them in her hands and stirred them into the stew.

There was a shriek from behind her, and she whirled to see Bone Look flying toward her, face contorted with rage. In a storm of words Carrie could barely interpret, the woman berated her for her stupidity, accused her of putting *pawahkapʉ* in the food, and wrested the rib bone from her hand before she could do any more damage.

Carrie tried to tell her it wasn't *pawahkapʉ*—she was certain of that—but she couldn't remember what it *was* called, and she could barely get in a word anyway. And her attempts to defend herself only seemed to further enrage the other woman, who brandished the carved stirrer in Carrie's face. Yelling that *pawahkapʉ* was taboo for her husband to eat and now the whole stew would have to be thrown out—and she would have to start over—Bone Look struck Carrie with the rib bone—once on the upper arm, and then again before Carrie could react.

Yelping with pain and outrage, Carrie reached out and grabbed the bone, preventing it from striking her again. Bone Look tried to wrest it from her grip, but couldn't. For a few moments the two women scuffled, trying to gain control, then Carrie saw surprise widen Bone Look's eyes as the weapon was wrenched from her grip.

Now Carrie brandished it, trembling with her long-pent rage at feeling powerless and sometimes oppressed. Words boiled out of her, but they were not in the Comanche tongue: "You know, I'm sick and tired of you! Of a lot of things! Do you think I wanted this?! I'm sorry if you had a rough time when you came here, but none of it is my fault, so back off! And as for that husband of yours, keep him—please! I don't know why you hate me, but—"

Bone Look—obviously unable to understand a word—lunged at the arm holding the rib and pinched it savagely with both hands.

Carrie bellowed in pain, felt the rage sweep through her body like a brushfire. *"Nʉ bʉa!"* she roared—pulling back the rib, ready to strike Bone Look—"Leave! Me! Alone!"

And the other woman fell back, raising her arms defensively. Such power surged through Carrie—strength and spirit and determination beyond anything she'd ever experienced—that suddenly she felt certain she could no longer control that arm and hand. She didn't want to control it. More than anything in the world in that moment, she wanted to strike Bone Look...hurt her.

But instead, she brought down the rib, grasped one end in each hand and—repeating, *"Nʉ bʉa!"*—smashed it down across her lifted knee. Who would think it was possible? But the power she possessed in that moment—and any weakness due to the deep carving—aligned, and the bone cracked with a huge report that carried around the camp. Everyone who heard it turned to stare—though of course, most of the women were already gathered there and riveted on the drama.

With the sound and the physical release, Carrie's rage swept out of her—leaving a sense of emptiness—and she stared down at the broken bones in her hands: the carved pieces of a gift from Bone Look's faraway father. A sick sadness rushed into Carrie, brought tears to her eyes, and then was gone.

She looked at the other woman, who stared back in shocked disbelief. "I'm sorry," Carrie said very quietly and with grave sincerity as she handed over the two pieces of rib. Bone Look took them, nodding as if to say she understood it was the natural outcome of their confrontation. For surely if the spirits gave Carrie such power, it was meant to be.

But it was not enough for Carrie. She couldn't bear knowing she had damaged such a precious gift. But then, what could be done? There was no way to mend what was broken. Yet she *must* do *something.*

She reached up behind her neck and undid the clasp of her locket chain, drew the silver case from its always-place inside her clothes. She held it a moment, remembering, and then told Bone Look, "This was from *my* father." As the other watched, looking both wary and baffled—Carrie demonstrated how to open it, showed her the tiny picture inside, answered the question on Bone Look's face. "Yes. That's me."

She snapped it shut, pressed the locket into the other's hand until Bone Look rearranged the way she was holding the carved bones and took hold of the necklace. Carrie found it difficult to let go of her treasure; her fingertips lingered on the filigreed case.

"I'm sorry," she said again and turned away. Through her tears, she saw Wading Bird and Red Moon Girl had returned and were watching her with sympathetic faces. Everyone was watching her, offering comfort.

But she needed to be alone, so she walked away from all of them, out where she could sit and watch the horse herd grazing. She could see Brandy and Pearl and many other horses she recognized, fattening on the rich grasses. There was something peaceful and replenishing about the scene, and Carrie sat a long time, thinking about what had happened and wondering what would come of it all. How the women—and Bone Look especially—would treat her now.

As it turned out, the changes were subtle. She seemed to inspire some new respect in the camp because of her daring and strength and generosity, and she learned that behind her back some people called her Bone Breaker. But Wading Bird assured her the nickname was a compliment and was not likely to last.

As for Bone Look herself, she left Carrie alone. They never became friends, but they were no longer enemies. They could work comfortably together, only speaking when necessary for the task at hand, and without any of the old tension.

Carrie had wondered how the woman would receive her gift, what she would do with it. Throw it away? Destroy it? Trade it? Wear it?

Bone Look chose not to wear it as a necklace. She took it off the chain—which she used as a decorative fastener around a drape in her tipi. But the locket itself she wore every day, sewn on a rawhide circle pinned to her dress.

And life went on in the camp of Old Otter. When the war party had been gone a month and a day, Carrie tossed all night in a storm of dreams: images of green grass and black buffalo, blue horses and white dogs, yellow flowers, grey birds, and skies the color of spilled blood. On the edge of morning she dreamed she lay warm in Blackhorse's arms, and he whispered to her, "*Kwasikʉ pʉetsʉku*...the day after tomorrow."

# CHAPTER ELEVEN: GRIEVING

Carrie awoke to the voice of the camp crier announcing the vision of Broken Tree, the medicine man: The war party would return the day after tomorrow. Such a bustle of excitement hit the camp as everyone prepared to welcome back the brave warriors with feasting and festivity.

Carrie's heart seemed both incapable of beating at a normal speed and permanently lodged at the base of her throat, making it difficult to breathe. She put Blackhorse's home in order, making sure all things were clean and aired and tidy.

On the second day, the camp waited expectantly, feasts prepared, all the people dressed and painted for welcome and celebration. They waited a long, anxious time, and when they first saw the few dark dots on the hills to the west, no one asked aloud the question in each mind: Why had they not sent a messenger ahead to tell of their coming?

And why were there not more of those dark dots? Even if they had been unlucky and captured no horses, each of the nearly twenty men who'd set out had taken two or three horses with him.

Carrie could barely hear the noises around her, so loud was her heart pounding in her ears, and when she realized she was about to faint, she remembered to draw another breath into her lungs. To her left, she saw Wolf-At-Dawn watching her with a mocking smile.

*Why? What can he see that I can't?* Then her eyes picked the black Appaloosa from the others. Yes, it had a rider, but he wasn't sitting tall and proud as she had expected. And where were his chestnut and his claybank dun?

As they drew nearer, she could see the men and horses were brightly painted, and there were many new scalps on their lances. But the party seemed so tired and grave; two of the horses drew makeshift *wʉtaràa*—and one of them was the grullo.

At the moment Carrie's eyes found the blue horse, she heard Red Moon Girl gasp beside her. Carrie reached blindly to hold the young girl's arm, but Red Moon Girl broke from her grasp and ran toward the warriors, followed by all the other women. All except Carrie, who felt frozen to the spot. For she could see in the way the body lay on the platform behind the grullo—whose head was painted black and whose long mane and tail had been shaved—that Red Moon Girl would not be wearing her new bridal dress. Not for No Feathers. Not for Laughing Fox.

The sound that came from Red Moon Girl as she touched the body raised every hair on Carrie's skin, set her teeth grinding against each other. The other women took it up, a terrible keening lament. Carrie watched Red Moon Girl take out her own knife and begin to hack at her hair, and women related to the five absent warriors began to do the same. Then there was a flurry of activity as they grabbed one of the riders and pulled him to the ground, beating him with shrieking fury.

Carrie wondered briefly who he could be, but her eyes were drawn to the rider of the black Appaloosa. For there he was—her captor, her husband—Blackhorse. Though he tried to straighten tall and proud as he rode up to her, his bright-red hand was pressed against his side, and even though Scar—who rode beside him—lunged to try to catch him, still Blackhorse fell and lay unmoving at her feet. *Just like the antelope!* Carrie thought in wild confusion. The one he had dumped, dead, at her feet two days before he left on the wartrail.

Scar was immediately down off his pony, and Still Water had pushed past her, and together the men lifted the limp body—*Oh, God! Is he dead?*—and carried it toward Blackhorse's tipi. But Broken Tree, the medicine man, was right behind them, so there must still be some hope.

Carrie felt herself move forward, take the Appaloosa's rein. He snorted tiredly, eyeing her. He also was wounded, she saw. It wasn't just paint but blood, too, on his white-speckled coat. She led him toward the tipi, turning her back on the scenes of grief, trying to close her ears to the cries. She saw the almost-smile in Wolf-At-Dawn's eyes, but she looked through him as if he didn't exist.

Outside Blackhorse's lodge Carrie tied his stallion, and, gathering up great handfuls of grass, she began to clean away the paint and blood. All around her the camp itself seemed to be wailing, there were so many voices lamenting those lost. From inside the tipi she could hear the chanting and the gourd-rattling of Broken Tree. Numbly, she continued to groom the horse, and she managed not to think about anything else at all.

After a while, Still Water and Scar came out the doorway, looking very grave, and seemed surprised to see her there with the horse. They took the stallion's rein and led the horse away, leaving her with no way to occupy herself. So she just stood staring at the tipi doorflap.

Wading Bird came out, carrying cloths stained with blood. For just a moment, Carrie could see past her...to where they'd laid Blackhorse on the bed robes she'd aired only that morning. He lay very still, and she would have thought him already dead if the medicine man weren't still making *puha* to save his life. Wading Bird frowned at her and started to shoo her away.

But Carrie could see Blackhorse's body begin to twitch and shudder on the bed, and Broken Tree called for Wading Bird, who dumped the rags and ducked back inside, closing the flap to curious eyes.

*He's dying!* Carrie thought, backing away from the lodge. *What will happen to me now?*

She backed into someone, stepped on a foot, started to apologize, but when she turned, she found it was Wolf-At-Dawn waiting there, arms folded across his bare chest, his face the perfect picture of cruel arrogance. She flinched back from him. He began to speak in a tone that sounded soothing and respectful. Lost in her own churning thoughts, she missed many of his words, but he seemed to be telling her not to worry; that if Fire Dreamer died, he—Wolf-At-Dawn—would take good care of her.

Carrie pretended she hadn't understood at all, pushed past him, and ran blindly, without purpose, wanting only to be away from them both—Wolf-At-Dawn and Blackhorse too. A few moments later, hardly able to breathe, she sank down behind one of the other tipis, pressing her fingers into her ears to drown out the sounds of grief in the camp. But the wailing came to her anyway—and the groans.

Puzzled, she pulled her fingers from her ears and heard them again. Groans. Nearby. She crept a bit farther and peered around the tipi...saw the *taiboo*....white man.

At first she was too shocked to believe what her eyes told her, so she stared, open-mouthed, at the man who was unaware of her presence. He had dark straggling hair and a full beard. He wore no clothing except the remains of woolen britches, which he had soiled. The fair skin of his chest and arms was not only blistered raw by the sun, but cut and bruised and showed the long red lacerations made by the Comanche women's fingernails. Carrie remembered then the rider pulled from a horse and beaten.

He groaned as he wallowed to a sitting position. Carrie could see the ropes about his wrists and ankles were biting into the flesh, and the blood there—and elsewhere—was drawing flies.

He saw her then, blinked dazedly, as if the pain and long exposure to the sun had half-blinded him. His voice came out in a croak: "Water?" The first English word anyone had spoken to her in five weeks.

At first she found she couldn't speak. She swallowed painfully, then said, "I'll get some." But she couldn't seem to move either. He stared at her more intently, squinting ice-blue eyes shot with blood. She knew he was seeing now past her buckskin clothing and sun-browned skin to her green eyes and hair that—despite being braided and darkened by its dressing of bear fat—was definitely red.

"You're white!" he muttered, as if unbelieving.

"Yes," she said and quickly left him. Her heart was pounding as she entered Still Water's tipi, found it empty. She took a turtle shell and filled it with water from a hanging bladder bag. Her hands trembled, and a little water splashed out onto the floor. Surely this was her chance at last! Surely this unknown white man would help her escape. Though it seemed he would need her help first. She took the water—and some jerky—to him, moving stealthily among the tipis.

She held the shell to his lips, and when he had drunk half the water, she put a piece of the jerky into his mouth. He watched her all the while as he tried to soften and chew the dried meat in his mouth. She had so many things to say to him, she found she was unable to speak at all.

He swallowed, said, "My name's Blake. Caleb Blake."

She nodded. "Carrie," she whispered, tears coming to her eyes as she said her old name. "Carrie McEdan." She fed him more jerky, then the rest of the water. His eyes never left her. He seemed to revive quickly, looking more alert and strengthened.

"Where are we?" he asked, his voice still rasping as if he had damaged his throat recently with too much talking—or too much screaming. "How far away from a white settlement?"

"I don't know," she had to admit. "I'm sure we're hundreds of miles from my home in Texas."

"How long've they had you?"

"About five weeks," she said, saw a subtle, unreadable shift in his eyes.

"Belong to one of the bucks, now, do you?"

Confused, she blurted, "In a way, but—"

"Y'started liking it yet?"

Carrie lurched back on her heels, aghast at his sneering rudeness. Part of her wanted to defend her honor, part of her felt white-hot anger pushing blood into her face, choking her speechless.

"Well, if yer man was in that war party, mebbe I did y'favor. Widdered you, so t'speak. That one that died just 'fore we got here—with the blue horse?—I did for him." No Feathers! "And the other one. The one that's dyin'. I put three bullets in him, personal." Blackhorse!

Inside herself, the feelings swelled and struck at each other like great warring storm winds, and Carrie felt like a lonely cottonwood leaf, tossed and helpless between those two forces.

This was the man who would help her escape? The man who had taken Red Moon Girl's happy dreams? The one who was making her—Carrie—more vulnerable by the moment to Wolf-At-Dawn?

"I thought you could help me escape, get back home," she said weakly, her eyes blinded by hot tears.

"Aw now, that's a good idea, lass! Be glad to, if y'll help me get free m'self. Cut me loose, get some horses and water fer us. I'll need a gun."

"You won't kill anyone?" The words slipped out before she could stop them—or even think about them.

His chuckling laugh was raspy too; the sound of it raised the hairs on Carrie's arms. "No one human," Caleb Blake answered. "Hell, they's jest savages. Ain't y'learned that yet? I rode with Chivington at Sand Creek. Now there's a man knew how t'deal with injuns." He spat and eyed her speculatively. "Sure y'want t'go home? How 'bout we go north? You keep me warm along the way, and when we get t'Dodge City, I'll put y'on the train and buy y'ticket to a new life either d'rection—east or west."

The feeling of horror grew inside Carrie, and she whispered, "What do you mean, new life?"

He grinned, showing newly broken teeth. "Y'sure you'd be welcome back home? Five weeks. Who'd want y'now?"

She leaped to her feet and ran, heard his voice call after her, "Hey, wait now! I'll take care of ya till we get there!"

She ran all the way to the river, sobbing out loud now, crumpled to the grass beneath the willows and trailing vines, which bent tenderly over her, seeming to echo her weeping.

*Oh, God! Is he right? Will they take me back?* Would Danny if he were still alive? How would her family treat her? Wesley and Papa and proper Aunt Emma? She would never be able to marry well now. What of the people in town and at church? Would they avert their eyes, avoid touching or speaking to her? Would they gossip and snigger when her back was turned? Would anybody ever love her again?

Gentle hands touched her, soothing words came to her, "You grieve too soon. There is life yet in that one's body. He may still live." Carrie crawled closer to Wading Bird, let the woman hold her like a child as she wept.

A long while later, when the tears were finished, Wading Bird told her, "Come. There's work to do."

*There's always work to do,* Carrie thought dully, but she followed the woman obediently. She was still barred from entering Blackhorse's lodge, but as she worked nearby, helping Wading Bird cook a meal, she could hear the medicine man entreating the spirits. Once Scar—who was now assisting Broken Tree—came out to get some more water, and told them that the bullets had been removed, but Carrie was not reassured by his expression.

There was a gathering that night to note the taking of scalps and the counting of coups, to honor the deeds of the brave lost in battle, and to deal with Caleb Blake. Carrie stayed away for a while, heard from a distance the heartbeat of drums, the eerie chanting and once, a horrifying shriek of pain. But at last, she was drawn by the hypnotic flicker of the firelight, the rattling gourds, and by the softly ominous, repetitive slap of dancing moccasins against the earth, the rustle of long fringes like the warning of a rattlesnake.

When she joined the Comanches, she saw that Caleb Blake had been stripped naked and tied standing between two upright poles, his arms and legs stretched wide. Near him, a cottonwood log shifted in the fire, sent up a spray of sparks, lighted him more clearly.

Carrie saw he had been scalped alive, and the area on his crown where the hair had been taken was raw and bleeding. He sagged from his arms, the muscles twitching in his skinny thighs, and a terrible groan slipped out of him. Here and there, arrows bristled from his skin, showing the marksmanship of those who could barely pierce his flesh, adding to the blood loss while keeping him alive. Carrie watched numbly as the dancing line of warriors, one by one, used their sharp knives to draw stripes of blood on his bare flesh.

Not really aware of how she came to be in line with the other women, how she came to have a club in her hands, Carrie found herself watching Wading Bird—that gentle spirit—strike the whiteman's side with such force that ribs caved beneath her heavy stick. Yet he seemed past all crying out. And then it was she—Carrie—who was face to face with Caleb Blake. He groaned, and his head rolled back. The relentless pain and blood-loss had begun to dull his eyes as he slid nearer death. But when he saw who stood before him, he called up some last reserve of pride or bravado or anger, tried to spit on her, but he had no saliva. "Lyin' bitch!" he grated.

She stared at him, weighing the club in her hand, vaguely aware of the impatience of Red Moon Girl who waited behind her, last in line. Carrie looked long into his insolent eyes, smelling the fear as it seeped from his pores. Caleb Blake, her last chance for rescue and escape.

She watched his mouth twist around the words: "Filthy, stinkin' injun slut!" The club dropped from her fingers, and her hand came up fast, struck his face with the sound of a pistol shot, a blow that rocked his head back as if it might leave his shoulders.

Carrie turned blindly away, bumped into Red Moon Girl, who was moving eagerly toward Blake with firelight gleaming on the knife in her hand. Carrie did not stay to see how Red Moon Girl took her revenge on Caleb Blake, but his screams filled her ears as she ran into the night.

She moved without plan, trying not to think at all. She found herself standing before Blackhorse's lodge, gazing up at the paintings touched by moonlight and lit from within by the fire that had been made in the center firepit. The soft light inside made the whole tipi glow like a giant golden lantern. Carrie realized no sound came from within. *Oh, God!* she thought. *He's dead!*

Gazing at the painted symbols, she allowed herself to remember exactly how Blackhorse had looked when she first saw him by the corral full of mares in that long terrified moment before she ran. How bold and self-assured and dangerous.

The tent flap rustled and a buffalo head pushed out—the headdress of the medicine man Broken Tree. He stepped through the opening, straightened, gazed at her with a face like stone beneath the crown of black-brown fur and curving horns. He did not speak but motioned her inside.

She did not want to go. Did not want to see what remained of that proud young warrior. Did not want to prepare the body for burial. She thought of how the body must be bathed and dressed in its finest clothing, the knees bent up to the chest and head on the knees, bound with ropes in this prebirth position. Carrie thought,

*I don't want to put the red paint on his face. I cannot seal those fierce eyes with red clay. Anyway, isn't it true a man should do these things, not a woman—not even his wife?*

But Broken Tree's gaze did not waver, and she saw suddenly how tired he looked. When he gestured again toward the doorway, Carrie bit her lower lip and entered the tipi. It was warm and fairly light inside because of the fire. Blackhorse lay on the willow bed, covered only by a light-weight skin blanket. *Where will they bury him?* she wondered. *Must they kill the black Appaloosa so he'll have a worthy steed to carry him across the sky to the place beyond the sun? And would there never be an end to all the killing?*

She moved close to Blackhorse, knelt beside the bed. How young he looked! Her eyes blurred with tears, so that at first she thought she had imagined the movement. Blinking her eyes clear, she saw it again—a ripple in his throat muscles, a flinching of the eyelids, as if in pain. Quickly, not daring yet to hope, Carrie leaned down and put her cheek near his lips and nose. Yes! Very faint, but very real, a feather's touch of breath upon her skin.

Another touch, soft on her shoulder, startled her, and she whirled to see Wading Bird smiling gently at her. The other woman held several items in her hands, but it was hard to distinguish what they were, because Carrie's eyes had filled with tears again.

"He may still live," Wading Bird told her. "But there is much that must be done."

Carrie nodded. Wading Bird knelt beside her and began to show her what to do.

# CHAPTER TWELVE: HEALING

For many days, Carrie did little more than care for Blackhorse. She was not asked to work on hides or harvesting or cooking, though surely her help was needed. She made broths for him there in the tipi, stirring highly nutritious mesquite meal into hot meat juices. She herself ate only when reminded, a handful of *tʉrayapʉ* or a bit of left-over stew that Wading Bird brought and insisted she eat.

Sometimes she was active: treating the three bullet wounds in his side with sliced-open prickly pear cactus and mysterious powders the medicine man gave her; bathing Blackhorse's body regularly; brewing special teas according to Wading Bird's instructions; propping him up to coax the liquids into him. Other times, she sat for hours beside him, watching for any change, considering this person whose life had so abruptly altered her own. Sometimes she held his hand and tried to think him well and strong again. And sometimes she prayed.

It didn't seem quite fitting, Carrie thought, to pray to the same God that Wes and Emma seemed to believe in. Somehow, she was never quite convinced that Papa believed in God after

Mama died so young. She thought, rather, that he was just hedging his bets. Carrie found she could no longer pray to that God in the white church house who allowed everyone to sin all week and beg for forgiveness each Sunday, but who would torture for eternity anyone who did not come to Him in just the "proper" way.

Nor could she quite bring herself to pray to the spirits Blackhorse must believe in. It was not her way. She still stood at the edge of a community that saw every single thing in creation—not just people or animals or even plants, but also rocks and water and wind and fire—as possessing a spirit. To these people, every thing was alive, and every act—from hauling water to solemn ceremony to taking an enemy's scalp—was an act of prayer. It was a life imbued with spirit, and though she recognized and admired this, Carrie couldn't see herself fully assimilating the same beliefs.

Instead she found her prayers went to what she had begun to think of as a Great Spirit, a Giver of Life. A being or force who was aware of and cared about each interrelated fragment—no matter how small—of a wondrous and complex universe.

Several times in the first long week, Blackhorse lay again close to death. For a while he burned with fever, rearing up wild-eyed on the willow bed to call out a warning to Laughing Fox; babbling about fire; trying to sing one of his medicine songs. Carrie bathed him with cool water and pushed the matted black hair from his hot forehead, memorizing the lines of this face that looked so different from that of the man who had captured her. This person seemed so fragile, so vulnerable and young.

Broken Tree came at the worst times, donning his buffalo headdress and dancing the proper steps on the swept-sand floor of the lodge. He used an eagle feather fan to waft sacred smokes—sage, cedar, sweetgrass—over Blackhorse's trembling body as he called upon his most powerful spirit helpers. Wading Bird assured Carrie more than once that no one was more respected for his healing abilities and successful cures than Broken Tree, but even Carrie could see he now wore sadness and futility like an invisible blanket across his shoulders.

After one of the worst nights—when Blackhorse was at last resting easier—Broken Tree spoke to the worried brother Still Water outside the tipi. Inside, tidying up after the treatment, Carrie strained to hear and comprehend the words. As close as she could figure, the medicine man said, "I have done my best, but my power may not be enough. I have stepped many times into the spirit world of visions, searching for that one who is lost, trying to call him back to this world."

Carrie went closer to the open doorway so she could hear better. She saw him shake his head before continuing. "I get close. Always I see a glow of fire beyond the next hill. I walk toward it, calling his name, but when I reach the crest, the glow is beyond the next hill...and the next. And each time it gets more faint."

"You will keep trying?" asked Still Water, and the healer nodded tiredly.

During those long days, Wolf-At-Dawn lurked outside the tipi, waiting for the news that she was free to marry. Seeing him there only made Carrie redouble her prayers and attempts at healing. She slept fitfully at best, there on the skins beside Blackhorse's bed, waking at the slightest noise, aware of his every movement. And when sleep did claim her, it was crowded with visions of locusts, hungry-eyed wolves, and *Muupitsʉ*, the bogeyman giant of Comanche legends.

And then there was the dream that came to her four times. In the way of some dreams, there were only the same brief images: first her hand holding a hank of black mane, and then, casting her eyes down, she could see her bare feet on one side of a dark abyss, and on the other, the restless hooves of a black horse stepping dangerously close to the edge so that it crumbled away. Leaning across the abyss, she tugged on the mane, but the horse hesitated and pulled away from her grasp, and then she would wake up. Each time she dreamed it, the abyss was wider and she had to stretch farther to touch the horse.

On the fourth night, though, she would not give up. She clung to the mane as tightly as she had to Brandy's on that first wild ride, speaking softly and lovingly, and tugged again. The horse shivered with nervousness and drew back even more, stretching her arm so she thought it might rip from its socket, but she would not let go. And then the horse shuddered one last time, and its hooves stepped over the abyss and stood quietly beside her feet. She awoke with a start, and seeing her patient sleeping peacefully on the bed above her, she let herself drown in another hour of precious—but this time dreamless—sleep.

It was later that same day—as Carrie sat beside him remembering the dream—that Blackhorse suddenly opened his eyes, stared at her, and asked for water. She brought it, propped him up for the trembling sips he managed to take. Then he gazed at her a long moment, said the Comanche name he had given her, and slid away into sleep again.

But it was like a sharp bend in the road of recovery, for he gained strength daily after that and spent less and less time lost in the wilderness of sleep and dreams. Her own dreams, too, improved. She began to see parfleches full of *tʉrayapʉ*, black horses winning races, new grass covering fire-scarred prairies. When Wolf-At-Dawn heard that Blackhorse would live, he promptly approached Still Water, saying, "I will relieve you now of the responsibility for Red Moon Girl."

Whereupon—Wading Bird giggled when she told this part to Carrie—Still Water had answered, "Thank you for this kind offer, but I must return the ponies you've tied outside my lodge. For in the time since Red Moon Girl's parents died and I have kept my wife's little sister, I have become very fond of her. My tipi would feel empty without her, and so I myself will take Red Moon Girl as a wife."

Carrie giggled too, not only at Still Water's diplomacy, but also because, she thought wryly, it must have saddened Still Water to pass up those fine ponies. Then she heard Blackhorse chuckle weakly from the bed behind them. Their voices had been low, and they had thought him asleep. Carrie felt a little stab of annoyance at him. It was all very well for him to chuckle—he didn't know how the prospect of marriage to Wolf-At-Dawn had haunted her, how very close she had come at times when Blackhorse had sunk low into the valley of fever.

By the time Carrie next went to the small private tipi in her time-of-the-moon, Blackhorse was much better and did not need such constant attention. Wading Bird promised to watch him carefully and make sure he was well fed. It was not until then that Carrie realized the woman had not been in isolation since Carrie had met her. Taking a closer look at the changing contours of Wading Bird's body, she asked the question.

"In *Ʉkʉ mʉa*....the New Spring Moon...our child will be born," Wading Bird answered, both shy and proud.

Carrie smiled and said, "This child will grow up to be strong and beautiful."

"And powerful," Wading Bird added with quiet confidence.

Once again, Red Moon Girl shared the Moon Lodge with Carrie. *She's changed,* Carrie thought, remembering the happy girl who had—only a month ago—chattered about her dreams. She was a woman now, a wife of one week. She seemed full of some mysterious wisdom, but Carrie wasn't sure whether that came from her great loss and sorrow or from knowing the secrets of sharing her body with a man. Her hacked-off hair was beginning to grow, but very slowly.

Carrie missed the youthful exuberance Red Moon Girl had once shown, and realized that it was gone forever. In its place now—after that intensely painful but comparatively brief period of mourning—was a kind of peaceful acceptance. Red Moon Girl had a kind and generous husband whose first wife loved and welcomed her, no less than what most Comanche women would wish for. It was not the life she had planned with No Feathers, but it was worlds better than being Wolf-At-Dawn's third wife.

Early in their time together, Carrie tried to convey to the other girl her own sorrow over the loss of Laughing Fox, but Red Moon Girl cautioned her not to speak his name. "He is on his journey now," she explained. "If we say his name, it can call him back. Sometimes then a spirit starts missing the ones he cared about, visiting their dreams and even trying to share in their lives again. This is not good. We must grieve our losses quickly and then release those spirits so they can follow the sun road to the west."

But it was more difficult for Carrie. During their numerous reflective hours that moontime, she wondered what filled Red Moon Girl's thoughts. She herself contemplated death in her own life—how much pain she still felt at her mother's passing but how practicality had forced her to numb any such feelings for the young man she had once loved. Here was a society that revolved around warfare—which itself had become progressively more deadly—what must these people believe that they could send their men so frequently to face death?

Carrie wasn't sure what she believed happened when people died. She knew she didn't believe in the Heaven and Hell that so awed Wes and Aunt Emma. But she knew without a doubt that there was *something* beyond this life.

When she broached the subject with Red Moon Girl, the other told her: "There is *this* world," she patted the earth on both sides of her, "and the Spirit World." Her hands spiraled upward from her temples in an evocative, ethereal gesture. "We can pass back and forth easily, especially when we dream or have visions. Brave warriors live on the boundary between the worlds, and the closer they live to the line between life and death, the more powerful their lives and their medicine. Sometimes they enter that world and do not step back across the boundary but continue on their journey toward a new place we don't know about yet."

Carrie herself slipped into that Spirit World of dreams every night of her moontime and knew she dreamed deeply and vividly, but always upon waking, the images fled away from her memory like water through her fingers.

Carrie left the Moon Lodge a day before her companion. Another time she might have wished to linger that extra day with her friend, glad of the respite—especially after the weeks of wearing anxiety. But she was eager to see how Blackhorse was progressing—though she'd had at least two reports daily from Wading Bird, who told of his steady gains in strength.

Carrie savored her bath in the running creek and sat humming on the bank as she combed out her long red hair. A sudden trill of birdsong—bright and precise as beading on a wedding dress—drew her attention to a nearby hackberry tree, made her wonder what bird had made the pleasant sound. Even as her eyes found it, the bird took flight, circled above her in the soft September light, calling out the sharp "Killy-killy-killy-killy" of the sparrow hawk. But this grey-and-black-and-white creature was not a sparrow hawk.

Startled, Carrie realized the bird looked just like the one she had seen in all those dreams, and in her waking state, she recognized it as a mockingbird. An odd feeling came over her as she watched the familiar wheeling, searching flight. As if she might be dreaming now instead of wide awake with her fingers tangled in her dripping hair.

The feeling of unreality grew and deepened when the bird suddenly alighted in the bush beside her, barely a foot away, and regarded her with one yellow-encircled dark eye. Carrie's mind filled with thoughts of vision quests—of animals speaking aloud to a seeker: giving advice, telling the future, bestowing *puha.*

*Surely that can't be happening to me,* Carrie thought with amusement. It was almost unheard-of for a woman to be given such powerful medicine visions until she was *pʉetʉpʉ.* She herself was still subject to the cycles of the moon.

Yet speaking seemed the mockingbird's intention, for his eye never looked away from her. And then his beak opened, as if—indeed—words would come out.

Holding her breath had made Carrie light-headed, and it seemed to her that her mind could float right out of her—like another kind of bird—and up into the treetops. Inside herself, she spoke: *So, Brother Mockingbird. What is your message for me? What secrets do you bring?*

The moment drew out between them like the most delicate filament of a spider's web, and Carrie was sure her heartbeat matched the quick rhythm she saw pulsing in the bird's grey throat just below the opened beak.

And she leaned slightly forward, so sure it would speak, not wanting to miss a syllable. But her movement—like a heavy raindrop on a web-strand—broke the moment. The bird exploded into flight—a wing-whirring kaleidoscope of shadow tones—swooping quickly out of sight with a last plaintive cry.

Carrie laughed shakily, chiding herself, "Silly girl! It was just an old mockingbird. No messages— no *puha*—for you."

She'd almost forgotten about the bird by the time she had combed out her hair, leaving it unbraided. *I do feel purified,* Carrie thought with a smile as she walked back toward camp and her tipi. She felt fresh and new and very strong. She liked the way the breeze felt lifting her damp hair, drying it as she walked. She wondered if Blackhorse would notice it.

He was propped against a willow backrest just outside the doorway of their lodge, basking in the warm rays of the late summer sunlight. When he saw her walking toward him, he smiled, and Carrie felt a great tenderness rise up in her.

He spent most of the next few days resting in the sun, though he did feel well enough to begin repairing his shield and repainting its mystical power symbols. Carrie returned to her usual chores: cooking, cleaning, harvesting—though she spent more time working near her tipi than she did with the other women. That way she was close if Blackhorse needed anything, and it allowed them to talk together at length. He seemed well pleased at her ever-growing ability to communicate in his language, though very often their conversations involved her listening to long speeches or stories and only making brief comments in response.

She did enjoy listening to him, learning about his life and the ways of his people, but sometimes she just had to get away for a time. It was good to work with her women friends again, but that, too, was an animated and talkative environment, making her seek a chore or two she could do alone.

But then, toting bladder bags of water from the river, she found herself drawn to the infants she saw along the way. She had caught herself thinking quite often of babies now—perhaps because of the new life expected in *Ʉkʉ mʉa*. A niece or nephew for Blackhorse. She stopped to smile at the fat-cheeked brown faces with solemn dark eyes peering out from the cradleboards. These protective sheaths on wooden frames—lovingly decorated with crow feathers or stuffed baby bats to keep away the evil spirits—were carried whenever possible and always hung very near the mothers' working places where they could be closely watched while the infants observed the workings of the community.

She found it interesting that, after spending many months in such a sheltered way, young children were free to roam and play as they wished with little supervision or interference, even when the activities were dangerous. They developed a self-assurance based on making their own mistakes, yet there were few real injuries, and they rarely disrupted the life of the camp, even unintentionally. It seemed that those early times of constant close contact gave them a sense of security that made it unnecessary to seek attention from adults. Carrie could not remember ever seeing children who appeared more relaxed, respectful, or happy.

Three days after Carrie returned from the Moon Lodge, she noticed that Blackhorse seemed especially quiet during their evening meal, as if his thoughts were all he had time for. After they'd eaten and she had tidied everything away, Carrie's eyes began to burn, and a cough tickled in her throat. The wind must have changed and now the smoke—unable to escape properly from the hole at the top of the tipi—was collecting inside the lodge.

She stepped outside, saw that the wind, indeed, blew from the south now. On each side of the lodge were two tall poles that attached to flaps—like the pointed ears of dogs—by the smokehole where the upper ends of the lodgepoles emerged like a circular fan of bare sticks. She struggled to reposition these tipiflap poles until she was sure the moving air would now properly draw the smoke from the lodge and leave it comfortable inside. She couldn't help feeling a ripple of pride. This simple-seeming task had been one of the most challenging to master.

Carrie took a moment to stand alone, there by the tipi with the black horse rider painted on it. Near the door on a pole tripod hung Blackhorse's flame-patterned war shield, its slightly convex face pointed toward the east to capture the replenishing power of the sun. Along its bottom edge, the eagle feathers stirred in a breeze that carried the gentle sounds of Old Otter's camp as it settled itself for the evening. Carrie breathed deeply the soft golden air of almost-autumn, but as the wind touched her cheek, she felt the warning hint of chills to come, and she shivered.

When she slipped back inside the tipi, she saw that Blackhorse's eyes now paid attention to her. He told her to close the doorway flap and put out the crossed sticks so that visitors would know they were not to be disturbed.

This she did, her mind full of questions, and then she went to sit, as he indicated, on the robes spread next to his willow bed in the spot where she had slept all those long nights he battled for his life. She kept her eyes down and waited for Blackhorse to speak.

"A vision quest is a very private thing," the warrior said at last, almost as if he were scolding her. "The songs a man hears, the powers he learns are only to be shared with the permission of his spirit guardian." He shifted restlessly on the robes and said in a proud voice, "I have never told anyone the most important part of my vision quest. But I am permitted to tell you. *You,* I must tell."

Carrie's eyes came up to meet his, and she listened carefully to his story, not interrupting when she didn't understand words or their meanings. But he spoke slowly—he was still very weak—and in the end, she felt certain she understood it well enough.

He had dreamed of fire, as everyone knew, but a spirit voice had come from the fire, singing his songs, giving him his secrets. And then it told him that one day he would find a woman who was very powerful—even though she was not yet *pʉetʉpʉ*—a girl on fire, with fire for hair and fire in her heart. That woman—weaponless—would strike him and draw blood.

But if he captured her and treated her well, that girl would save his life one day. As her husband, he would be happier than with any other woman, but more important, if she chose to be his wife, he would gain a very powerful medicine to protect him during dangerous times in the future.

But she must *choose* to be his wife. He could not ...must not...force her.

Carrie sat listening to the whole story, saw him gaze upward at his medicine bundle where it hung at the top of the tipi drape—a buffalo hide package containing secrets she had not ever seen, would probably never be allowed to see. All the while, his hand touched at the amulets about his neck: a thong strung with elk's teeth, a silver ring, the little buckskin bag she now knew contained small pieces of flint—source of his *puha*, his personal power: Fire.

*Perhaps I'm not really the one who saved his life,* Carrie thought. There was the work of Broken Tree—and Blackhorse's brother, Still Water, who had given all those fine ponies and the proper gifts required by the healer spirits—and what of the teas and powders Wading Bird had prescribed?

But then Carrie remembered the long hours she had spent thinking him well and strong. And had not her prayers lifted so constantly and fervently to the Great Spirit that perhaps, she thought—almost smiling—He'd had no choice if He wished to have any peace again. And she remembered the dream, leading the horse to step back to her side of the abyss. So perhaps she could, after all, take credit for saving his life.

For a long moment after Blackhorse's voice had stopped, neither of them spoke, but Carrie's heart felt like a bird fluttering high in her ribcage. For surely she knew what must come next.

He gazed at her as intently as he had in their early days together, and his hand moved as if he might reach over and touch her hair, but he made it sink, instead, onto the soft buffalo robe. "So, Girl-On-Fire," he said at last, and Carrie thought his eyes and voice seemed suddenly shy. "Do you choose to be my wife?"

Looking deeply into his dark eyes, she did not think about love, but wondered, instead, at the forces that had drawn them together, that had foretold their meeting and her own actions, that had set the guidelines for them to follow. How could she hope to ignore or reject such a destiny?

"Yes," she said softly. "I choose it."

# CHAPTER THIRTEEN: WAITING

The long, beaded fringes of the white buckskin bridal dress whispered about her as Carrie stooped under the flap and entered Blackhorse's tipi. She was alone, glad for the time to make a few last minute preparations on her wedding night. The round room was warm and fragrant, dimly lit by the smoldering fire. As she moved, the light glinted on the yellow and blue glass beads she had sewn on the yoke of her dress, and some of the silver beads on the fringes tinkled together like tiny bells. She wore nothing but knee-high leggings and a breechcloth under the dress, for her white-lace undergarments lay packed away at the bottom of one of the rawhide trunks.

She cleaned and put away the bowls and spoons she'd brought, then moved the narrow wooden bedframe well away so that she could arrange a larger sleeping area for two—soft with buffalo robes and tawny antelope hides and pillows made of otter pelts stuffed with sweet-smelling grasses.

She took the porcupine tail hairbrush down from where it hung on the lodgepole, tugging the soft leather thongs from the ends of her braids. She sat down on the bed of robes and began to unbraid her hair, listening to the voices outside the tipi: Blackhorse and Still Water talking together about the move tomorrow. At dawn, the camp would pack up and begin its journey to the canyon of the river they called *Pia pasiwahunu* ...Big Sand Creek. They would be making winter camp there, joining Quanah and the others who refused to believe the lies of reservation life—Comanches, Kiowas, some Cheyennes.

Irritated, Carrie tugged harder against a small snarl in her hair, thinking how riding with Quanah had almost gotten Blackhorse killed last time. Now the whole band would be joining Quanah's followers, sharing any danger he might draw to him.

When her hair was completely combed out, she left it loose, like a red-gold cape over the yoke of her creamy-white dress. She knew Blackhorse liked it best that way and tonight, especially, she wanted to please him.

But where was he? She listened carefully, certain now his voice outside the tipi was growing fainter—as if he and Still Water were moving *away*....

Carrie sighed in exasperation. Didn't he remember she was waiting? Talking of war was no way to spend a wedding night. But what could she do about it? Surely she couldn't call after him to come to bed! She would never hear the end of the teasing, and he would be angry, and she didn't want to get a reputation for nagging before her marriage had even begun.

So all she could do was behave as a good Comanche wife and wait for her man to come home. *I hate waiting!* Carrie thought and glanced about their living area to make certain every item was impeccably placed. Then she bent to fuss with the fire, even though it was already burning perfectly.

Despite her annoyed anticipation, Carrie felt tired. And her muscles ached again from riding. In the eight days since she had agreed to be Blackhorse's wife, she had begun to ride again—for pleasure, not as a part of her work or travel. He had suggested it himself when he saw her watching the horses longingly.

"Do you not ride the red mare?" he had asked, propped against the backrest in the warm sun outside the tipi. She had glanced up from pounding mesquite beans into meal, thinking, *When do I ever have time?* But she only said, "No."

Blackhorse filled his stone pipe with the mixture of tobacco and sumac leaves, lit it, and said, "She is your horse. I gave her to you when I caught you in the canyon; I could see the bond you shared. You should ride her often to keep that bond strong."

Part of Carrie wondered when she'd ever find the time; there was so much work to do if their household was to be comfortable all winter. But the other part of her could only think how it would feel to ride a galloping horse again, certain it would be better now, for she'd be in control and not running for her life. Even her Aunt Emma had occasionally said, "Some things, Carrie, you just have to *take* the time for." Of course, Emma had been talking about reading Bible verses, but Carrie had to agree with the sentiment.

So for the next eight days, she found a little time each day to catch Brandy and ride her near the camp. The young boys seemed almost always to be on horseback, constantly finding new games to test and develop their skills for hunting and warfare. Carrie still watched awestruck at times as they performed stunts that her disbelieving mind told her must be impossible. Yet they made them seem almost too easy to be challenging.

At first the boys acted amused that she should want to spend time riding horses for no apparent reason. Though Comanche girls were quite accomplished on horseback—so they could easily flee an enemy—they usually were more interested in toys and dolls and learning from their mothers how to take care of a household and family.

One of the boys, Bear Growling, stared at her each day with arrogant unwelcome when she came to catch up her horse. And so, today, on the eighth day, when she had looped the jawrope in Brandy's mouth and swung easily onto her back, Carrie had looked boldly at Bear Growling and suggested, "Race?"

What Comanche boy could resist such a challenge? He turned to his friends with a swaggering air, as if asking them to share this great joke. Then he nodded to her, and she was quick to point out the course: all the way to the persimmon grove, then back again. Carrie saw him hesitate. They both knew he'd prefer a shorter course. His pure white pony—what the Comanche called a *tosa pukurua*—was famous for its swiftness in short bursts of speed, but it didn't have the stamina for longer races.

She smiled at him, letting him know she enjoyed his discomfort. Sometimes she got very tired of the lordly way Comanche males could act and the way the women quietly accepted, even supported, their self-importance. Of course she remembered what Wading Bird and Cricket Song had said about humility and how women were the truly powerful ones. "Men know this too," Cricket Song said once,"and we women ease their embarrassment by treating men as if they were just as important and as powerful as we are."

*Still,* Carrie thought as she sat Brandy, watching Bear Growling consider his predicament and feeling her own power as she rarely had before,

*I guess I just don't have enough humility to be a good Comanche woman yet.* And she waited, refusing to be stared down by a boy who had yet to go on a vision quest.

He didn't look happy as he accepted the challenge. He rode well, quirting the *tosa* as it lagged behind, but the Kentucky mare had the long-distance speed, and she won easily. Bear Growling made a gesture of honor to Carrie and rode his white pony away to nurse his damaged pride.

Carrie laughed to herself, heard her name called. Glancing around, she saw that Blackhorse beckoned her. Would he disapprove of—or appreciate—the warrior spirit in her? she wondered as she rode Brandy to where he sat cross-legged by their tipi. He no longer used the backrest, but it was near at hand should he become tired. He did look stronger now and rested, handsome and young in the soft autumn light. Carrie found herself wondering how soon he would feel well enough to share his bed with her, to take her at last as his wife. The bold thoughts pushed color up into her cheeks. She watched him study her, and she waited, sitting as tall and proud as she could for his inspection.

He rose slowly, as carefully as a young colt first finding its legs, stood beside Brandy with one hand on the jawrope to steady himself. "You ride well," he said at last, a smile lurking in his voice and eyes. "Even better than the day I caught you."

His hand came up to touch her hair, which—even braided—hung past her waist. He took one of the braids in his hand and held it as he might the rein of a powerful and responsive warhorse, so that they were both aware of that delicate, trembling tension between them. "Tonight," he said, "we are invited to feast with my brother's family." He looked long into her eyes and told her, "Wear that whiteskin dress you made."

As his meaning came to her, she felt the heat rise in her cheeks again, and she looked down at her hands resting on Brandy's mane and asked, "You are well enough?"

He tugged the braid to bring her gaze back to his, and she read his answer—his promise—in those dark eyes.

*And where is he now?* Carrie fumed. Off smoking his pipe and talking of war while she sat waiting to finally learn the mysteries of lying with a man.

Well, she was used to waiting, and she had no other choice, but the hour was very late, and she lay back on the buffalo robes, resting her tired body. She made sure her hair was arranged all about her in a becoming fashion, patted the beads and fringes of her bridal dress into alignment, and then closed her eyes. She sighed tiredly, trying not to think about how soon she'd be pulling down the tipi cover and building a *wʉtaràa* with the lodgepoles. Already she could hear some people moving about, dogs barking, horses whickering. Surely it was too early to be packing. How far was it to the canyon of the *Pia pasiwahunu*? And what was in store for her and her people there? She lay half-dozing, dreaming of tall grass, clear water, and more buffalo than she could count; of strong ponies, smiling sisters, and children with plenty to eat all winter.

She thought of babies, the one growing in the womb of her friend Wading Bird. *What will my own children be like?* Carrie wondered. *Will they be strong and smart and will I be a good mother? Will I be a good wife?*

And making love. Would she like that? Would a Comanche lover be so different from any other man? She thought about kissing. She had never seen or heard about Comanches kissing. Remembering the sweetness of that one kiss she'd had from that grey-eyed boy—ages ago, it seemed, and worlds away—she knew she didn't want to forget about kissing. Perhaps she could teach Blackhorse? If she must learn the ways of his people, could she not teach him a few of her own? The thought amused her, and she smiled to herself.

She heard the tentflap rustle as he entered, but she didn't open her eyes, pretended to be asleep as if waiting had not mattered at all. But her heart speeded up as he drew near, knelt beside her, touched her cheek and said her name. "Carrie?" It was not the name she expected to hear.

Her eyes flew open. Nor was it the face she thought she'd see. The last face in the world she had expected to see gazing down at her was that of Danny Bonner.

To Carrie it seemed that time dragged to a stop all around her as she stared up at those cheekbones she remembered, the curly black hair, the grey eyes that looked as if they hadn't laughed in months. Finding she could not look away from his face, she opened her mouth to say his name, but no words came out.

He looked at her in the old way, as if he were drinking in the sight of her, touched her gently on her cheek, her hair, her shoulder. Said in a trembling voice, "Thank God I've found you." And he gathered her up in his arms and held her as if she were the most precious thing in all the world.

She felt like a block of wood in his arms, and it took all of her inner strength to make her own arms come up and fasten around his neck. In her numbness, she heard a tiny voice repeating again and again—like a fist beating against an unyielding door—"But he's dead! He's dead! He's dead!"

He held her a little away from him, searching her eyes. "You look well," he said, like a question.

She nodded, her eyes falling to his hand, finding there the impossible: the silver ring with the pattern of arc and waving lines, the darkened half-circle. Her voice came out in a small rusty whisper, and the English words felt strange in her mouth, "I don't understand.... "

"There'll be time later to talk," he promised, rising to his feet. "We must leave now." He paused, reaching down to her. "If you *wish* to return with me."

She stared at his hand—the one with the impossible ring—and struggled with her thoughts of that other world: the dim faces of Wesley and Papa and Emma, the sod-brick house with the corral behind, the white church with its bell calling worshippers. And she told herself, *Of course I wish to return!* Hadn't she spent the last long weeks waiting for just this opportunity? She told herself again, *Of course I wish to return.*

She reached up to Danny, allowed him to help her to her feet. He seemed much older, somehow, and he hadn't yet smiled. Where was Blackhorse? Carrie wondered. How was it this young white man could come here so boldly and take away that warrior's new wife?

When she asked, she used his Comanche name, "What about Fire Dreamer?"

Apparently Danny knew that name. "He's getting your horse. I told him you were already *my* wife." Carrie couldn't imagine how that could possibly matter, but before she could think of a way to ask the right question, Danny glanced about and said, "We should hurry. Is there anything you want to take?"

Was there? Carrie wondered. The beaded toilet case for the face paints she hadn't yet used? Her sewing awl and sinews? Her hide scraper? She pulled her rawhide belt around her waist, leaving behind her sewing kits, but keeping the knife where it hung by her right side. A good, sharp skinning *nahuu* should always be within reach.

Danny touched her arm, gently urging her toward the doorway. She glanced back over her shoulder, but every item in the room was already caught in her memory forever. Carrie knew that if she lived to be a hundred, she'd still be able to describe the willow bed and rawhide trunks and tell exactly where hung the horn ladle that Still Water's wives had decorated with plaited porcupine quills.

Carrie stooped under the doorflap and stood up outside, saw the faces watching her. At first, she avoided Blackhorse's eyes, looked instead at Still Water and Red Moon Girl and Wading Bird, memorizing their faces.

Red Moon Girl kept looking thoughtfully from Carrie to Danny and back, as if remembering the Moon Lodge conversation where Carrie had admitted being in love, perhaps realizing now Carrie had spoken of a romance before she met Fire Dreamer.

Wading Bird came to her, wrapped a buffalo robe about Carrie, trying to sound stern as she warned, "Keep the dew from that soft-tanned dress or it will stiffen and you'll have to start over."

"Thank you for buffalo robe," Carrie murmured, looking deep into the other woman's eyes, saddened by the thought that now she'd never see the child that would be born in the New Spring Moon.

How Carrie longed to embrace this woman—and her sweet sister! But she knew such behavior would be considered unseemly. And certainly she wanted to say good-bye, but the phrase—*Nah nʉ tʉasʉ ʉ punitui*—would not come from her mouth, for she was achingly aware of its literal translation: "Maybe I'll see you again."

"Carrie?" Danny prompted gently, and she turned away. He'd taken up the reins and was mounting his bay stallion Pirate, who seemed weary-looking and thin after months of searching travel. Beside him stood Blackhorse, holding the jawrope of the sorrel mare, Brandy.

As she moved toward them, Carrie no longer avoided Blackhorse's gaze. Instead, part of her cried out to him, *Oh, read my eyes! Make me stay! Don't let this stranger take me back to the land of square houses!*

But if he could read her heart through her eyes, Blackhorse never showed it. He stood very straight and proud-looking, as if her leaving meant nothing to him. *Why doesn't he stop me?* Carrie wondered desperately. *Doesn't he care?*

She moved near him, gave him the buffalo robe to hold while she swung herself onto Brandy's back. He handed up the robe to her, and she wrapped it about her, glad for its warmth in the near-dawn chill. When she took the rein from him, their hands touched and then their eyes. In leaning toward him, her loosened hair fell forward, brushed red-gold across his hand. Blackhorse said only, "Thank you for my life."

Carrie had so many things to say to him that they all seemed to crowd together in her throat at once, blocking the way, so that it was Danny's voice that took Blackhorse's attention. A voice she felt she had never heard before.

For the formal Comanche speech flowed from this Danny Bonner—this Texas rancher's son—as if it were his own tongue. "Thank you, brother, for keeping care of my wife. I regret the imposition on your household." As if the other hadn't stolen her in the first place. It was like saying, "Forgive me for your burns" to a clumsy guest who had upset the stewpot.

Blackhorse nodded, careful it seemed to keep his eyes on Danny's instead of hers. "She was little trouble," he said. "She works well."

"Good journey to your winter camp," Danny said, turning Pirate, moving away.

With her heart hanging like a stone inside her, Carrie tried to believe the voice that said, *If I don't do a thing to make Brandy follow—if I just sit here and don't move—then we'll be able to stay. Won't we?* But the red mare seemed tired of waiting, and she started off—without a cue—trotting eagerly after Danny's bay.

Blackhorse's voice followed them, "And good journey to you, brother."

All the way to the hills, Carrie kept glancing back over her shoulder at the four figures beside Blackhorse's tipi. None of them waved to her, and though she wanted very much to wave to them, she found her hands did not obey her but continued to clutch at the heavy robe about her shoulders, at the rein, and at Brandy's mane as she turned to look behind her.

Part of her kept trying to believe it was all a bad dream—she'd wake in a moment and it would be over. But she knew better. It was happening. Why didn't someone make it stop? Why didn't Blackhorse come running after her? Why didn't she do something herself? *He doesn't want me,* she realized. She had chosen to be his wife, but now, for some incomprehensible reason, he was throwing away the commitment between them. *Otherwise he wouldn't let me go. How can I shame him by going back and asking to stay?*

Soon the figures were too small and distant to distinguish in the dim light. Just before Danny and Carrie moved into the hills, she took a last, long look at Old Otter's camp. A few tipis were still dark, but most looked like cone-shaped lamps aglow with golden light. Several showed only as skeletons of poles leaned together, for women were already dismantling their homes for the move to the *Pia pasiwahunu*. Cook fires smudged blue against the salmon pink of the eastern sky, and Carrie heard the faint voice of the camp crier calling for haste from those still abed.

When they'd taken the easiest route through the hills and found a long stretch of flat country before them, Danny turned south and pushed the horses into a canter. Carrie was surprised since Pirate was clearly near exhaustion and there seemed no need to hurry. But the pace also made conversation difficult, so Carrie remained as silent as Danny. When they'd cantered for four or five miles—the bay was slick with sweat and glassy-eyed—Danny reined him down to a walk, and when he glanced over at her, Carrie asked, "What day is it? What month?"

"September," Danny answered, considered a moment. "Must be around the twenty-second or so."

Carrie realized her seventeenth birthday had come and gone. "My family?"

He turned a bit in his saddle to better see her face. "They're well. That Wesley like to drove me crazy over trying to find you. He rode with me the first two days, but then I had to take him back home. He's just too green. Never knew one person could ask so many questions and get in the way so often."

*Danny's changed,* she thought. *He's more serious and assured. Like he's all grown up in this short time. Well, I'm changed too. How can I possibly go back to the same life I had before? I've seen and heard and felt and learned too many things. She thought of Blackhorse and the others. None of us is the same. Or ever will be.*

"You called him brother," Carrie said aloud.

Danny turned his dark-skinned, wide-boned face toward her, and he said, "That's mainly formality. Though we once were closer than most brothers get to be." He drew a deep breath, as if he had something difficult to tell her. "Actually, we're cousins." And he watched her face closely before he went on. "Our mothers were sisters."

"I didn't know...." Carrie breathed.

His face moved into an expression that was a little like a smile, a little like a grimace of pain. "No one knows. My father always felt ashamed he fell in love with a Comanche girl. Called her Rosa instead of Wild Rose Opening. Let everyone think she was Mexican. But she was strong in her own way. Made sure I learned her language too. Called me by my Comanche name when we were alone." He leaned forward to stroke the bay stallion's neck, but he seemed unaware that he did it, his face reflecting some old sadness. "She died when I was twelve. Made my father promise to let me stay that summer with her sister's family."

Danny looked off into the distance, as if he could see across years instead of miles. "That was the happiest summer of my life. With Fire Dreamer's parents and my old *kaku*...my grandmother."

Danny was thoughtfully quiet for a time, and Carrie tried to picture him—and Blackhorse—as young boys of twelve and fourteen. Still Water would have been eighteen. Carrie could envision the whole family—even their old *kaku*. Wading Bird had told so many stories about her. Such a fierce old woman she must have been, becoming in her late years a powerful and highly respected medicine woman.

"Rains-All-Night," Danny said softly, as if his thoughts had been paralleling hers but he was also aware he shouldn't be speaking the name of someone who was *kehe wainahai*... no-longer-with-us. "That was her name. I was afraid of her at first—you could see the power in her just looking at her face—but she was good to me. Determined that I would learn as much as I could about my mother's people." He sighed. "Well, I learned so much I didn't want to go home when Pa showed up in the fall. He couldn't wait to get me out of that camp. But Rains-All-Night didn't give up so easy." Danny's gaze dropped to his hands on the reins.

"You see, Fire Dreamer's father—my uncle —had a Mexican captive who'd been a silversmith. Well, Rains-All-Night had him make each of us a ring with her name symbol on it, binding us together as brothers. But it was mostly for me, so I would always have safe passage among the Comanches. And—I suspect—so I would not forget their ways when I returned to my father's house."

*Two rings,* Carrie thought. *As simple as that.* They rode for a long time without speaking. Danny seemed lost in memories of the past, and Carrie was tangled in thoughts of the future. In trying to avoid thinking of what lay behind her, she found what lay ahead even more disquieting.

Try as she did to shut them out, still her ears filled with Caleb Blake's rude insinuations. Who would want her now? Perhaps not even Danny, for he hadn't yet spoken about his plans for her. In truth, he'd never quite proposed to her, and perhaps he had no intention of doing so now. Maybe he was only "doing the right thing" and would forget all about her once he'd returned her safely home. She tried to imagine herself readjusting to her old life with Papa and Emma, sweet-but-pious Wesley and the other white-church folk.

Why, she might live the rest of her life without ever finding a man willing to marry a girl who'd lived among the Comanches. She might have to share that same back bedroom with her aunt until she was as old and dry and bitter as Emma herself.

Then she became aware that Danny had spoken, had mumbled shyly, "You don't need to feel bound by it."

"What?" Carrie asked, wondering if she'd missed part of a conversation.

He avoided her eyes. "Telling them you were my wife. You don't need to marry me." Then just as her heart sank even lower—sure that Caleb Blake had been right—Danny's voice started up again, the words coming out fast now as he brought his shy gaze up to meet hers, "Of course, I want you to be my wife. More than anything. If you'll have me."

Carrie looked away from his eyes, down at her own hands resting on Brandy's mane. In the now-bright morning light, she saw something sparkle, tied there among the coarse red strands: a charm of blue and silver beads strung on black horsehair and a tuft of small blue feathers. Had he tied it there—Blackhorse—when he caught up the mare for her? Sending her off to a life with another man but wishing her well? The ache swelled up in her like a wound that might take forever to heal.

Danny shifted restlessly in his saddle, like a Comanche youth who'd tied his best ponies outside a girl's tipi and now awaited a verdict. But Carrie had no answer for him yet. She cast back in her memory, trying to recapture the feelings she'd once had for him. Were those fires truly extinguished? Could they not be rekindled when her heart had time to heal a bit?

This was the same handsome young man she had once loved, offering not only the home and prosperous life she'd anticipated—surely the highest goal she might attain in the wilds of Texas—but also now protection and support and honor as she returned to white society. For surely he among all others could foresee the difficulties that faced them. Could she not, after all, make a life with him, share his bed, mother his children? Might she not, still, be happy?

*Nahkia*...Perhaps. But how could she possibly say yes to him now? Only hours from the bed of Blackhorse, still clothed in the bridal dress she had made and worn for that other man? It was impossible! Yet she could find no words to tell him so.

"I don't expect you to decide just now," Danny assured her, though she was certain she detected disappointment in his voice. "A lot of things've changed, and you'll want to think about it."

He matched her silence until they stopped for a late-morning meal and rest. Mesquite bushes had grown to tall trees along the banks of a small creek, providing welcome shade. Carrie and Danny knelt side by side to drink, but still neither spoke, as if they each were alone in the world.

Danny unsaddled Pirate, inspecting him carefully, and at last said, "We'll rest here for a few hours." He handed Carrie a plump *wosa* from behind his saddle, telling her, "Still Water's wives sent along food for our journey." While Danny rubbed the horses down, checked their backs for sores and their hooves for stones, Carrie unlaced the folded rawhide package. Her fingertips lingered, tracing the familiar patterns Red Moon Girl had painted on the sun-cured leather. Inside she found not only ample dried food for their journey, but tucked to one side were Wading Bird's little buckskin spicebags.

"Hey, is that *ʉrayapʉ?*" Danny asked. Carrie glanced up at him and nodded, unable to speak around the knot in her throat. He sat beside her in the shade, and after the first few bites he told her wistfully, "Tasting this sure takes me back. This is just the blend my aunt used to make—none of the other women in camp put chokecherries in their *tʉrayapʉ*. It has more crunch because of all the seeds mashed up in it." She saw him almost smile as he looked back into that vanished summer. "Hoofprint used to fill a little bag with it when we'd ride out, pretending to be on a raid. You know...*tʉkʉ noopʉ̱*...kind of like a picnic lunch."

She nodded, repeating, "Hoofprint?" She wasn't sure why she hoped he'd keep talking, but the thought of him falling silent disturbed her.

"That was Fire Dreamer's boyhood name. Before his vision quest. His head was full of raiding that summer, 'cause his big brother was away on the wartrail most of the time."

"Still Water," Carrie prompted.

"Yeah. They were very close, and Hoofprint was real lonely without him. Then I showed up, and it was like having his own little brother, I guess. Someone to teach and brag to, show off for and confide in. Even then he was too fond of long speeches."

Carrie gave Danny a tiny smile to encourage him, and he returned it with a rueful laugh. "What a couple of hellions we were that year! Into everything. Can't tell you how many times we upset the drying racks and played practical jokes on the elders in council. He stood up for me when I lost a bow I'd borrowed, and I rescued him after his pony fell in a buffalo stampede."

She watched Danny eat another handful of *tʉrayapʉ* and drink from a freshly filled canteen. The smiles were gone from him when Danny said, "He changed some toward the end of the summer, though. Went off on his vision quest and came back kind of serious and grown-up. Got his new name Fire Dreamer. Close as we were, he'd never tell me about his medicine dream. I felt left out. Couldn't wait till I was a few years older and could seek my own medicine...get a warrior's name."

He rose suddenly. Carrie knew he was thinking of his father when he said, "But then *he* came after me and took me back home." And Danny walked away, back to the horses, and began to rummage about in his gear, as if he'd totally forgotten her.

The words echoed again and again in her mind: "But then *he* came after me and took me back home." Carrie leaned back against the tree, squeezing her eyes shut as she tried to clear her mind of all thoughts, all questions, all voices, hoping to ease the pain in her. Failing.

A few moments later, she heard Danny say, "These might be more comfortable for riding." When she opened her eyes, she saw him standing above her, holding out some trousers and a shirt. "Wesley sent them for you. Said to tell you he wished he'd let you have them sooner." Danny's tone told her he found the message puzzling and hoped it would be clearer to her.

She took the faded clothes, and when she recognized her own careful stitches where there was mending, quick tears came up in her eyes. Behind their blur, she pictured how Wesley's face must have looked when he gave the clothing—and the message—to Danny. "Yes, thanks," she murmured. "I'll change into them."

He returned to the horses, keeping his back to her as he saddled up his bay and folded the buffalo robe—no longer needed for warmth—across Brandy's back to make a kind of saddle for Carrie.

When she slipped into the shirt, the cloth felt rough against her skin after the softness of buckskin, but she was pleased by the almost-forgotten scent of her own lavender soap that came up to fill her nostrils. Because they were clothes Wes had outgrown more than a year ago, they fitted her fairly well. She kept her own rawhide belt and comfortable moccasins. With great care, she folded her bridal dress and leggings. Then Danny packed them away in one of the saddlebags—as if they were just any old clothes, instead of the wedding dress of a stolen bride.

Riding away from the creek toward the south, with her eyes still caught by the saddlebag, Carrie was reminded of the white-lace dress in her cedar trunk at home—the one her mother had worn when she'd married Papa; the one Carrie had intended to wear for Danny. Images drifted before her, and when she thought of that wooden church in town—remembering how Danny sat as solemnly as Wes through the long sermons—she wondered whether Danny really believed in the White Church God. Or did he pray to the many spirits all around him, attending church as an act of community? Or was his God the Great Spirit she had come to recognize? And if it was necessary for her to sit again every Sunday on one of those wooden pews, could not her God hear her prayers even from inside the church house?

She and Danny spoke little during the long afternoon, though the horses jogged comfortably side by side. When she glanced at Danny—drawn from her own thoughts long enough to wonder about his—she always found the same expression on his face: what seemed an uneasy blend of indecision, worry, guilt, sorrow. *Is he having second thoughts about his offer?* she wondered.

Carrie did get Danny's complete attention once when she chose to jump Brandy over a deep arroyo rather than slide down one steep bank and scramble up the other as the tired bay was forced to do. Watching for any trace of disapproval, she saw instead the admiration in Danny's eyes. Knowing how easy and graceful she'd made it look, she waited to hear what he might say. But when he began, "You ride well" it seemed an echo of another voice. Sadness rose thick and sudden in her, making it impossible to answer, and the silence drew out between them once again.

They camped in late afternoon on the bank of another small stream with the familiar shelter of mesquite and cottonwood trees. Danny went off with his rifle, returned with a plump, speckled prairie chicken, which Carrie prepared and roasted over a small fire. All the while she worked, a bold mockingbird flirted about high in one mesquite tree, filling the air with his varied calls, repeating himself tirelessly.

As they ate the prairie chicken, Danny pointed out with a wry smile, "Don't guess my Comanche relatives would approve of this meal, but I do like the taste of a good gamebird. And fish. I like to eat fish too."

It was then that Carrie realized, *He's caught between two worlds too. The same two worlds.* Being back among his mother's people must have stirred up a lot of things his father hoped he'd forget. She wasn't sure why, but Carrie felt certain Danny would never be able to put those things aside again. They were even more a part of him than they were of her, and she knew she could never live her life quite as she had planned before she met Blackhorse and his people.

Later, at sunset, after Danny had helped her with the cleaning-up, Carrie found herself standing, gazing back the way they had come, though she couldn't have said what she was watching for. Deep inside herself, she didn't really expect to see the black Appaloosa with its proud rider coming for her. Still she stood looking back, and was hardly aware when her hands came up and began to braid her hair.

Though he didn't speak at first, Carrie realized that Danny had come to stand beside her, and something in the way he leaned slightly toward her made her think he was trying to find just the right words. "Carrie...." he began at last, and then faltered in that familiar way of his. She looked into his troubled grey eyes. His hand came out and took one of her braids in a gesture that made hot tears flood up into her eyes, and she had to look quickly away. "Carrie," he said, "I think I've made a mistake."

She closed her eyes tight, tears squeezing out from under and escaping down her cheeks as she thought, *Oh, God. Now he'll tell me he can't marry me after all, and I won't have even that to go back to.*

She didn't want to hear any more, wished for the return of his long silence, but his voice went on, "Listen, Carrie. I have to say this fast before I lose my nerve. I came looking for you with only one thought: to rescue you and get you home and marry you. It never occurred to me you might want to stay. That you might fall in love with one of them."

The pain in his voice forced words past the tightness in her throat. "I thought you were dead," she whispered, then swallowed painfully. "I thought that was *your* ring he was wearing."

"Oh," Danny said softly, as if that answered some question which had troubled him. He stood a long moment, his eyes—perhaps unseeing—caught by the silver ring on the hand that still held her braid. "Well," he said, then seemed to remember her and the strand of conversation. "But when I got there, saw my cousin again, sat smoking and talking in that round-feeling warmth of a tipi, I remembered how a person might come to prefer such a world. Though he tried to hide it, I could see how much he cared for you. I didn't want to think that you might care for him. I arranged it so he'd lose face if he didn't let you go—especially since I'd saved his life that time his pony fell."

Danny's voice had turned bitter as he spoke of these deeds and motives. "I told myself I must give you the choice of staying or returning. And I did. But I took you by surprise and hurried you out of there before you could think or change your mind. It's just that when I saw you lying there—waiting for him in that wedding dress—I couldn't stand the thought of losing you to anyone. No matter how you felt about him."

Danny sighed, let go of her braid, releasing her. "I was wrong. It was selfish to take advantage of you, and I'm truly sorry. I'll take you back if you want me to."

"You could find them?" she asked quickly and was at once ashamed of the eagerness she heard in her voice and the pain it caused in Danny's eyes.

He drew himself up taller, nodded. "By tomorrow night they'll be in Palo Duro Canyon on the *Pia pasiwahunu*. If we travel to the west all day tomorrow, we can meet them there by nightfall." Then he said, "Now, I'm not telling you this to keep you from going back, but I think you should know it's sure to be dangerous to be with them."

She glanced quickly up at him, and he explained, "The government's hell-bent to catch Quanah. He's outfoxed the cavalry too many times, and that Colonel MacKenzie won't rest till he's put him away on the reservation for good. I'm afraid time's running out for Fire Dreamer and all my mother's people."

"You warned him?" Carrie asked, thinking of Blackhorse's warrior pride.

"I warned him," Danny told her, "but they're going anyway." He sighed. "There just aren't too many choices left for them. They hope to be safe for the winter in the Palo Duro."

Carrie gazed now to the west where red streaked the evening sky like stripes of warpaint.

Or blood. The singing in her heart told her that the threat of danger could not keep her from returning to Blackhorse, but still she did not say this to Danny. For she was thinking of her children. What she did with her life was her own choice, but could she bear the possibility of having her babies murdered by her own people as Blackhorse's first child had been? For that matter, did she really want to raise her sons to be warriors—send them off to fight and die in battles against the Utes, the whites, the Tonkawas?

"You'd best take some time to think it over," she heard Danny saying. "In the morning, you let me know what you decide. We can go west to the *Pia pasiwahunu* or south to our valley. If we go south, you can choose to return to your family or to be my wife. It's entirely your decision. I promise I won't try to influence you in any way." He left her standing there, facing west.

Carrie slept that night beneath the buffalo robe Wading Bird had given her. And she dreamed. At first, she seemed to float along and she found she couldn't open her eyes. All about her was the stench of blood and black powder and burning. She heard loud noises—hoarse voices, bugles, gunshots—echoing as if in a deep canyon. She felt danger press close against her like the hot breath of *Muupitsʉ* on the back of her neck. Then her moccasins touched down and her eyes flew open, seeing only dark smoke all around her.

When it cleared somewhat, she saw him: the great black horse with eyes of fire—though now those eyes held sadness, too, in their proud depths. For she saw that he was captive—his forelegs bound together with rawhide hobbles, and about his proud head was the whiteman's silver-studded bridle, a steel bit forced between his jaws, the reins tied up short and unyielding to an iron hitching post.

And perched on his back was the mocking-bird she had sometimes seen circling in her earlier dreams. It sat still for the first time, gazing fixedly at her with one yellow-rimmed dark eye, as if trying once again to make her understand something. Then it burst up into flight and away in a flurry of dark and light feathers.

And for the first time, the great black horse spoke to her. "You must go with the Mocking-bird," he said, his voice filled with certainty and sadness. "You and your children must be free. My children can be nothing but captives."

Carrie reached out to the horse, tried to speak, but found she was being pulled backwards, away from him, and the smoke came between them like darkness falling at the end of a long day. She opened her mouth to call out to him, and she awoke coughing with the acrid taste of burning in her mouth and nostrils.

Danny had a small fire going, and he called to her, "Sorry for the smoke. The wind shifted. Well, this is the last of the coffee."

She rose stiffly in the cool dawn and went near the fire's warmth, accepted the cup he offered and drank. Something in the rich, remembered flavor—or perhaps in the way Danny's throat moved when he drank from his own cup—stirred lost memories in her, threatening her eyes again with tears.

*I hope he doesn't ask me what I've decided,* Carrie thought, *because I don't know yet either.*

As they ate jerky and dried persimmon cakes and drank the last of the coffee, Danny chattered away with forced cheerfulness, not seeming to notice her silence, acting as if he had forgotten she was making a decision that would so affect his future and his happiness.

She hardly heard his words, which jumped back and forth between news from their home valley and recollections of his summer among the Comanches, as if by talking of both he would keep his promise not to influence her. Instead, she listened to the voices inside herself as they argued about which life, which world, which man to choose.

By the time they were packed and mounted, Carrie still had not decided. *Is it only coincidence,* she wondered, *that I'm sitting here on Brandy and she's facing west toward the Pia pasiwahunu? Have I already decided, but I just can't admit it?*

Danny moved the bay up beside her, saying, "Well, I guess we're all ready to travel." He didn't voice the question echoing in her own mind: *Which direction? Which direction?* But she was sure he'd noticed she was facing west. She made herself gaze full into his eyes—as she had done so many times with Blackhorse before they could use words to communicate. In Danny's eyes she read a confusion of love and hope and fear. *Oh, God! Which direction?*

A sudden bubbling of birdsong—repeated once and then again, followed by the perfect imitation of a mewing kitten—drew her eyes up to the mockingbird in the tree above her. He leaped about, flashing the white sides of his black tail, cocking his head to better see her with his bright yellow-and-black eye.

"You must go with the Mockingbird," the black horse had said in her dream. Inside her mind she asked, *So Brother Mockingbird, which direction? West to the Pia pasiwahunu or south to the valley of square houses?*

The bird was suddenly very still, perched on the mesquite limb and watching her as if it had understood and now pondered the choices. Then it flew—a smudge of grey with white-splashed wings and white-sided tail—it flew straight as a warrior's arrow toward the west.

Carrie's heart flew up inside her—like the bird itself—when she saw this, but still she did not move or speak. Hadn't the decision been made? Was it not as the dream had told her? Why then did she hesitate?

*Because,* one of the voices inside her said—and she had never known any of the voices to sound so clear, so strong, so absolutely sure—*Because my path does not lead to the west. My direction is to the south, back to my own people, with this young man who stands—as I do—between two worlds.*

It seemed to Carrie that she could feel the decision in every fiber of her body. As if every bit of bone and blood and muscle were saying a calm and certain "Yes." She sat very still, feeling the peace—and a kind of acceptance—seep into her. And because all of the voices inside her were now quiet, she realized that Danny had begun chattering away again.

She watched his anxious face, seeking just the right words to tell him her decision, wishing to ease the terrible pain she saw in his eyes. A tender warmth began in a forgotten corner of her heart, and as she felt it growing, some of his words penetrated, and she interrupted in a startled voice, "What? What did you say?"

"The mockingbird," he said. "Didn't you see it fly away? I was saying I used to be embarrassed to be named that. Thought I should have a more heroic Comanche name."

"Mockingbird," Carrie said.

"Yeah. That's the name my mother gave me. She heard one singing outside her window as I was being born. I'd hoped to get a warrior's name that summer in the Comanche camp, but I made the mistake of showing off what a mimic I am, and the name stuck for good."

Carrie sat on the red mare, and for the first time in many, many hours, she felt like smiling.

Meanwhile, Danny jabbered on as if he couldn't stop. As if then he might have to hear the decision he dreaded. "I always thought, if I had to be named for a bird, why couldn't I be called Sparrow Hawk? They're such brave and fast little birds with those fine, handsome markings."

Carrie gazed down at Brandy's mane. She touched the glittering charm of blue and silver beads where it still hung—for neither of them had removed it. Then she lifted her rein.

Danny's voice rushed on, trying to hold the moment, push away the future: "Don't you think Sparrow Hawk is a better name for a Comanche boy?"

Carrie turned Brandy across in front of the bay stallion, nudging her into a trot, heading south. She saw the surprise in Danny's grey eyes and the dawning of something more. Over her shoulder, she gave him a smile. True, it was only a small smile, and it didn't try to hide the sadness in her, but it was a smile, nonetheless. Her voice drifted back to him, low and lilting, the words Comanche: "So, Mockingbird," she said. "Perhaps we will give that name to our first son."

# AFTER IT HAPPENED
## Texas ◆ September, 1874

The story of Quanah and his white mother, Cynthia Ann Parker, is true. And so is what happened to those who joined him in Palo Duro Canyon, Texas in late September, 1874.

**1999** marks the 125th anniversary of the Red River War, which began with the June 27, 1874 attack on buffalo hidehunters at Adobe Walls, a conflict in which Quanah proved a prominent figure.

But the most significant event of the year-long war must be the battle in the Palo Duro. Through this canyon runs a watercourse known to Texans as the Prairie Dog Town Fork of the Red River. The Comanches called it *Pia pasiwahunu* or Big Sand Creek.

(This is not to be confused with Sand Creek, Colorado, where, in 1864, the troops of Colonel John M. Chivington shot and mutilated some 123 Cheyenne people, who had already submitted peacefully to the government and were camped under both an American flag and a white flag of surrender. Ninety-eight of the Cheyenne were weaponless women and children. Chivington—a former Methodist minister—had ordered, "Kill them all, big and small; nits make lice.")

Quanah and his followers chose the safety of the Palo Duro Canyon for a winter camp and rendezvous with New Mexican traders, confident that the area was little visited by whites and the terrain too difficult for Army supply wagons. So it was that in the last few days of September, there were hundreds of tipis and some 1400 horses and mules spread out near the junction of North Cita

Canyon. Quanah himself was absent from the camp when it was surprised by the September 28 dawn attack of Colonel Ranald S. MacKenzie's 4th Cavalry (who had left their supply wagons some distance away in the canyon of Tule Creek).

As was customary, the Comanche men held the troops at bay until the women and children could escape up the steep sides of the canyon. During a stand-off that lasted most of the day, only four Indian people were killed, but they had to flee without their homes, winter stores, and most of their animals.

Having already been bested on several occasions by Comanches, MacKenzie knew he would have to take drastic steps to bring about their surrender to reservation life. He ordered the burning of all that was left behind: tons of lodgepoles and tipi covers, robes and winter clothing, tools and utensils, and food—jerky, pemmican, dried roots, fruits, and vegetables. It was, in fact, all that those people had managed to harvest and preserve during that drought- and locust-plagued summer.

Remembering how, two years earlier, his troops had captured 3000 Comanche horses only to have them stolen back that very night by Quanah's raiders, MacKenzie made another difficult decision. After awarding his officers and scouts with several hundred of the best of the captured horses, he had all of the other animals (more than 1000) shot at Tule Canyon and left as a powerful message to a people whose very lives depended on the mobility provided by horses.

The winter of 1874-75 was formidable, indeed, for the Comanches. Little could be salvaged from the burned rubble, there were few resources for food-gathering so late in the year, and little time before the snows began. With the few horses they had left and without their winter-resistant tipis, it was impossible to live as Comanches. Many of those who survived did so by wintering in damp caves cut under riverbanks, and eating half-rotten foods, tree bark, grass seeds and foods they considered taboo.

Small bands of Comanches drifted onto the reservation all through the winter and spring. But Quanah had managed to gather over 1000 horses and find buffalo to hunt, and his people held out until summer. Still Quanah must have realized just how futile it would be to continue resisting removal to the reservation.

On June 2, 1875, Quanah led his people into Fort Sill in what is now Oklahoma and surrendered. For all intents and purposes, this marked the end of the Red River War. Though perhaps as many as fifty Comanches remained at large and some reservation Indians slipped away to raid while under permission to "hunt," Quanah's surrender was definitely the end of a way of life for all the Comanche people.

Who knows how long it could have lasted anyway? Railroads and barbed wire and windmills were changing the face of the prairie, and within four years the rest of the buffalo—their greatest source of food, clothing, and shelter —would be gone from the Plains. In fact, when Quanah was allowed to take a hunting party off the reservation in 1878, after weeks of searching they found not one buffalo where once had roamed an estimated 30-90 million.

But surrender at Fort Sill was not the end of Quanah's story. It was, instead, a kind of beginning—for he reasoned, "If my white mother could learn the ways of the Comanche, then I can learn the ways of the whites"—and the rest of Quanah Parker's story is very interesting indeed.

**THE END**

# Author's Notes

Researching is both a fascinating and frustrating experience. Sources frequently offer contradictory information, and often one can't tell if an agreeing source has only relied upon material as written, without further/independent verification.

I found numerous accounts of the battle of Palo Duro Canyon (often citing the date as September 27) and how many horses and mules were destroyed by the U.S. Government afterward. Most (including the historical site marker inside the Canyon as well as the small museum in the Visitor Center) agree there were around 1400 captured and some 1048 shot, but in an article called "The Livestock of the 1874 Red River War and Alleged Genocide During the Late 19th Century Indian Wars," author Edwin F. Quiroz maintains only 732 horses were shot, the others given to officers and scouts or later sold at auction. His sources appear reliable, but given the political slant of his arguments, personally, I find myself unconvinced.

Various historians place differing emphasis on the role and prominence of Quanah Parker, especially before his surrender to the reservation. My references to his notoriety during the Red River War allow me to set an historical frame for my story.

There may also be some disagreement about certain Comanche words and terms I've included. Comanches were ever the ones to do things their own way: different bands sometimes had different words/pronunciations. My language resource for **Girl-On-Fire** has tried to provide a majority view. And beyond that, one can always say, "Well, that was the way it was said in the band that adopted Carrie."

For those who know enough about Comanche healing practice to say, "a young woman would not be allowed to remain in the tipi with the medicine man,"

I've been assured she could have if she'd been needed to assist him (and there's reason to believe Wading Bird may have assisted her husband's grandmother, a medicine woman).

My **Girl-On-Fire** adventure began in February of 1982, and, over the years, I've immersed myself in countless books about Comanches and other Plains tribes. I've pored over maps and studied photos with magnifying glasses. It would be impossible now to list all the books and materials that formed a basis for **Girl-On-Fire**, but the main source for cultural detail was the book *Comanches: Lords of the South Plains* by Ernest Wallace & E. Adamson Hoebel, which (along with others the tribe considers credible) may be found at the CL&CPC website below.

For those interested in learning more about
(and/or those wishing to support efforts benefiting)
the Comanche language and culture,
please contact:

***Nʉmʉ Tekwapʉha Nomneekatʉ***

The Comanche Language and
Cultural Preservation Committee
P.O. Box 3610
Lawton OK 73502-3610

www.skylands.net/users/tdeer/clcpc/

***The CL&CPC Mission Statement:***

"To foster a cooperative relationship among federal, state, and tribal agencies, schools, parents, and others for the preservation and promotion of the Comanche language and culture, to change the direction of the Comanche language—from near extinction—and take our language of heritage into the future."

***Currently, CL&CPC is completing a new dictionary of the Comanche Language, and donations to assist the publication are greatly appreciated.***

**Vicki Hessel Werkley**
—flanked by (at left) **Sky**, a Morgan,
and **Charley**, a mustang/Appaloosa cross—
at the Onstad Ranch in Lower Lake, California,
November, 1999. Photo by **Tom Werkley**.

# About the Author

**Vicki Hessel Werkley**, a writer since second grade, has won numerous awards for her non-fiction, poetry and short stories, including a National Scholastic Writing Award. Her articles have appeared in various newspapers and magazines, including several with international readership. She enjoys researching and writing about many different topics, but favorites include: history (especially of the American West), animals and science fiction. Psychology, dreams and the world of the spirit figure prominently in all her work. **Girl-On-Fire** is her first published novel.

Born into an Air Force family stationed in the Panama Canal Zone, Vicki later lived in Texas, Arizona and very briefly in Japan, but has been a Californian since 1957. During fourteen years as an educator in Mendocino County, Vicki both taught and wrote curricula for a wide variety of subjects; she's worked extensively as a peer counselor and mediator and has been editing other people's writings for many years—even during a time she was legally blind.

Now enjoying better eyesight, Vicki lives in Lake County, California with Tom, her husband of thirty years, and Lani (short for Hokulani, which is Hawaiian for "Star in the Sky"), a parakeet who thinks she runs the household.

Since 1987 Vicki has taken a very active role in Spotlight Starman International—an organization dedicated to promoting socially and environmentally conscious television—and has served as Co-Editor-in-Chief of its newsletterzine *Blue Lights* since 1991. This involvement has also piqued her interest in screenwriting.

Having longed for her own horse since she was two, Vicki enjoys riding at the Wild Horse Sanctuary near Shingletown, California, and still hopes to someday adopt a rescued mustang.

# Haven Books

*Erin Gray's*
*&*
*Mara Purl's*
Act Right

*Congratulations, you got the job. Now what?*
A step-by-step guide for the professional actor

**$19.95**

INCLUDES:
a complete glossary & anecdotes from
well-known performers & professionals

I am blown away by the clarity and completeness of Erin Gray & Mara Purl's book.

– Joan Van Ark
Actress ("Knots Landing")

I have nothing to add – except my endorsement of "Act Right": a must read.

– Dan Hamilton
Emmy Award-winning Director

***AVAILABLE AT ALL SAMUEL FRENCH STORES,***
***AT AMAZON.COM, BORDERS.COM, BN.COM***
***OR***
***DIRECTLY FROM THE PUBLISHER***

Haven Books
10153 ½ Riverside Drive
North Hollywood, CA 91602

Havenbks@aol.com
Phone 818/ 503-2518
FAX 818/ 508-0299

www.havenbooks.net

LaPorte County Public Library
LaPorte, Indiana

# *Mara Purl's riveting Milford-Haven Novels*

*Travel to America's favorite little town...hardly the spot for a hotbed of controversy – or is it? A murder mystery, a romantic adventure, a compelling tale of intriguing relationships and complex issues unfold as Mara Purl shows the lines being drawn between those who want the town to expand, those who want to keep it the last pristine haven, and those who have their own secret agendas....*

| | | |
|---|---|---|
| BOOK ONE | *What The Heart Knows* | 0-9659480-1-3 |
| BOOK TWO | *Closer Than You Think* | 0-9659480-2-1 |
| BOOK THREE | *Child Secrets* | 0-9659480-3-X |

AVAILABLE THROUGH YOUR FAVORITE BOOKSTORE
OR ORDER FOR OVERNIGHT DELIVERY

*$11.95 $11.95 $13.95*

**Haven Books http://www.havenbooks.net**
10153 ½ Riverside Drive
North Hollywood, CA 91602
818/ 503-2518 phone
818/ 508-0299 FAX
Reya@havenbooks.net
Havenbks@aol.com

LaPorte County Public Library
LaPorte Indiana

*Discover*

# Haven Books

**http://www.havenbooks.net**

*Fiction with vision*

*Mara Purl's*
Milford-Haven Novels

*Vicki Hessel Werkley's*
Girl-On-Fire

Coming Soon
*Katherine Shirek Doughtie's*
Indigo Sage

*Non-fiction with purpose*

*Erin Gray & Mara Purl's*
Act Right

*Coming Soon*
*Deena Mannion & Mary Sunkenberg's*
Back to Basics

**Haven Books** **http://www.havenbooks.net**
10153 ½ Riverside Drive
North Hollywood, CA 91602
Reya@havenbooks.net
818/ 503-2518 phone
818/ 508-0299 FAX
Havenbks@aol.com